DUTY OF CARE

JC RYAN

VINCI
BOOKS

By JC Ryan

Rex Dalton K9 Thrillers

Dedicated to my good friend Mitch Pender, a military dog trainer, for giving me the idea for this series and guiding me through the intricate and amazing capabilities and psychology of those majestic four-legged soldiers.

Mitch has a lifetime of experience and exceptional depth of knowledge as a military dog handler and trainer.

Vinci Books

vinci-books.com

Published by Vinci Books Ltd in 2025

1

About Duty of Care

It's Rome. It's August. It's early morning. It's going to be a perfect day.

Rex and Digger, his former military dog and best friend, are in Rome. They are at a trattoria not far from the famous Spanish Steps. Rex is hoping that Catia Romano, the woman he fell in love with four years ago, would make an appearance.

It's been two years. Rex's memory stirs. He can see her auburn curls fall across her face, her blue eyes sparkling beneath her lashes, and he wonders if her smile still reaches them.

But then her image fades from his mind's eye as his hand reaches for the vibrating phone, and within seconds he knows that his plan to see Catia will come to nothing, as he listens with growing alarm to Rehka, his IT expert in India, telling him that former CRC colleagues of his came to her apartment and wanted to know where they could find him.

My cover is blown, my extended vacation is over, and John Brandt could be in perilous danger.

John Brandt, the CEO of CRC, whom they all referred to as the Old Man, has been abducted, and CRC needs Rex's help. It's a matter of life and death.

Do I have a duty of care?

Just when he puts the phone down, Catia is there. Stunning as ever, breathtaking, more beautiful than in his most romantic dreams.

His eyes flick to her hands, no rings.

Damn!

"Come on Digger." He stood, grabbed Digger's leash, and walked away.

Damn!

Thus, begins another nerve-wracking quest for Rex and Digger to save someone. This time, someone from Rex's past. A past which he is trying to escape from.

Chapter One

John Brandt was a former warrior of the Cold War era, an experienced spook with more missions under his belt than he cared to remember. After retiring from the CIA, he'd formed Crisis Response Consultancy - CRC. He might have been too old, according to the federal government, to be useful as a field agent. But he was not too old to train his own team in the old ways and make a lot of money doing what the 'new' CIA was expected to do but couldn't because of the interference of politicians. Outsourcing to private contractors was the only alternative.

CRC – Crisis Response Consultancy, nominally commanded by the CIA, was a private military contractor under the command of John Brandt. The name, Crisis Response Consultancy, was one of those nondescript names that simultaneously said nothing and everything about the activities of the organization. You had to be one of them to know what crises they were consulted about and how they responded to it. CRC was a Black Ops organization.

Every few months Brandt would take an overseas trip to

visit some of the countries where CRC agents on missions were operating and meet with them, in secret of course. Some of the trips were to touch base with his 'boys and girls' and some were to evaluate them while on a mission.

On these trips he always traveled under pseudonyms, and there were only a few people who knew about it—among them, his second in command at CRC, Chris McArdle, the CIA's Deputy Director of Operations—informally known as Clandestine Services, and of course the agents whom he was visiting.

To attract as little attention as possible, he was usually accompanied by a small group of 'friends' in a tour group, ostensibly interested in sightseeing and the stuff tourists are usually interested in seeing and doing. They stayed in tourist class hotels, ate at tourist class restaurants, and did the things tourists did. In other words, they blended in and went to great pains to attract as little attention as possible. These 'friends' were an old network which he'd cultivated as informants in his days in Russia and France. He kept in contact with them and from time to time used them for surveillance work. They were also among the most talented field agents Brandt ever had the pleasure of working with.

After all this time and so much hands-on experience, they also had the added advantage of being among the invisible ranks of the late middle-aged to elderly. No one paid attention to an old woman knitting a sweater on a park bench, or a pair of old men engaged in a chess match at a picnic table, or a single old man feeding pigeons. An elderly woman waiting for a bus or staring mindlessly at the passing crowds wouldn't excite a moment's curiosity.

What made his 'friends' even more exceptional were that they were lifelong students, now masters, of the science of human behavior. Their particular talent was that they could follow a target for ten to twenty minutes and then predict the target's next or even final destination and be there in advance.

Tailing a subject who had a highly-trained security detail was dicey. It was so amusing to know that the target was taking extreme precautions, long and circuitous routes, and other countermeasures to avoid being followed, only to arrive where they were expected and their 'tails' waiting there for them. These wily old spies could do it without the target's knowledge and get it right with astounding accuracy.

Brandt and his cronies called themselves the Old Timers. He, in his late sixties, and his friends, ranging from his age into their mid-seventies.

Athens, Greece

Day of abduction

They were in Athens, at the Apollo Hotel, Karaiskaki Square, a two-minute walk from Meraxourgio Metro Station allowing for easy rail access from Larissa International Train Station five hundred meters away, and bus access, with convenient reach to Plaka (the Old Town of Athens) and the Acropolis. Being so centrally located enabled Brandt's party to move easily around the city, enjoying the sites of the ancient city and keeping an eye on the agent Brandt was evaluating on his trip.

That night, they all bundled into a taxi and took a food tour of Athens, which took them on a three-hour excursion to ten different restaurants all over the city for a tasting of authentic Greek food. They got back to their hotel at about ten p.m. After the unusually-heavy dinner, the rest of the Old Timers were tired and went to their rooms, but Brandt said he was going to take a stroll before bedding down for the night.

He went to his room first, put on his jacket, and took his wallet. As usual, he looked out the window at the street below to see what was going on before leaving. There was nothing of note.

When he exited the elevator, out of habit, he scanned the lobby and noticed a man with his back to him in a chair reading a newspaper. Besides the chair in which the man sat, there was a couch and two empty chairs. He noted the man was in a strategic position, but that could have just been the most comfortable chair.

However, it's the seat I would've chosen if I wanted to monitor who's coming and going through the lobby.

When Brandt passed him, he noticed the man glancing at him briefly. Brandt nodded, the man nodded back and then turned his eyes back to the newspaper.

The small things. Enough of them and trouble is the next thing on your doorstep. Paranoia? Maybe. That's what kept you alive so far.

He headed for the front door and stepped out. Before proceeding, he stopped and scanned the street outside, first left, then right. There were three cars parked on his side of the street, two to the right and one to the left. Across the street, there were four parked cars. He'd seen them from his room before he'd left. None of the cars had occupants.

Nothing to be concerned about.

He glanced back inside at the man in the chair. He was still reading, showing no interest in Brandt. He ticked the man off his list.

The sidewalks were empty, not unusual for ten-thirty p.m. in this part of the city, where there were only small hotels and apartment blocks. Brandt took a deep breath of the fresh night air, turned to his left, and started walking.

He was about five hundred meters away from his hotel when an African man blocked his way and tried to sell him a handcrafted, collapsible wooden basket. Brandt couldn't understand a single word, but he'd seen peddlers selling those baskets all over Europe. The cleverly-designed baskets were spiral cut and mounted on a circle of wood, with a handle that rotated to lift the bowl part and keep it standing, causing it to drop the spirals into a bowl shape.

Over the years he'd bought them from immigrants trying to make a living in Italy, France, Germany, and elsewhere. He had about a dozen of them in various shapes and sizes at CRC headquarters, serving as vessels for anything from fruit to paperclips.

He sighed, smiled at the man, and said, "I've never bought one of these in Greece before," as he reached into the inside pocket of his jacket to retrieve his wallet.

In the next moment, Brandt knew something had gone terribly wrong. Three men in police uniforms came rushing toward him from the foyer of the apartment building where he and the hawker were doing business. They were screaming at him in English to drop to his knees and put his hands behind his head.

A sting? But…

He heard tires screaming and engines roaring as vehicles came rushing toward him from both sides of the street.

In seconds, he was surrounded by at least eight men and two cars. He was on his knees, hands behind his head, and staring down the barrels of two SIG Sauer P226 guns in the hands of the two men directly in front of him. A third tapped a baton into his opposite hand, and to his left was a man with a Taser X26 gun.

It took him less than three seconds to figure out these men were imposters. The Hellenic police's standard issue handgun was not the SIG Sauer P226 but rather the Heckler & Koch USP 9 mm, or Beretta M9, or Smith & Wesson Model 910, or Ruger GP100. They didn't use tasers, and they didn't wear hiking boots with their uniforms.

Brandt was hopelessly outnumbered, that much he knew very quickly. In days of yore, if it were two or three attackers facing him, he'd put up a fight and would've given himself a better than even chance to beat the crap out of them. But he was sixty-eight years old, and there were eight attackers he could see. There could have been others as well, but there was no point in looking for them. All he could do was to go along with whatever it was these men wanted, for now. He didn't get much more time to think through his situation when the hooks from the taser gun embedded in his chest and his body was jolted by 50,000 volts. He never felt the prick of the needle that was plunged into his neck before his world went dark and quiet.

Chapter Two

Arizona, USA

Fourteen months previously

He'd never had a mission go so badly, though he'd lost men before. At least they'd always had a body to bury, or a reliable witness who saw what happened, some closure—they'd never left a man behind, dead or alive. He'd never cried over a loss before, but now he gave in to the grief and let the tears come.

He loved Rex Dalton as if he were his own son.

Those who were not in the know about CRC's business would probably refer to Rex as a consultant. Those who had an inkling of what was going on would have thought of him as a field agent or an operative. His enemies, and some others, would have used the word assassin.

Rex was CRC's most coveted asset; a stone-cold killer with a grudge against bad guys, especially terrorists, who had killed his family when they blew up a train in Barcelona in 2004.

After ten minutes of stunned inaction upon hearing the news from the director of the CIA, Bruce Carson, that Rex and his support team were missing, probably dead, Brandt pulled himself together.

The others had to be informed. He called in Rick Longland, his company's resident psychologist, to help him plan what to tell the others and how to commemorate the best agent CRC had ever had. Rex Dalton inspired great loyalty among his teammates, and a paternal feeling in Brandt. He deserved a memorial, at the very least.

Longland was there within minutes and saw the devastation in Brandt's face. "Dalton?" he asked.

Brandt nodded. "It appears he and the team he took with him may have been ambushed."

"What makes them think it's our men and not the drug lords Dalton was supposed to dispose of?" Longland asked. "Isn't there any hope?"

"Right number of bodies, according to the operational plan Rex submitted before he and the others headed out. Rex must be dead. He'd never leave me hanging like this if he weren't dead or worse."

"What's worse?" Longland asked.

"Do you need to ask? Worse would be if he were in the hands of the terrorists. Remember, the Taliban were supposedly at that meeting. I pray if the team was ambushed that they were killed rather than captured."

"John, I can't tell you how sorry I am."

"What are we going to tell the others, Rick?"

Longland had no answer to the rhetorical question.

Brandt prepared a few remarks, and then he abandoned them when the time came. For the sake of the entire team, he had to be as strong as he ever was in these situations. He decided to inform them at dinner, after he'd had a chance to compose himself. There would be a formal memorial later, when there was a body to bury or at least incontrovertible proof that Rex was really gone. As soon as it appeared that most of the men were finished with their meal and about to leave, Brandt stood up. Everyone went quiet and every eye turned toward him.

"Men, I have some unhappy news. Rex Dalton, whom most of you know, is believed killed in action in Afghanistan. He was a brave man, a great agent, and an excellent soldier. We will all miss him. He wouldn't want you to grieve. Dalton was a man of few words, but those words spoke of his devotion to this country and the missions we take on. The incident was such that there is no body to recover.

"You all know that shit happens, and in our line of work some of us get killed. Nonetheless, Dalton, like you, signed up for this. He knew the risks and never hesitated to take them. None of us is invincible. We bleed and die like any other human. Rex has paid the ultimate price, and I can tell you I know without a doubt he paid it willingly for the safety and betterment of our country."

He turned and left abruptly and with the certain knowledge that Rex had not *willingly* given his life. Not in that sense. He'd willingly gone into danger, he'd willingly gone to the battlefield to fight, but he'd never willingly gone to be betrayed. If he'd failed, it wasn't because he hadn't given it his best shot, he'd failed because of treachery.

Chapter Three

Present time

Unknown location

The blow to his stomach would have hurt less had he known it was coming. He could have hardened his muscles. He tried to hit back, and that was when he realized his hands and arms were immobile, wrapped in duct tape to the arms of a chair. The most uncomfortable chair he'd ever sat in.

I'm ready for you now, you bastard. Come on, come at me again.

It was dark—he was blindfolded. He tried to remember where he was, how he'd come to be there, when and how he was taken.

A blow to his jaw rocked his head back.

"Shit!"

He willed his right leg, the stronger one, to move and sweep the attacker's legs from under him, but his legs were also immobilized. Brandt shook and threw his head back, preparing to head-butt his assailant—if he'd only come close enough.

He muttered something, believing he was coherent and snarling a credible threat.

The next blow, contrary to all reason, cleared his head.

John Brandt, The Old Man his underlings called him, found himself in a situation he hadn't encountered since his youth. But he was no longer the formidable hotshot CIA agent he'd been then. Now, even if he hadn't been tied to the chair, chances were, he'd be getting the worst of the beating; back in his youth he would have left his attacker with something to remember.

John Brandt was sixty-eight years old, and if this beating didn't stop soon, he might not make it to sixty-nine. He'd have doubled over with the next blow to his stomach, but yeah, his chest was also duct-taped to the back of the chair.

There was no way to protect himself against the blows he couldn't even see coming. It would have to be his wits that kept him alive, or if not, at least it would safeguard the knowledge in his brain. He knew enough to get a lot of people killed or worse.

The question now was which knowledge this was all about. Bringing his decades of training and focus to bear, he tuned out the physical pain of the blows still raining down on him and assessed his mental condition. The lingering fog around the corners of his mind and the vulgar taste in his mouth told him he'd been drugged.

Had I been questioned?

Had I said anything?

He didn't think so, but the possibility remained.

And then, mercifully, the beating stopped. He estimated the voice he heard next was about a foot to the side and a couple or three feet above his sitting position.

"He should be softened up enough to talk now. Any more and he'll be out again."

The next voice came from farther away. Six feet maybe? No way to tell and no way to use the knowledge anyway.

"Mr. Brandt, I'm sorry to have to resort to these methods, but you haven't been very cooperative so far."

Good. Exactly what I hoped for. Thanks for the confirmation, asshole.

Brandt noted the accent, New York upper-class, but with a hint of something else underneath, indicating it was either affected or perhaps the questioner had lived somewhere else in his youth. Southern?

"I have it on good authority that you were the person who ordered the destruction of our stockpiles of opium product in Afghanistan. What can you tell me about the person or persons who carried out that order?"

Brandt stayed silent. He'd given no such order.

What's this guy talking about?

He got a stinging slap to his bruised cheek. Truthfully, he was confused by the question, and he didn't think it would hurt to say so, though he was shocked at the croaking sound of his voice and the slurred words that he uttered.

"Ah doan nuh wha ur 'alkin bow."

"Oh, I'm certain you know what I'm talking about. We know you had contractors in Kabul at the time. Who gave you the contract? What are the names of your operatives who did it?"

He shook his head.

Wasn't us. That much I know. So, there's nothing you can beat out of me, shithead.

Speaking very carefully, making an effort to enunciate, he answered, "I din' gi' order. Mah org din' do it."

"Gentlemen, I think your assessment was wrong. He

hasn't had enough incentive to talk yet." It was the New York voice again.

Brandt barely had time to clench his core when the next blow knocked the breath out of him. The blows came hard and fast, giving him no warning of where the next strike would hit him, and mercifully everything went dark again.

When he resurfaced, it was to the sure knowledge he was drowning. Wave after wave of ice-cold water hit him in the face, and he swallowed some with each gasp as he tried desperately to breathe.

"Enough," said the voice. It was the one who'd questioned him before. The water stopped, and Brandt sat shivering and shaking as the man began to question him again.

"I'll give you a minute to compose yourself," the unseen man said. "And then, I want to know about the operation that slaughtered our opium suppliers. It happened after the raid your men attempted to perform outside Kabul over a year ago. We know you killed ours in retaliation for them killing yours and that the CIA ordered the destruction of the warehouses. You will tell me who raided the compound of the head of our organization, beheaded him and several of his colleagues, and made off with a fortune in gold and his computers."

Rex Dalton did that.

I 'know' he did, despite all evidence that he's dead. And if they want to know about him, then they too must think he's alive. Well, they won't get anything from me, because I don't know anything. But I can do something to keep them occupied, son. That I'll do for you even if you don't trust me enough to report in.

Brandt took a deep breath and spoke with a labored voice. The effect of the drugs was wearing off.

"Okay, you've got me dead to rights. I cannot tell a lie." His tongue firmly in cheek, he spun a story close to what he thought was the truth. "You're right. We're the ones who took out your guy's – Usama was his name, right? We took out his warehouses on a contract, sure. But it wasn't the CIA who ordered it.

"We're a private company, an international organization, and we don't care who we work for as long as they pay. We take work where we can get it. In this case, it was a Pakistani outfit." Assuming it would mean nothing to his questioner, Brandt uttered one of a few Urdu phrases he'd learned to pronounce well. He was naming the fictional organization, the Urdu equivalent of 'Shock and Awe'.

He went on to explain. "They call themselves Shock and Awe, wanted to break into the drug market in the US and Europe. Apparently, your guy, Usama, wasn't as loyal as he could have been. He'd been talking to them, but the talks broke down, so they decided to take him out of the equation by destroying his warehouses. We did that. But we didn't take *him* out. I have no idea who did that."

It was all a lie, of course. Like any good lie, it held an element of truth. The organization he'd named was real. The relationship with Usama was a figment of his imagination, but his interrogator didn't know that. It would take time to verify everything, and time was what Brandt needed. Time would allow him to prepare himself mentally, and it would give his agents opportunity to find him. He knew that all men broke eventually, and he intended, if he was not rescued before then, to come up with such a whopper that they would kill him before he broke down and talked, endangering all of his agents, many CIA operatives, and— not to put too fine a point on it—many spies and informers across the globe.

A bonus would be if he could confuse and misdirect them to the point where they'd doubt and mistrust their own. He doubted he'd ever know how successful he was at it. At least the lie he just told them had the desired effect. The beating stopped and the questioner left the room.

A prick in his arm was the only warning before he drifted into unconsciousness.

When he woke, he was alone, still in a dark room, but now on a thin mattress in a moving vehicle. Having the time to think, he tried to recall the incident they questioned him about.

Chapter Four

Unknown location

Present time

If he'd been honest with himself, he would have been both ashamed and disgusted by his weakness. Somewhere in the darkest recesses of his mind he knew that having other men do the dirty work while he stood back, stayed clean, and then tried to have a civilized conversation with a brutalized man was the act of a coward.

But he would never admit it. He hadn't risen to his position of power and wealth by being honest with himself or anyone else.

In the end, he left it to the people he paid. He traveled some six thousand miles back to New York to watch the proceedings through a closed circuit, in a secret room, in his Manhattan mansion. He was a brutal man who wouldn't hesitate to kill, or rather order a killing, but this was too close, too personal—he just didn't have the stomach for it.

While he sent out feelers to substantiate Brandt's story about the Pakistani outfit, 'Shock and Awe', whom he had never heard of, the professional he'd hired to kidnap Brandt told him an ugly truth.

"It's going to take more than a beating or two to get anything out of him. He's a pro, and he's tough, even though he's old. You need an equal pro to work on him. I suggest we move him offshore and you let me take over the interrogation."

He waved tiredly, and in an unconscious imitation of a popular TV character said, "Make it so."

The 'pro' nodded.

"I think he is sending us on a wild goose chase with this story about the Pakistanis. But let's investigate it, and if he is lying, punish him. I'm going home. You know what I want, get it out of him."

"I will Mr. Hathaway, you can bet on that."

———

Manhattan, NYC, NY, USA

Fourteen months previously

Winston Reginald Hathaway was the man who instigated the chain of events which led to the betrayal and killing of Rex's team in that ambush in Afghanistan. He did it in retaliation for Rex destroying his 'livelihood' - a stockpile of drugs earmarked for the Mob in the USA. He didn't know the name of the man or men who had done it nor the outfit they belonged to. Hathaway was the American Mafia's sole source of Afghani heroin. His customers would not be pleased when they learned their supply had been jeopardized by an American operation targeting the warehouses. He had to nip that in the bud.

Neither of them knew it at the time, but the phone call Hathaway made to the senior senator from Georgia, chairman of the Senate Intelligence Committee, who in turn made a call to the Director of the CIA, Bruce Carson, had been the first salvo in the war between Winston Reginald Hathaway and Rex Dalton.

Among a lot of other self-serving traits, Hathaway was also a narcissist who liked to look at himself in the mirror, usually smirking at his youthful image and, without fail, telling himself, *not bad, for an old duffer of sixty-something*.

Hathaway actually believed his own legend, which was the mark of a great con artist. His home, his bank account, his wardrobe, and even his accent proclaimed him 'old money' in the rarefied environs of New York's *nouveau riche* social circles. By carefully avoiding the real scions of old money, he'd clawed his way up the ladder of wealth and respectability despite his humble beginnings.

Hathaway's real name, long lost to time and expensive eradication, was Joe Fink. Not Joseph—Joe. He'd spent his formative years in orphanages and foster homes, where he'd learned to bully back when other kids bullied him about his name. In the streets of the poor neighborhoods where he'd been housed, 'fink' meant snitch, and snitches died. However, Joe was one tough cookie, and his mission in life, since a very tender age, was to get to the top, by any means.

At first, he headed in the wrong direction thinking violence, stealing, and robbery would get him to the top. But by the age of eighteen, with a juvenile record longer than he was tall, he'd committed his first adult felony and landed in prison. There, the good-looking youth, in return for favors he'd never spoken of or cared to remember after his release, had turned his life in another direction. He learned from a much older felon with an upper-class British accent the fine art of the con. Fink was released at the age of twenty-one and had never looked back. His upbringing might have been deficient, but there was nothing wrong with his mind.

He went through several changes of identity while pulling off more and more sophisticated scams, finally achieving a semblance of respectability. By the age of thirty, he'd married wife number one, the first of three, a former Miss Georgia and the heiress to a minor fortune. His philosophy was that it is not your fault if your dad is poor, but it definitely is if your father-in-law is. Her untimely death in an auto accident fueled his rise to fortune.

His second wife, the love of his life, died giving birth to their second child. He married the nanny, with a watertight prenup in place, only a few months later, simply to save her salary. By then he had all the money he needed, though he never felt he had financial security until he'd become a major importer of Afghani heroin.

How he escaped with his life when he muscled into his status as supplier to the Mob, no one could explain, and no one who was alive knew to ask. To the world, he was a man of leisure, overseeing his fortune and that of his late wife held in trust for his two adorable children. The nanny was wise enough to get the message when he started treating her like dirt. When the children were in their late teens, she divorced him and moved on. So, he became the most eligible bachelor and playboy in New York. His social circle loved him, foibles and all. Sixty was the new forty, his age was no hindrance, even if he hadn't had several plastic surgeries to disguise it along with his previous identity. What he lacked in looks and youth, the money made up for. He discovered that some women found his money, the world's number one aphrodisiac, overwhelmingly sensual.

Less than forty-eight hours after making the call to the senior senator from Georgia, Hathaway and his cronies were celebrating the deaths of those who dared interfere with their drug empire. Hathaway even traveled to DC to join the celebrations with his business associates.

Chapter Five

Koh-e Shir Darwaza, Kabul, Afghanistan

Fourteen months previously

His mission for CRC ended in tragedy when an Afghani drug lord arranged an ambush that killed Rex's entire team. All except Digger, the military dog trained and owned by the former Australian SAS operative, Trevor Madigan, Rex's good friend. Digger was now Rex's trusted companion only because of a promise Trevor extracted as he lay dying. Rex had been afraid of dogs before that, and even as he promised to care for the pooch, he hadn't known how he'd do it, or whether Digger would accept him.

Rex and Digger had teamed up in the aftermath of the ambush and had gone in pursuit of those responsible. They soon caught up with them, and from the interrogation of the drug lord and his cohorts Rex gathered enough information to conclude that the strings had been pulled from

America. The ambush was set up with the sole purpose to kill him, and now he was presumed dead in the attack.

That was the night Rex decided to walk away from CRC and what he'd thought was his life's work. That night, he took an oath that he'd determine who betrayed him and his men, and he'd then go back to America and take care of it. In the meantime, to stay alive he had to remain 'dead'.

Accompanied by Digger, who he passed off as his service dog, they started a new life. A life intended to be one long vacation until he was ready to exact his revenge. He would be a nomad, searching out places that interested him because of their history, living nowhere and traveling where the wind blew him and Digger.

Washington D.C., USA

Fourteen months previously

At the time of their revelries in DC, Hathaway and company were unapprised of the grisly fate that had befallen their suppliers 7,900 miles away to the east, in Kabul, Afghanistan.

The partyers had barely emerged from their drug- and alcohol-induced hangovers, when the news reached Hathaway's ears. He was in his hotel room, still in DC, when the call came through. Apparently, the Afghani drug lords were also in a celebratory mood about the demise of their enemy known as The Ghost or *Alshaytan*, the Devil.

The difference between the two parties was that the one in Afghanistan got gate-crashed. Unfortunately, no one at the party in Afghanistan survived to tell who the uninvited guest or guests were. Speculations about who did it ranged from rival drug lords, Taliban antagonists, religious zealots who had a gripe about drugs, and many others.

Hathaway wanted to know from his informant, "What kind of a sick monster would kill and behead people like that and then burn the place down? Some people just don't know where to draw the line between taking care of business and barbarism."

His informant made no reply.

Hathaway obviously neither spared one moment to think about what kind of a sick monster would betray his countrymen and have them walk into an ambush which he instigated, nor what kind of a sick monster would smuggle drugs into the US and Europe and destroy more lives than any war in human history.

He was too self-absorbed to see his own hypocrisy—for him it was all about money and Winston Reginald Hathaway, 'Winnie' to his friends, of which he had few of the true variety, actually none.

Nonetheless, if he were to be honest about it, it was not the gruesome killings that bothered Hathaway at all. The truth was, he was scared out of his wits. Those who were able to track down the drug lords and kill them could also track *him* down and could very well come knocking on his door soon.

Not even in the wildest of his drug-induced psychedelic euphoria could he have contemplated that this was the work of one man and a big black dog.

Hathaway and his business were in great jeopardy—in one fell swoop his suppliers had been wiped out and business would soon come to a screeching halt. He didn't need any reminder that the drug trade was a hazardous kind of enterprise. Participants were a trigger-happy bunch, and missing delivery deadlines, such as he had with the Mob as their sole supplier, would not just earn him a slap on the wrist—his head was literally on the block now.

An ice-cold shiver ravaged his body when that thought crossed his mind.

He'd have to call another meeting with his American business associates, and they'd have to make crisis decisions. Not only did they have to establish new supply arrangements, they'd have to come up with a way to keep the Mob happy and do it proactively. Unless they could find new suppliers, and very quickly, which was highly unlikely, they'd have to run their business at a loss by buying product from other drug dealers and forsake their smaller, less lethal, clientele to remain in favor with the Mob.

And it was not only that he had to deal with. Hathaway knew that he'd never have another peaceful night's sleep as long as he didn't know who'd tracked down their suppliers and exterminated them.

Although Hathaway's accomplices were high-ranking people with a wide sphere of influence, none of them were as well connected as Hathaway himself. With the senior senator from Georgia in the back of his mind and by extension the Director of the CIA, Winnie would pull out all the stops to get to the bottom of it.

Chapter Six

Fourteen months previously

Two days after the dreadful news of the ambush in Afghanistan, Bruce Carson, the Director of the CIA, met with John Brandt in DC and told him that four top opium lords in Afghanistan had been executed in a particularly brutal fashion, and the home of the top guy where they'd been meeting was destroyed by arson. It happened to be those same four guys who were supposed to turn up at the house where Rex and his team had set up an ambush for them two days earlier and been caught in an ambush themselves.

Carson told Brandt, "Whoever did it managed to kill several servants, a security advisor, and six guards, along with the principals." He wanted to know from Brandt if

CRC had anything to do with the killing of the drug lords, specifically his super-agent, known as the Ghost.

Brandt assured Carson that CRC had nothing to do with it, and to think that such an operation could have been the work of one man, was preposterous. Not even his man, Rex Dalton, whose name he didn't give to Carson, could pull off a stunt like that.

But Brandt lied, his mind working overtime to figure out *how* Rex had done it.

It was as good as getting a personal call from Rex saying, "I'm alive and well, and I'm on my way home, but don't stay up for me. I'll come in late." For the first time since he'd gotten the dreadful news of the ambush, his heart grew lighter.

Is it possible? Could Rex be alive? But then, why....?

Brandt couldn't get the insufferable Carson out of his face quickly enough and return to CRC headquarters, where he immediately summoned Josh Farley, one of his best agents whom he judged to be nearly as good as Rex Dalton, to his office.

"I have a special assignment for you. Go pack your stuff. Wheels up in half an hour."

A few hours later and several hundred miles to the east, Brandt introduced Josh to his best female agent, Marissa Bisset. Over dinner, Brandt gave them their orders, finally satisfying the agents' curiosity. Before doing so, he gave them the history and explained in no uncertain terms that Rex Dalton was a dangerous man to cross swords with. They should avoid it at all costs. He gave his assessment of what was going on if Rex was still alive, and why they needed to not approach or confront him in any way.

Their priority was to find out if he was still alive. If they found him, they were to stay out of his sight and get in touch with Brandt immediately. He'd take it under advisement from there.

"Do not, repeat do not, approach or confront him in any manner without my say-so," Brandt told them. "Rex Dalton is an exceedingly dangerous man, and there are only a couple of explanations for him not contacting me if he's alive. Either he has lost his memory, or he blames us for the betrayal. After all, it was my orders that sent him into that ambush. I'll have a conversation with Bruce Carson about that, but you must stay safe while I figure out how to approach him and let him know it wasn't us."

Thus, the two agents began a global search for Rex Dalton, the man around whom many rumors had been built. Among his enemies he went by many names. *El Gato*, the cat, in Spanish, *Alshaytan*, the Devil, in Arabic, the Ghost, and many others. Whatever name they used for him, one thing was sure – just the mention of him gave his enemies the jitters.

Chapter Seven

Unknown location

Present time

The next time Brandt regained consciousness, he knew instantly he was in trouble. The thin mattress had been replaced by a hard surface, and what was worse, he was lying on his back, his arms and legs stretched to their limits and shackled to something immovable. A cold breeze informed him he was naked, and an unpleasant rocking motion indicated he was now on a ship or boat. He ached in places he didn't even know existed, like the roots of his teeth. A noxious odor came from some kind of covering over his face.

His memory came back more slowly, as he exerted all his control to avoid retching and adding to his discomfort from the putrescent tangs of vomit, snot, and sweat emanating from the bag enveloping his head and face. He remembered a beating and questioning, but then he was seated in a chair, albeit a damned uncomfortable one. He thought he'd had clothes on at the time, and he didn't recall the movement of a boat.

What had happened to land him in an even worse situation?

Gradually, he remembered lying to the questioner. And he had a vague memory of being overpowered by... Greek policemen?

What the hell?

However, at the moment, he had a more urgent problem. He shouted, "Hey, assholes, I'm awake. I need to take a piss! And I need water."

The reply was a deafening silence.

He shouted again and again and got the same reply.

Well, if that's the way you're going to be...

He let go, creating a big puddle of urine around him. At first, he welcomed the bit of warmth as it registered that he was uncomfortably cold. As the warmth receded, he wished he'd thought it through. But then, what else was he to have done?

To keep his mind off his misery, he began working at the mystery of who had him. In his almost seven decades, Brandt had made more than a few enemies, so there were plenty of possibilities. Radical Islamic terrorists, Russians, drug dealers? The list of bodies attributable to him personally or to his agents was impressively in the hundreds. Organizations, friends, family members—it could have been any of them. It could even have been his own countrymen. Remembering some betrayals that led to him punishing the perpetrators, he wouldn't have put it past even one of the alphabet-soup agencies in the government.

The next question was why?

Revenge?

Probably.

But before exacting that, they'd want some information. He reflected on the previous questioning, which was beginning to come back to him.

It's about Rex. Has to be. And I wouldn't give him up, even if I knew the answers they wanted. And once they know about Rex, would that be the end? Will they kill me, or will they want to know the rest of what I carry around in my head? I bet they'll want that.

What are my options?

It boiled down to three.

Option One, just give it to them and keep this short, not sweet, but if he was lucky a bullet to the head kind of short. Tell them what they want to know and get it over with. But that was treason and he was not a traitor.

Option Two, don't give them anything, tough it out, annoy them so much that they'd lose it and kill him in the process.

I'm an old man, I might not last as long as when I was young.

This was much better than option one, though painful without a doubt. But definitely not treacherous. The problem with this option was, in the end they'd still get the information out of him, if they didn't kill him too early.

Option Three was a combination of options One and Two, mixed in with as much deceit and misdirection as he could endure. Options Two and Three involved pain, a lot of it. If they were professionals, and the way they'd snatched him off the street in Athens gave him the impression they were professionals, they wouldn't kill him right away. They wouldn't overdo his torture—they'd do it slowly and painfully and make it last for a long time, weeks, months if necessary, but the torment would not end until he gave in. And he knew eventually he would. The human mind under duress had its limitations before it would just open up and let the secrets spill out.

The only difference between option Two and Three was that option Three was going to take much longer. Time in which he'd pin his hope that his CRC agents, the CIA, the FBI, and others would pull out all stops to find and rescue him.

In a hopeless situation, it was sometimes only a small thing, such as the hope and belief to be rescued, that would keep a person alive. And he knew *that* was going to be the first thing they'd try to take away from him—his hope.

It is said that everyone breaks in the end. But Brandt was not everyone. Yes, he was sixty-eight years old. Admittedly, he'd lost the strength and mobility of his youth, but he had full control of his mind, and it was loaded, not only with some of the most damaging secrets the intelligence community of the USA had but also the experience of more than forty years of spycraft.

I'm going to screw their minds with so much misinformation they won't know what to believe. They'll start arresting, torturing, and killing their own people before this is over. They'll have nightmares about traitors in their midst, spies in their own camps. I'm going to have a ball with these suckers.

Option Three it was.

He was going to start by playing meek and mild, *oh please don't hurt me, I'll tell you anything you want to know, please don't hurt me.* Brandt grinned into the filthy bag over his head and pledged to fight them every step of the way, to cause them more damage than they'd have ever imagined possible. And if they'd either intentionally or accidentally kill him, it would be a victory.

Then he heard loud metallic clanging sounds of a door

opening and got the impression he was in a shipping container.

Must be a freighter I'm on.

Chapter Eight

Manhattan, NYC, NY, USA

Twelve months previously

Within a few weeks of the raid on Usama's compound, Hathaway had his hands in his hair, threatening to pull it all out in frustration. Not only did he have to deal with the reconstruction of his drug enterprise while at the same time having to appease the angry Mob bosses, he also had to establish a new network of contacts and collaborators among politicians and government officials. It had frustrated him to no end to learn about the very inconvenient disappearance of the CIA Director, Bruce Carson. That was the man who'd kept him abreast of what the CIA was doing.

One of the big concerns was that Carson, when he reported the massacre of the drug lords before he'd gone AWOL, mentioned that whoever did it also cleared out

Usama's safe, took the hard drives of the computers, and his laptop. Hathaway and his cronies could only speculate and agonize about the information that could have been kept on those and how much of it could lead back to them.

At the time of the news of Carson's disappearance, Hathaway was at his wits' end, but, over time, he'd come to think of it as a blessing in disguise. It meant one less person who could eventually stab him in the back—so long as Carson remained missing. He'd contemplated putting a contract out on Carson to make sure of that, but he was too busy putting out other fires—Carson had to be dealt with later. And maybe, if he was lucky, Carson's disappearance meant he was in fact already dead.

There were many days when Hathaway considered retirement. He'd changed name and identity before. With the millions he'd stashed away in offshore accounts, it would be much easier now than before. But those were just fleeting thoughts. Winston Reginald Hathaway was an egomaniac, and he would not admit defeat, not even with his last breath. He was not going to give up, he would rebuild his empire or die trying. It was not about the money—he had enough to afford a life of extravagance even if he lived for another sixty years or longer—this was about the humiliation he'd suffered at the hand of an unknown rival.

And he would not rest until he had his revenge.

He became obsessed to find out who those people were and get rid of them before they followed the chain back to him and his council of evildoers. Though he didn't care much about his council—they were expendable. After all, they were on the council by his invitation. If he had to sacrifice them to save his own hide, he'd do it in a heartbeat. But, as long as they were useful, he'd use them for their money, contacts, and influence to achieve his own goals.

The senior senator from Georgia was another worry. The man's drinking habits made him a catastrophe just waiting for a time and place to happen. However, not long after Carson's disappearance, Hathaway's strains were somewhat relieved when he learned of the sudden, but as far as he was concerned, very timely and pleasing, death of the bourbon-guzzling senior senator from Georgia, chairman of the Senate Intelligence Committee.

A few months later, his mood improved yet again with the tiding that Bruce Carson had also swapped the ephemeral with the eternal by jumping out of his apartment window in Valparaiso, about sixty miles outside of Santiago, Chile.

Thanks Carson, you saved me the trouble of sending a hitman after you. I can now only pray that all my enemies would take their cue from you and die in one big calamity, so I can go back to living my life. That would just be dandy.

But Hathaway was a devoted atheist, so no deity responded to his entreaty—he had to do it himself.

Hathaway and his council of five met in secret on a regular basis in different cities and venues along the eastern seaboard of the US. They agreed that first and foremost they had to make sure they stayed in the good books of the Mob. There was product stockpiled in warehouses across the country, but it was not going to last very long.

"In other words," Hathaway said after studying the stock level reports, "we've got less than two months to get new suppliers and stock our warehouses."

"Ain't gonna happen," growled a big, hairy, very obese council member, the man in charge of distribution. "We'll have to buy or steal or take by force, if necessary, product from our competitors until we can get new suppliers."

A long discourse followed between the five, and their

schemes ranged from raiding their opposition's warehouses, to hiring a team of mercenaries to get rid of them and confiscate their product or just meet with them and make a deal. The latter idea was accepted as the first option, the other options to be considered if the deal-making failed. They all understood that to start a drug war on US soil was not going to work out well for anyone, but if necessary, to save their own hides, they would not shy away from it.

Thus, began a deadly process to establish contact with other drug cartels, with the view of making interim supplier arrangements. But they soon found out that they didn't have the necessary people skills for it. In the business world, corporations generally welcome the opportunity to explore mutually beneficial arrangements with others, even competitors sometimes. In the illicit drug industry however, the main players tended to see the other participants as archenemies, not to be trusted, not to be partnered with, vermin, best to be eradicated. The cause of the culture of distrust and violence among the people in this industry probably had something to do with personality traits such as glibness, heartlessness, manipulativeness, narcissism, deceitfulness, and a grandiose sense of self. In short, they were, almost without exception, a bunch of sociopaths with no respect for human life or the law.

Therefore, Hathaway's council soon found themselves in a tangled web of duplicity and distrust. It was all but impossible to make any headway. Any freshman psychology student would have told them they were attempting the impossible—mutual trust was a prerequisite for any relationship to work. But their sociopathic nature, of course, prevented them from seeing the logic.

Turning up at meetings armed to the teeth, surrounded by an entourage of hulking security guards dressed to kill and then getting upset to learn their counterparts returned the favor by turning up equally armed and protected, was not only futile and frustrating, it was downright dangerous. One wrong move by any one of the idiots, and truth be told, all of them were idiots, had the potential to start a war from which very few, if any, would walk away. Mutually assured destruction is what kept the west and the Soviets from obliterating each other with nuclear weapons during the Cold War, but in the drug business people just didn't have that kind of insight—they would be happy to start a shootout in a confined space and keep at it until they ran out of ammunition or were dead, whichever occurred first.

Chapter Nine

Manhattan, NYC, NY, USA

Twelve months previously

In the end, after weeks of repeatedly coming dangerously close to annihilation, Hathaway's group was out of time, out of patience, and virtually out of product.

Hathaway realized they had no choice but to play open cards with the Mob. He had a good relationship; well, as good as one could hope to have with a Mafia boss in New York. Fortunately, the man was sympathetic to Hathaway's supplications and offered to facilitate a meeting between the prospective business partners to see if he could break the impasse.

And this time it worked. Mainly because the Mafia boss brought his own security guards to the meeting. They scanned, searched, and disarmed all participants on arrival. Then, when all were unarmed and seated in the meeting room, surrounded by the heavily armed Mob henchmen, the boss stood, pulled his gun out, cocked it, and started talking in an authoritative voice while wielding the gun in the faces of his audience. He told them to stop this bullshit and make a deal. He told them there were hordes of people out on the streets of the US in desperate need of their drugs, and he was not going to let those people suffer because they, the traders, couldn't come to an agreement while all the product required was sitting in their warehouses.

He left no doubt about his deep desire for them to play nice, make a deal, shake hands on it, and start delivering. If not, he was going to get very upset with them—to the point where he would start shooting one of each of the parties every fifteen or so minutes until they had reached an agreement or none of them were alive. At which point he was going to take over their warehouses and hand the stock over to other willing and motivated traders.

That worked well. Obviously, *that* was the protocol to follow to get sociopaths to work together.

After this meeting, the word must have spread like wildfire through the drug dealers' community, because over the next few months many more such meetings were called, were well attended, and mutually beneficial deals were forged, in quick time.

The drug traders were happy to be alive, happy to be of service, and the Mob was happy that their supply lines were reestablished.

And the drug users on the streets of America were none the wiser about the calamity that was prevented.

Chapter Ten

Washington D.C., USA

Eleven months previously

A few weeks after Josh and Marissa started their manhunt for Rex Dalton, news out of Saudi Arabia about the untimely demise of one prince Mutaib bin Faisal bin Saud broke the news headlines in the Middle East. The news never reached the headlines of the mainstream media in Europe or America, but quite a few security agencies across the globe, among them, MI6, the Mossad, and the CIA, took note and were elated with Mutaib's death and the chaos it had caused among his customers.

Mutaib was an illicit arms dealer who supplied terror groups and drug dealers.

Through the CIA, news of Mutaib's death came to the attention of John Brandt. A sixth sense made him wonder about the details that weren't being given. He requested more information about the circumstances of the death from the CIA, and he wanted it warts and all—not the media version. Only Brandt, who was still looking for Rex Dalton, gave a care about the details. The other agencies only cared to know Mutaib was gone—grateful to whomever it was for clearing a bit of trash off the international lawn.

Reading through the report, which included the statements of witnesses, some eyewitnesses, others hearsay, it first struck him that they mentioned only one man doing all of this.

Rex Dalton, if he is alive, could've done this. But why would he have? Has he gone rogue? Or maybe working for another country's security agency? Israel's Mossad? The UK's MI6, The French DGSE?

He kept on reading and then came across the mention of a big black dog accompanying this man. It was unclear to whoever had interviewed the women in Mutaib's official harem whether the dog was a djinn or a real dog. The women were too agitated to be clear on the subject, and only one claimed to have seen it. The others were repeating her assertions.

Nevertheless, Brandt couldn't help but think that if Rex were alive, this was a mission he would have been assigned. An audacious stunt like this would have been exactly his style, and he had the skills to get the job done. But the enigmatic thing was Rex had never worked with a dog on any mission.

In the end, Brandt decided to inform Josh and Marissa and let them decide whether it was worth investigating or not. However, they thought Brandt was a bit too desperate to find Rex—there was no way he could have pulled off a mission like that on his own. Besides the mention of a big black dog, which the witnesses thought was a djinn, tainted the credibility of the story.

They had other, more plausible, explanations such as a fanatical religious sect or a business deal gone sour or a covert operation by Mossad or another security agency, but definitely not Superman and a djinn in the manifestation of a big black dog.

Therefore, Josh and Marissa parked the idea that this could have been Rex Dalton's doing.

Chapter Eleven

Manhattan, NYC, NY, USA

Eleven months previously

There was no shortage of opium suppliers in Afghanistan. Hathaway could get a dozen of them lined up within a few months if he wanted to. But as long as those party crashers who killed their suppliers in such a brutal fashion were still out there, they were running the risk that the same thing would happen again once they'd setup a new supplier network in Afghanistan.

Hathaway and his council members were well connected throughout the American law enforcement and security communities. On their rolodexes could be found the names and contact details of a two-star Air Force general, a deputy director of the NSA, a deputy director of the CIA, and a high-ranking FBI officer. And, it almost goes without saying, quite a few influential politicians from both parties in both the Senate and the House, over whom they held sway because of generous campaign contributions or the dirt they had on them.

So, they launched a project to re-establish their supply network, and they also discussed what their exposure might be and how they could find out who had put them in this position. Whoever it was needed to learn a very important lesson which would end in the culprits' termination with extreme prejudice.

During a few brainstorming sessions the council reconstructed, as best they could, what could've happened in Afghanistan.

The first part was easy. Hathaway had organized it and knew how it went down. He'd received a phone call from Usama, the person in charge of the Afghan suppliers at the time. Usama had told Hathaway about the raid on their drug depot. Hathaway had then contacted the senior senator from Georgia who in turn had contacted Bruce Carson, Director of the CIA. Carson had outsourced a job to someone who he, Carson, believed were the perpetrators who blew up the depot with tens of millions of dollars' worth of opium in it. But Carson never told Hathaway or anyone else the name of the contractor to whom he'd outsourced the job.

The 'mission' Carson had sent the men on was what Hathaway and company believed at the time a huge success; the ambushers had walked right into an ambush themselves and were all killed. That was where the good part of the story ended.

Two days later, their fortunes were reversed when their entire syndicate of opium suppliers was killed in one night.

The council had to reach out to their contacts and get the information about who did it, and they knew, although it would be relatively easy to get the information, it was going to take time to get it without raising suspicion.

Chapter Twelve

Washington D.C., USA

Nine months previously

Once they'd set their minds to the project, it took about two months or so to find out who did the contract job for the CIA. Carson had disappeared, and the Senator from Georgia was dead, so the delicate inquiries needed time to work their way through the system via their own contacts, who didn't know the answers right away. Within a couple of weeks, the information was fed back to them. It was a private military contractor by the name of Crisis Response Consultancy – CRC – with their headquarters in an undisclosed location in Arizona.

Finding out more about CRC was more difficult. The person who told them who it was would not say more, citing a healthy regard for his own skin. When they threatened to kill him if he didn't tell them all he knew, he just said he'd rather be killed outright than what would happen to him if CRC found it was him who'd spilled their secrets. But Hathaway's outfit could be very persuasive if necessary. So, they explained to their informant that he was already a dead man walking. He was either going to be killed by CRC agents, when they heard about his treachery or by Hathaway's men.

The informant didn't need a lot of time to think about it before telling them the rest.

John Brandt, they learned, was the CEO of CRC, the man they assumed would know about the follow-up revenge operation to kill the drug lords.

Hathaway and cronies were burning to take their own revenge, and their first reaction was to consider killing Brandt. They reckoned it would not have been too difficult a task to set for a professional assassin and would cost them in the order of half a million dollars max—not much for them. But once they'd all vented their spleen, they realized it would've been the wrong order in which to go about it. They had to first get Brandt in their hands, interrogate him for the information, and then kill him.

One of the worrying aspects of their information gathering mission so far was that it had turned up no indication of what had happened to the contents of Usama's safe, the hard drives of the computers, and his laptop. In fact, their contacts in the military, CIA, NSA, FBI, and politicians all shrugged their shoulders. None of their organizations had sanctioned an operation to kill Usama. They knew about him and his cronies and their roles in the Afghan opium trade, and all were under strict orders not to interfere in their business. Therefore, they neither had an idea of what exactly happened when Usama and company were killed, nor what happened to the contents of Usama's safe, the hard drives, and the laptop. Nor did they care. Despite being under the thumbs of powerful people above them, most members of those agencies had no love for the drug trade and were either neutral or happy it had been interrupted, even if temporarily.

The council of five didn't know if it was good or bad news. Nevertheless, they decided to play it safe and regarded it as a big risk that those devices were out there with all the damning information on them and therefore critically important to retrieve them, second only in importance to re-establishing their supply chain. This was by no means an easy or quick decision. It took them about four months to even get a unanimous decision on the solution.

The next step was to assemble a team of wetwork specialists to abduct John Brandt and take him to a place where he could be thoroughly interrogated and killed.

But this was not the type of thing in which Hathaway and his associates had much experience. In fact, they had none.

However, they had enough brains between them to know it would require extreme circumspection. One wrong word at the wrong time to the wrong person could unleash a deluge of trouble for them, which could very well land their asses in prison for a lengthy period.

Hathaway, as chairman of the council, got tapped to find out how to go about this and hire the team of specialists. And to make sure that he left no trails back to the group.

It was not one of those types of jobs where one would place an ad in the papers, or employ a recruitment agency, or that could be researched on the internet without setting off alarm bells somewhere. But he was firmly embedded in the high-class society of Manhattan. Among the people in his social circle, there were quite a few unscrupulous people and a good number of psychopaths.

Psychopaths are often thought of as cold-blooded killers, with lack of empathy and lack of interpersonal skills. But very seldom is it realized that not all psychopaths are killers and that many of them have other, less frightening traits in abundance—impulsivity, heightened attraction to rewards and risk-taking. It is not uncommon to find psychopathic traits in businesspeople, CEOs, politicians, and other powerful people. They often have such a strong draw to reward—to the proverbial carrot—that it overwhelms the sense of risk or concern about the stick—the potential punishment. And that is what often makes them very successful in business and power roles.

Hathaway had no way of knowing which, if any, of his psychopathic friends had any experience in abducting, inter-rogation, and killing people. Very subtly, he started putting out feelers in the form of hints that he had a problem that required some specialist skills. Then, after a few weeks of subtle hinting, one of his friends, at a party one night, pulled him aside and whispered into his ear that he knew of a trustworthy person who would keep his mouth shut.

His friend had given him the business card of this person and said they should meet the next day, maybe over lunch, so that he could explain to Hathaway how to go about dealing with this person.

Looking at the business card, Hathaway reflected that maybe he had been too discreet. He thanked his friend very politely and said he'd call him the next day to set up the time and place. But he had no intention of doing so.

Chapter Thirteen

Arizona, USA

Nine months previously

Despite Josh's and Marissa's misgivings about Rex, over the course of the ensuing months, whether it was intuition or being attuned to the best agent he'd ever had- the man he'd thought of as a true son, John Brandt's thoughts kept turning to Rex Dalton and the odd story out of Saudi Arabia. He'd always been skeptical about one man operating on his own with no support team behind him overcoming a Saudi prince and his entire security team, and still managing to escape.

But then again, unreal as the whole story may have sounded, he'd never known anyone else but Rex Dalton who had the brains and guts capable of pulling off a stunt as audacious as that one. In the past, he'd reluctantly dismissed it as a clue to whether Rex was alive, mainly because of the report of that dog or djinn being involved.

However, with nothing but his strong feeling that Rex was alive and the lack of other clues behind it, he finally decided he had to settle the matter once and for all. So, that's when he called in a favor from a former colleague at the CIA who agreed to help.

A few days later, his ex-colleague called with information. He got it from the Saudi General Intelligence Presidency who in turn got it from the Mabahith, the Saudi Secret police.

Mutaib was a known illegal arms dealer, but his status as part of the royal family protected him. However, he was an embarrassment to the King, so the official investigation didn't go far. It was the Mabahith that dug for details, then buried them and had to dig the file out of their archives to provide it to the General Intelligence Presidency. The file contained proof that prince Mutaib had an official and an unofficial harem. Whoever the individual was—for they still had no clue who it was—raided the residence, killed Mutaib and all his guards, and took some valuables, along with half his harem—the unofficial half. Well, not all of them, but most of them. Seven women and a little girl. And apparently the dog, or djinn, whatever it was, helped this mysterious hero.

And there was no question it was only one man.

When Brandt shared the information with Josh and Marissa, predictably, she was cynical. She'd been cynical about it from the beginning.

"It could have been Rex." Brandt said. "Do you know of anyone else, ours or internationally, that could have pulled that off?"

Marissa had waved her hand in a dismissive gesture.

"I've never met Rex, I only know what you and Josh told me about him. Admittedly, by all accounts, Dalton seems to be a very capable man. But let's be realistic, this is not Hollywood.

"Djinn?

"Are you serious? C'mon John, this is a fairy tale. It's been exaggerated by the witnesses to absolve them of any blame.

"Why would Rex have been involved in something like that? If he's alive, and you know that's a big if, he'd be hiding. For what reason on earth would he get involved in a high-profile crime in a country where getting caught would mean a death sentence? Why would he abduct a bunch of civilians, and maybe get them killed too? It doesn't make sense."

Josh wasn't so sure. "Well, look. Rex Dalton specialized in the impossible. Remember London? And come to think of it, Naples and..."

Brandt held his hand up to stop Josh and brought Marissa up to speed on the missions she hadn't known of, when Rex was sent to terminate a problematic Russian expat, and not only did so, but in the process implicated a child pornographer that hadn't even been on MI5's radar. He also told her how Rex went to Naples and prevented a major arms deal between a terrorist group and the Camorra, the mafia group operating out of the Campania region in Italy with their headquarters in Naples.

Then, Josh speculated that if Rex had somehow hooked up with a well-trained military dog, the Saudi incident would be even more possible for him.

"You think it was a military dog, not a djinn?" Marissa asked, the sarcasm clear in her tone.

Josh turned to stare at her in disbelief, then saw from

her expression it was a rhetorical question. She was still talking.

"So, what do you want us to do, go hunting stories of evil spirits in the Saudi desert? If this was Rex, he's long gone. It's been months."

"Of course not," Brandt said, taking her question seriously, though she'd asked it with heavy sarcasm. "Look. Mutaib was a known arms smuggler and dealer. If it hadn't been for what I learned of his family life, so to speak, I'd think the raid was carried out by some official agency. The CIA, MI6, the Mossad. He was high on all of their hit lists. It could also have been one of his rival arms dealers. However, whispers are that the bastard had a few more wives in his harem than the authorities had on record. Those on record are all alive and well, still in the country, and now being taken care of by the Saudi government as is their right." He paused for breath, and Marissa jumped in.

"And?"

"And the ones not on record, but mentioned by the others, are the missing ones. And from what the Mabahith learned, all of them were foreigners who were there against their will. Naturally, the Saudi government doesn't want to know anything about these women—it could cause an international incident if the world learned that a member of the royal family had been participating in human trafficking."

Marissa made a derisive noise, and Brandt raised his eyebrows.

She said, "As if they weren't all…"

"Irrelevant," Brandt said firmly. "My point is that the household staff must know something. If nothing else, they know what the missing women looked like, and probably something about where they came from, maybe. I want you to go over there and talk to the staff, see if you can pick up a lead on the women, and then find and question them."

Brandt observed that both Josh and Marissa were looking uncertain. He went on. "I'll arrange matters so you won't be stopped. Trust me on that. See if you can find out who these women were, where they came from, maybe get pictures of them or use ID software to make sketches. Find out about that dog, and most important of all, show them Rex's picture and see if anyone recognizes him.

"You may as well be prepared to stay on this mission indefinitely, because you're looking for a needle in a haystack."

"And that's worth it to you, John?" Marissa made her voice tender as she asked.

Brandt ignored Josh as he captured Marissa's eyes with his. "You know it is. If he's dead, I can accept that. But if he's alive, I want to know why he hasn't reported in. Maybe he thinks we were involved in that ambush. I don't know the reason, but we don't leave our people behind, ever. I'd do the same for you, or Josh, or any of us. I need closure, Marissa."

Chapter Fourteen

Eastern Europe

Seven months previously

Rex had been searching for some peace and quiet ever since leaving Saudi Arabia with seven of Mutaib's pleasure wives. He'd sent them on their way to their homes, scattered across Western Asia and Eastern Africa, then escorted Rehka Gyan home to her parents in India, the original purpose for his raid on Mutaib's harem. From there, he'd traveled to Thailand and then Peru. In both he found trouble or trouble found him—he wasn't sure which.

After Peru, a vacation to the southern Pacific island paradise of Vanuatu was also interrupted, when he had to help a French girl, Margot Lemaire, the paramour of the French president, avert a major scandal which threatened to become a major international incident.

By the end of the saga, as a token of their appreciation

for what Rex did to help them, a grateful Margot Lemaire, the French president, and his prime minister insisted on rewarding him with a commission in the French Foreign Legion and French citizenship by *Français par le sang verse*, 'French by spilled blood'. It could have been dicey—his face in international news clips—but Margot had understood and made sure it was all done in secret on the Lemaire family estate in Lyon, France.

Landing in Austria after his flight from Lyon, he told his canine companion, Digger, that all he wanted was a nice vacation with no drama. His plan was to explore historical sites in several countries before deciding what to do with his life next.

Digger, the big black Dutch Shepherd he'd inherited from his friend Trevor Madigan in the aftermath of the Afghani ambush, yawned widely, as if to say, "What's a vacation with no drama?"

Or maybe he just didn't understand what Rex was going on about, and in any case, it was time for food. In Digger's mind, it was always time for food. Or his kong, his favorite toy, especially when it was stuffed with a treat such as chicken or jerky or some other delicacy. The kong was an oddly-shaped item, part cylinder, part cone, with indentations that made it look like a hard-plastic snowman, with a hole running through it from top to bottom. The only toy ever known that a Dutch Shepherd couldn't destroy in a few minutes, according to Trevor Madigan, Digger's previous owner.

Rex delighted in Digger's absolute ecstasy whenever he saw that kong. It was a special treat, reserved for times when Digger had done especially well, and given sparingly. Digger worked for praise, not treats.

Although Rex understood Digger much better now, he

was often still surprised by a talent or skill he hadn't known the dog had.

"Want to find a park and play, buddy?"

Digger's grin was all the answer Rex needed.

Rex had no particular itinerary. He had no end destination in mind and all the time in the world to get there. He rented a car at the airport, using his new French passport in the name of Rowan Donnelly, tickled that it was a legal document which would stand up to close scrutiny—no need to use one of his expertly-forged ones. He'd landed in Salzburg, with the intention of taking a leisurely tour around the country visiting the World Heritage sites. They ranged from the historic architecture of the Habsburg Empire to prehistoric 'pile dwellings', or stilt-houses in and around the Alps.

Ski season was ending, but the Alps were just as beautiful in spring and summer. Rex thought he might even get in some fishing. He'd enjoyed camping and fishing with his family as a kid and had managed a few fishing trips over the years since. It was a bitter-sweet activity, though. It always reminded him of his family, all lost in the 2004 Madrid railway bombing. That had been the fulcrum event in his life, propelling him into the lifestyle that, now that he thought about it, was the reason he could never have a peaceful vacation. Trouble had an attraction to him like iron filings to a magnet.

Surprisingly, his dread proved unfounded. Rex and Digger romped through Austria into the modern-day Czech Republic, Slovakia, Romania, and Hungary without incident for an entire month. The rich history of the region spanned millennia, and Rex, ever the history scholar, soaked it up. His original interest had been pre-history, and there were plenty of sites to satisfy that interest. Lately, he'd been more interested in how the world had gotten itself into the mess it was in at present.

He'd been making his way clockwise in the region, but he had no interest in visiting Serbia or Bosnia and Herzegovina. Those countries were too troubled for his liking, and he wanted to avoid being sucked into another fight to interrupt his peace.

Another consideration was the likelihood of running into old enemies. Although the chances were slim, why tempt fate?

From Hungary, Rex decided to take a vacation from his vacation. His head was stuffed full of historic sites, and he thought he'd like to get a taste of the beach again, though he had no desire to return to Vanuatu. So, he turned in his rental car in Romania and hopped on a plane to Croatia.

Chapter Fifteen

Manhattan, NY, USA

Seven months previously

Whether it was wisdom or providence no one would know, but Hathaway again approached the Mafia boss, the one who helped them before to keep the supply of drugs to the Mafia going. This time, however, the boss was not so friendly.

The boss greeted Hathaway curtly, didn't ask him to sit, and told him to state his business. Within less than a minute after Hathaway started speaking, the boss lost his temper, took the Cuban cigar out of his mouth and shouted, "Hathaway, stop beating around the bush. I don't have all day to sit and listen to your sulking. Spit it out!"

Hathaway spat it out.

"I can't help you. We don't go around whacking people anymore. In the old days we did, but now we don't." Of course, what the boss said was not true—they still did, and both of them knew it. "I miss the old days."

Hathaway explained that he was not looking for the Mafia to help him in that way, all he wanted was a contact that could be trusted to find the right people and hire them for the job.

The boss glowered at Hathaway through the clouds of cigar smoke for an uncomfortably long time. "Oh, that's what you want. Why couldn't you just say so?" The boss growled.

Hathaway made no reply.

Wordlessly, the boss thumbed through a stack of business cards on his desk, apparently found the one he was looking for, grabbed a pen, and scribbled on a yellow sticky note. He ripped the note off the stack and handed it to Hathaway saying, "Go see this guy. Tell him you have exactly four million two hundred and fifty bucks with you, no more no less. Tell him you want to pay him three sums of money, the first sum is exactly one and a half million, the second is exactly one and a half million one hundred and thirty-five, the third exactly one million one hundred and fifteen. Got it?"

Hathaway nodded and asked, "Then what?"

"What do you mean then what?"

"Well, what happens after I've told him that?"

"How thick are you? You pay the money; the man will ask you what you want done. The money you pay is a non-refundable introduction fee, and the sums are the signal that I sent you. I get half and this man gets half. You tell him what you want done, he will think about it for a few days, tell you how much it's going to cost and his terms and conditions. If you agree, you'll pay fifty percent of the contract price up front, non-refundable, and the balance when the job is done. I get ten percent of it. Any more stupid questions?"

Hathaway shook his head, thanked the boss, and left.

He sighed in relief when he got outside.

Then for the first time he looked at the scribbling on the yellow sticky note and took a deep breath—what were the odds? It was the same name and contact details as on the business card his 'friend' at the party a few nights ago gave him.

Hathaway's mind immediately went into overdrive, *I wonder if I should have that lunch meeting with my friend and find out what his 'introduction fee' would be?*

But he realized that would be a very unwise move, not conducive to his long-term health prospects at all.

Chapter Sixteen

John F. Kennedy Airport, Queens, NY, USA

Six months previously

As he boarded the plane for Vienna, Hathaway was not a happy man. He was unused to being given the runaround, and he hated being at the mercy of other men, especially men who were more powerful than he was, or at least in a position to make him jump through the hoops he normally made others jump through.

It had taken him a month to get an appointment with the banker in Vienna, despite asking the Mafia boss to give him an introduction and speed up the process. He'd heard nothing from the boss, and it pained him to realize that the month had probably been spent on the part of the banker to fully vet him and check out his background.

He felt exposed, irritable, and put out that his request had to be made in person—and in cash—causing him the inconvenience of travel to the supposed bank haven. *Supposed*, he reflected, because he needed no reminder that banking secrecy in Switzerland and Austria was a fallacy. He had enough firsthand experience with so-called offshore and secret banking to know that anyone who told you otherwise was either lying, inexperienced, or stupid. Bankers in those countries would cooperate with any law enforcement agency that turned up at their banks with a proper warrant.

However, Hathaway was not going to Austria to set up bank accounts or deposit money. He didn't have any bank accounts in Austria. But he did have four million, two hundred, and fifty dollars in a false, lead-lined bottom in his suitcase. It was not for deposit. It was for a coded message to the banker to negotiate a contract he wanted executed.

At first, he'd been surprised to realize that the banker was actually the broker, or middleman, in this deal. But then again, when he gave it more thought, he comprehended what an ideal cover it was, not only that no one would expect a banker to be in this line of business, the banker would also never get his hands dirty. His main job was to receive and distribute money, and for that he had the backing of the Austrian banking privacy laws and could decide which law enforcement agencies he'd cooperate with.

Vienna, Austria

Six months previously

After more than eight hours in the air to dwell on his grievances, Hathaway was ready to throw his weight around and hard put to repress the urge, knowing that if he burned this lead, it might take months to develop another. But, to his surprise, the banker rose to greet him pleasantly by name as Herr Hathaway before he had a chance to introduce himself. He automatically shook the other man's hand when he extended it and felt somewhat mollified by the polite greeting.

The man mumbled that his name was Uwe Krause.

Krause was a small man, thin to the point of looking anorexic. It took only a moment for Hathaway to reassess the greeting as correct, not friendly. He never smiled, nor did his eyes behind thick hornbill glasses show any warmth. It was all business.

Hathaway immediately let the smile fall from his face and became just as correct and polite. He responded to the tilt of Krause's head by reciting what the Mafia boss had told him to say. He handed over the cash in a briefcase, correctly divided into three bundles as directed. Only then did the banker offer him a seat and a cup of coffee, which he accepted.

It was probably the most expensive coffee ever—forget about Kopi luwak, a type of coffee literally made from mouse dung. Luwak, Asian mouse-type creatures living in palm trees, consume the coffee berries, but their digestive systems leave the coffee seeds undigested in their droppings. The luwaks' coffee seed droppings are collected, cleaned, roasted, and ground to make the most expensive coffee in the world at $700 per kilogram.

Hathaway had just paid $4,000,250 for one cup. He wondered if he collected his urine in an hour or so if he would be able to turn that into some kind of exotic beverage and sell it to recoup some of his money.

Without becoming any more nor any less friendly, Krause assumed an interested expression and said, "Now, tell me how I can help you. What is your problem, and how do you want it taken care of? However, before you speak, let me give you my terms. I have the right to walk away from the deal at any time until I accept the down payment for the contract, which we will negotiate at a second meeting. Also, we don't do heads of state, coups, the Pope, the Dalai Lama… in other words, high-profile contracts. I will maintain your confidentiality if one of those is your request. You've bought my silence. However, if your target is on my proscribed list, you can turn around and leave right now—there'll be no refund."

Hathaway did his best to maintain his composure, though the implication that he might have paid over four million dollars for nothing incensed him. Nevertheless, in for four million, in for the rest. Sullenly, he gave the banker Brandt's and CRC's details, such as he had. He didn't include information about his motives, and the banker didn't ask.

"I'll be in touch."

With no other choice, Hathaway left for his hotel to wait.

In keeping with the legend he'd built for himself, he would make the best of it by visiting a few cultural sites in Vienna. There was a lot to see and explore in the capital of Austria, on the Danube River, home to many famous artists and intellectuals such as Mozart, Beethoven, and Sigmund Freud. The city was also known for the illustrious Schönbrunn Palace, the Habsburgs' summer residence, and the Hofburg, which was the official seat of the Austrian President. In addition, there was the St. Stephen's Cathedral, the Spanish Riding School with its famous Lipizzaner horses, the Belvedere Palace, Vienna Zoo (Tiergarten Schönbrunn), and others.

Late on the evening of the first day of waiting, just before implementing a plan to find some company for the night, Hathaway remembered the banker hadn't asked where he was staying or his number. He realized the banker probably knew everything about him and that he was probably being followed, his every move being checked out. He had no tradecraft skills, so he had no idea if that was the case or not. But just in case, and to give the impression he could be trusted to keep the banker's secret, he'd better be on his best behavior—no hookers or booze on this trip.

Two days later, he returned from a late breakfast to find a typed note in an envelope in his hotel room.

The note read, "Tomorrow 10:03 a.m. same place. Be on time."

What a weird time, not 10:00 or 10:05 or 10:15 or 10:30 or a breakfast or lunch meeting—after all, he just paid the guy more than four million—a breakfast or lunch would have been... *nah, not with this guy... it would be more fun having breakfast or lunch with a corpse. So, this guy wants a meeting at 10:03. The banker is a weird man in all manners, not just his looks.*

At the meeting Krause was the same as before. Polite, but distant, not friendly, all business.

"The contract price is five million dollars US; half now and half when the job is done," he said.

Hathaway started to complain about the more than four million he'd already paid. "I understood what I already paid would be the price," he began. "I don't have another two and a half million with me, and another five is outrageous."

Krause, for the first time, had what someone with good detective skills could possibly have interpreted as a smile.

"In my experience, once people have used my *banking*

services, ninety-five percent of them return for more business because of the impeccable service. The four million you paid before was an introduction fee. It was a one-off, and you won't have to pay it again if you want to use our services in the future. The five million is for the contract you want done. If the price is too high—if you cannot afford it —then we have nothing further to discuss."

Disgruntled, Hathaway allowed that he might be able to get the money, assuming it could be done in a way that international banking law or security agencies monitoring financial transactions would not find suspicious. The banker assured him that of course he was competent to arrange it.

With the financial arrangements agreed, he offered Hathaway another coffee, and Hathaway accepted again, reckoning at least that way he had halved the price of the first cup. But he never got around to turning his piss into a drink, so he was still over four million out of pocket for two cups of shitty coffee and just seeing this man's face.

For that kind of money, I should have at least gotten a look at a more beautiful countenance and maybe two cups of mouse-shit coffee.

The rest of the instructions were straightforward. All communication would go through Krause and would remain anonymous through encrypted phones and websites until Brandt had been abducted, and then Hathaway would be notified by the same means. He would then return to Vienna to pay the balance of the contracted price, and, after he'd paid it, he'd be told where he could collect Brandt. Failure to pay the balance would result in 'the package's' death, and he would not be able to use the banker's services in the future.

Chapter Seventeen

Croatia

Two months previously

Rex and Digger landed in Zagreb, the capital of Croatia. He'd explore the country as he drove southwest from Zagreb toward the famous islands of Croatia in the Adriatic Sea. He'd heard Croatia was pleasant at this time of year, warm enough to soak up some sun on the beach, maybe even get some ocean swimming in.

There are between 1,185 and 1,246 of these islands, depending on whose definition of what constitutes an island in Croatian terms one adheres to.

The Hydrographic Institute of the Republic of Croatia categorizes all landforms surrounded by water as an island (*otoci*) if it's bigger than 1 square kilometer, an islet (*otočići*) if it's between 0.1 and 1 square kilometer, or a rock (*hridi*) if it's smaller than 0.1 square kilometer. By their definition there are 1,246, covering a total area of approximately 3,300 square kilometers in the Adriatic Sea on the western side of Croatia.

The tiny Adriatic island of Olib seemed like just the ticket for peace. Very few full-time residents, private beaches, and quaint places to stay—a paradise by all accounts.

It was just unfortunate that a murder occurred there during his visit. Murder investigation wasn't his bailiwick, but the injustice he saw about to happen compelled him to take Digger's opinion into account. Digger knew they had the wrong man and let Rex know about it. Rehka had helped, and eventually the matter was settled to everyone's satisfaction. Everyone's except the victim's, of course, and her hapless lover.

Nevertheless, the incident had spoiled Rex's holiday, and he was anxious to get on with something else to take his mind off the senseless murder. He had finished his business with the perpetrator in Zagreb and moved to Santorini, Greece for another attempt at relaxation, when he received the birth announcement via a special email address.

Margot Lemaire had delivered a baby girl, naming her Rowena after Rex, the man she'd only known as Rowan, who'd helped her avoid an international incident over her little one.

He was oddly pleased by the honor. Rex had never considered he'd be a father, and to be sure, having a child named after a false identity was certainly nothing like being a father. Nevertheless, it touched him. He would send a gift, just as soon as he could get some advice on what would be appropriate for a newborn baby.

He was pretty certain if he'd asked Digger's advice, the answer would have been, "Give her a kong."

Thoughts of fatherhood and how unlikely it was that he'd ever become one turned to thoughts of whether he'd ever have a permanent relationship with a woman. There had been a few whose company he'd enjoyed, a few more who he was certain would be lifelong friends, such as Rehka. He knew Rehka had a sort of crush on him, but he was sure it was simply hero-worshipping, because he'd rescued her.

But one woman, always on his mind, was different from all the others. He'd met the mysterious Catia Romano in Rome, one of the contacts he'd been introduced to through MI6 during his training with CRC. He'd known at the time that there was no romantic future for them. It would have been prohibited, if he'd acted on the attraction he felt for her. He hadn't expressed it at the time, neither did she, but it was there, they both knew it.

It wasn't until he'd met her for the second time, while on a mission in Naples, that he knew she felt it, too. Kissing her goodbye at the end of the mission, neither knowing if they'd see each other again, Rex had promised himself, *maybe another time, another place, when there was no mission.*

Now there was no mission, and he wasn't very far away. But that last meeting had been four years ago. A lot could have happened in four years. She could have left the business. She could be married, even have children by now. He had no way to contact her except in person, and no guarantee he could even find her by now.

But the only way to find out was to go.

After aimlessly wandering for several months, he finally had a purpose. He'd go to Rome and see if he could find Catia. But he wouldn't approach her directly. He had no wish to cause her a problem. He'd disguise himself, watch the *trattoria* where he knew she was a frequent patron, and see what would progress from there.

But he saw no reason to hurry. He spent a few more days planning his travel.

Chapter Eighteen

Dammam, Saudi Arabia

Six weeks previously

It had been nine months since The Old Man again brought up his belief to his agents Josh Farley and Marissa Bisset that there was a chance Rex Dalton was operating on a one-man basis, based on the strange story out of Saudi Arabia. They'd dismissed it then, and had been on the hunt elsewhere, off and on ever since. Off when another mission required their urgent attention, or the attention of one or the other of them.

Josh and Marissa were both pulled off the search for Rex to hunt down Bruce Carson and make sure he would keep his mouth shut about sensitive information he'd learned as head of the CIA. Carson's 'suicide' left him free to return to Brandt's pet project.

Mostly, they now worked as a team because they'd proved so effective on missions requiring a couple. Brandt had taken on more of those since he first put Josh and Marissa together to find Rex and then realized such an asset expanded his potential contracts. But no matter what they were pulled away to do, they always returned to the search for Rex.

Brandt's hope had become an obsession, and he'd finally insisted they check out the Saudi story. There had been more dead ends than they'd cared to remember in their quest to find him, when Josh and Marissa arrived in Saudi Arabia.

They'd started in Saudi Arabia through semi-official channels. Even rival security groups sometimes cooperated when they had aligned interests. Of course, officially, the Saudis wanted to find the man who killed their prince and the women to silence them. Unofficially, the Saudis wanted the whole episode buried and forgotten. Josh and Marissa knew they had to go about it in a very circumspect manner so as not to give away the real purpose of their mission. So, they created the impression that they were interested in Prince Mutaib's business dealings.

This was the last lead they'd follow. Every one of their previous endeavors, nine months of sporadic searching in India, Pakistan, Afghanistan and other places in the middle East, had produced nothing. They still had no clue if Rex was even alive, much less where he was hiding if so. Both were highly doubtful about their chances of turning up anything better this time. To be honest, they were reluctant to even go to the Kingdom of Saudi Arabia to investigate what Marissa called "a fairytale about a super hero and a djinn."

They only did it because The Old Man insisted and because they thought it might just serve the purpose of proving to him that Rex was indeed not among the living anymore and had nothing to do with Prince Mutaib's death.

Prior to their arrival, the Old Man had pulled all the strings to assure the cooperation of the Saudi authorities.

They didn't give their real names or their real employer's identity and didn't even appear in their real appearances. So much could be done with cheek inserts, hair dye, contact lenses, and a slight change to vocal pitch, inflection, accent, and gait.

The men to whom they spoke appreciated Marissa's modesty in both her clothing and demeanor, which was what gave her access to the legal widows of Mutaib. And it was that which gave them their first breakthrough in all the months of fruitless efforts. Over the next two weeks, Marissa was able to question the widows.

Marissa had photos of Rex with her, and two of the women recognized him from the images. One was certain, as she'd been the official hostess for the early part of the dinner party the first night Rex visited—before Mutaib offered 'special entertainment'. The other had only glimpsed him from a distance as he, the dog, and the women who'd escaped raced through the halls of the harem.

It was the first lead they'd had that this wasn't just the Old Man's wishful thinking. Rex was indeed alive, or he had been when he annihilated Mutaib and his henchmen and took seven pleasure wives out of the harem. The narratives about the big black dog or djinn, which the widows confirmed was there with Rex, were still a puzzle. But Josh and Marissa soon realized it didn't matter much, they had the confirmation they were looking for—dog or djinn or none of those, Rex was alive at the time of the raid.

The Old Man's joy was poignant when he got the news. So much so that Marissa told Josh after they'd ended the call that if she didn't know better, she'd think Rex was Brandt's own son.

Further questioning of the women pieced together some vague descriptions, information about the names of the seven, and the nationalities of a few of them. It turned out that the legal wives weren't very interested in the pleasure wives. They saw some of them as rivals, and below their notice.

Josh was able to extract more useful information about the seven women from his contact in the Mabahith. It just so happened that Josh had helped Saleh al-Mufti, a Mabahith agent, escape a life-threatening situation a few years before. For his forbearance, Josh had earned Saleh's debt. It was time to call in that marker.

From Saleh, Josh learned a lot more about Mutaib. It seemed the Mabahith kept secret files on the international arms dealer. His business was quasi-legal. That is, he had a license to sell weapons in Saudi Arabia. However, he'd used that privilege to expand his business far beyond legal limits, and the Mabahith kept records in case it became necessary to bring him down one day.

Their records had names, pictures, and country of origin for all seven of Mutaib's pleasure wives who'd escaped as well as those who didn't. But, unfortunately, no physical addresses, except for the hometowns of three of them; Hande Avci from Bolaman in northern Turkey with a population of a little over 5,000, Zoya Egziabher from Addis Ababa, the capital of Ethiopia with a population of

3.8 million, and Rehka Gyan from the village of Bilaspur, in central India with a population of a little over 300,000.

According to the files, Hande Avci apparently arrived in Saudi Arabia six years before, as a young, naïve, and inexperienced seamstress in search of a better life. A man had come to her village to recruit factory workers, and Hande had responded. But the agent told her many lies, wooing her with tales of independence and a good living in Saudi Arabia. On arrival, the agent sent her to a factory owner under the *kafula* system, meaning the factory owner had paid the agent, and she was now obligated to pay the owner back for her passage to Saudi Arabia and the room and board he provided. The long and short of it, it seemed, was that she couldn't pay and was eventually sold to prince Mutaib bin Faisal bin Saud as a pleasure wife. The information from that point onward was a bit murky, but seemingly Hande had displeased Mutaib for some reason or another and had been relegated to entertaining the prince's guests.

As for Zoya Egziabher there was no more information, other than that she was from Addis Ababa.

Rehka Gyan's information on file indicated she was a graduated software engineer. Apparently, she'd borrowed money from a loan shark to pay for her university studies. She couldn't repay her debt and entered into an indentured servitude agreement with the loan shark. It was a practice forbidden in India, but that didn't prevent it from happening. In fact, it was alive and a thriving part of the Indian economy.

The loan shark in turn owed a lot of money to some big shot, by the name of Kabir Patel, in the gang known as the D-Company or Dawood Company. They were a Mumbai underworld organized criminal syndicate founded and controlled by Dawood Ibrahim, an Indian mafia don, drug dealer and wanted terrorist who had built a powerful transnational crime-terror organization, in part from drug proceeds.

The loan shark couldn't pay his debt to Kabir Patel, so the latter had taken Rehka Gyan as payment. Then, as a favor to a visiting Saudi friend, prince Mutaib bin Faisal bin Saud, Patel sold her to him as a pleasure wife for a special price.

How the Mabahith came by all that information while those women were kept in hiding in Mutaib's compound, Marissa and Josh didn't know, didn't ask, and didn't care. They were just grateful that the women, evidently, were free from the bonds of sex slavery and hopefully would be able to help them—if they could find them.

Marissa thought the airports with their security cameras could be a good starting point to find out where and when Rex and his group would have left the country—if that was the way they left.

Josh however, said "Nah, don't think that's how it happened. Rex would never have led his entourage of fugitives and a big black dog through any of the Kingdom's international airports. At least not in one big group, maybe one or two people at a time, but that meant those women would have had to travel without male chaperones, a big no-no in Saudi Arabia. Otherwise it would have taken days while he traveled back and forth to escort them, and that would have risked discovery while they were all still in Saudi. They'd be in prison or worse by now."

Marissa conceded that Josh was right and agreed that there was no point conjecturing about where and how Rex and his charges would have escaped. The fact of the matter was there was a zero percent chance that any of them would still be in Saudi Arabia.

So, Marissa and Josh agreed there was nothing more to be gained by hanging around in the Kingdom of Saudi Arabia, a country neither of them wanted to spend any time in unless they had to. They would have to track down the women and question them as to Rex's whereabouts or plans. They could only hope at least one of them would know.

Chapter Nineteen

Santorini, Greece

Four weeks previously

Rex's original travel plans from Croatia had been to take a ferry across to northern Italy, starting in Venice, and spend some time traveling south to Rome. He told himself that it had been that way, even before he'd thought of checking up on Catia. If he'd been honest with himself, he'd have known Catia's presence in Rome was a stronger magnet than even the historic sites that awaited his exploration.

However, the unpleasant business on Olib had sent him back to Zagreb, in the interior, and thence to Santorini by air. Since deciding to start a tour of Italy in Venice and make his way to Rome via some of the historic cities on the way, he'd discovered that driving wasn't going to be his best option in Italy, as the historic parts of the cities didn't allow cars and were very walkable. That suited him just fine, and

Digger as well. They'd take the train system and make no firm plans.

The other issue was how to get to Venice. He could fly, but where was the adventure in that? He could take a catamaran to the mainland and then drive, but that took him through Serbia, where he'd already determined he didn't have an interest in going. He could even fly to Rome and take his trip backwards, but since he wanted to see what would happen with Catia, he wanted to *end* with Rome, not begin.

In the end, he decided to do what would have made no sense to anyone but him and take that ferry trip he'd planned a few months ago. It departed from Split-Acona, Croatia and took a leisurely nine hours to get to Venice. There were shorter times for the ferry and closer routes, but he was in no hurry.

Furthermore, what amused him was that he could actually fly from Santorini to Split – via *Oslo*! Or he could fly to Zagreb and drive or take a bus to Split. The flight would take about the same length of time either way. Driving would add about four hours, but again, he was in no hurry, and neither was Digger. However, they'd already driven through the most interesting parts of Croatia when traveling to Olib. Oslo it was.

"What do you think, Digger? We're about to travel over twenty-seven hundred miles to get from here to Venice – a distance of nine-hundred and twenty-four miles as the crow flies."

Digger's expression might have meant, "That makes about as much sense as flying over the North Pole to get from New York to Hong Kong." Rex smiled. Of course, Digger's expression meant nothing of the sort. That was his own fancy, and in fact, it did make more sense to take the polar route in that case. In this case, maybe it was crazy, but it was in fact the quickest way, even though, as he reminded himself once more, he was in no hurry. His plans were all set. It was time to make the reservations.

It was only later that he asked Digger to help him figure out exactly *why* he was in no hurry and why he was making all these convoluted travel arrangements.

Chapter Twenty

NSA Bahrain, Manama, Bahrain

Three weeks previously

Before leaving the region to search for and interview the women who'd escaped from Mutaib's harem, Josh and Marissa made a side trip to Bahrain, where they'd previously interviewed a surviving member of the ill-fated Phoenix Unlimited group, seven of whom had died in the ambush thought to have killed Rex Dalton.

If it was true that Rex was now working with a dog, the question was where, how, and why had Rex acquired a canine companion? But the answer was surprisingly simple to find. All along, they'd been tracking down and questioning any former employees of Frank Millard's outfit, Phoenix Unlimited, the outfit that had been contracted as Rex's support during his Afghanistan mission. They hadn't asked about a dog before, but now they returned to some of the people they'd already questioned and asked the obvious question.

Had Rex had a dog before the ambush?

One of them had been a friend of Trevor Madigan, Digger's original handler, and he'd mourned both Trevor and Digger after the attack. When Josh and Marissa asked him, they got a question in return.

"Why are you asking?"

Josh looked at Marissa, who raised one eyebrow. He turned back to the man and said, "We've got a lead on Rex Dalton. It seems he may have survived that attack. We don't know whether he has amnesia, or whether he has his own reasons for not reporting in, but we have reports that the man we think is him is traveling with a big, black dog. We're trying to figure out when he got it."

The man, a rugged-looking Aussie with a scar across his left cheek, a shock of dirty-blond hair, and a wild look in his blue eyes, choked back a sob. "Fair dinkum that's him! It's that dish licker, Digger, I'd bet my life on it."

"Digger?" Marissa prompted.

He smiled, "Yes, Digger. He's a Dutch Shepherd, a big black one. And a nasty son of a bitch if he doesn't like you." The man showed with his hands about two feet above the ground. "In Australia the troops are called 'Diggers'. It comes from World War One with the trench warfare – the Aussies, because of their skills as miners, were the ones who designed and dug those trenches. And although way back it could have been a derogatory term, it isn't anymore. The Aussies love and respect their Diggers just as much as you Americans love and respect your troops."

Josh and Marissa nodded.

The Aussie continued. "But let me tell you about the best friend I ever had. Trevor Madigan. We were in SAS together, and we mustered out together. He was allowed to keep his dog, Digger. That was the smartest dish licker I've ever seen. Smarter than a lot of humans I know. Would you believe it? He could climb trees! And he had a vocabulary bigger than a kid's. Knew hundreds of commands."

"And you think the dog Rex has now is Digger? Why would Madigan give it away?"

Their informant wiped a big hand down his face and shook his head, obviously gripped by a powerful emotion. "He wouldn't have. That dog was like a brother to him, or a son. But Trevor was on that mission. The only thing that would make Digger be with anyone else would be if Trevor was killed, which we all believed he was. So, either the man you think is Rex Dalton is actually Trevor Madigan, or Trevor is dead, and Digger is now with this Rex Dalton you're talking about. Digger wouldn't be with anyone else if Trevor were alive, that much I'm sure of."

He looked up, hope in his face. "Could it be Trevor you're following, instead of Rex?"

"What did Trevor look like?"

"A bit like me, I guess. Light brown hair, blue eyes." He smiled and added, "Not as handsome, though. He didn't have this decoration." The man winked and ran a finger down his scar. "Looked like a kid, he did."

Marissa liked the guy. She liked most of the Aussies she'd ever met. They were a happy-go-lucky lot, for the most part. Good-natured at least, always up for fun or cracking a joke. A bit mischievous at times. And that Aussie slang some of them used was always amusing.

She hated to burst this one's bubble.

"I'm sorry," she said regretfully, shaking her head and showed him a photo of Rex.

They left the man crestfallen after his moment of hope.

As they turned to leave, he asked if they'd let him know if they found Digger. They promised they would but knew they probably couldn't. If Rex were alive, dog or no dog, he clearly didn't want to be found. They'd honor that wish as far as outsiders were concerned. Only they, John Brandt, and whoever Brandt or Rex chose to tell would ever know. But they'd pass along the request.

It was up to Rex.

Chapter Twenty-One

Bolaman, Turkey

Two weeks previously

Josh and Marissa caught an international flight from Manama, the capital of Bahrain to Istanbul, Turkey and after a day's layover caught a domestic flight to Ordu–Giresun Airport. The airport was one of three airports in the world built on an artificial island in the sea. They rented a car at the airport and drove the thirty-six kilometers to Fatsa, only a few kilometers away from Bolaman. There were no hotels in Bolaman, so they booked into the 3-star Yildiz Apart Hotel in Fatsa.

The confirmation that Rex was alive and the information about the pleasure wives they'd collected in Saudi Arabia had invigorated the two of them. That night, over dinner, Marissa expressed the hope that they'd be able to track Hande Avci down quickly, within a day or two, have a chat with her, and soon be on their way to find Rex Dalton and his dog or djinn.

Josh tried to share in her optimism but couldn't help to point out that in his experience, missions seldom work out exactly as planned.

And of course, Marissa, although she was a trained CRC agent and knew he was right, couldn't help but admonish him for being negative.

They were up bright and early the next morning, had breakfast in the hotel's in-house restaurant and then drove the twelve kilometers along the Black Sea from Fatsa to Bolaman.

Josh wondered out loud why it was called the Black Sea if it wasn't black but a rather unappealing greyish blue. "I see no black. Do you?"

Marissa smiled and launched into a brief history lesson. "Due to the difficulty navigating it and the hostile tribes inhabiting its shores, the Greeks originally called it the 'Inhospitable Sea'. However, over time as they tamed and colonized the shores, they'd changed their minds and renamed it to the 'Hospitable Sea'.

"As for the reason it's called the Black Sea today, there are two hypotheses. The first one is that metal objects, plant, and animal matter that sunk in these waters soon become covered with a black sludge, which is due to the high concentration of hydrogen sulfide in the sea. The second one is that sailors called it the Black Sea due to the severe storms experienced in winter. During the buildup to those storms the water is so dark it looks black."

Josh smiled and nodded. "Thanks Marissa, that was very instructive. I get the impression you can be a teacher if this CRC job doesn't work out for you."

"Yeah right," she retorted, "I can just see myself in front

of a class full of rebellious, supercilious, all-knowing teenagers. I'd much rather stick needles into my eyeballs or hang a millstone around my neck and throw myself into the Black Sea."

Josh chuckled. "Okay, okay I get it, we won't inflict you upon the poor kids then."

A few minutes later they arrived in the coastal town of Bolaman in the Ordu Province of Turkey. According to Marissa, the town was named after Polemon, a governor of Ordu during the era of the Roman Empire.

They'd decided the night before that the best place to start the search for Hande Avci or her family would be at the markets, of which there were a few in close proximity to each other.

It turned out to be easy to find the markets but not so easy to be understood by the locals. The Turks don't speak Arabic, which both Marissa and Josh could. And in this remote location almost no one spoke English either. Turkish was part of the Ural-Altaic linguistic languages, related to Finnish and Hungarian.

Marissa's plan to use a translation app on her phone to translate from English to Turkish and show the translation to the person they were talking to on the phone's screen quickly landed them in hot water.

The first man they approached looked at the screen, tsk-tsked, turned away, and mumbled a string of single syllable words, which they didn't need to understand in order to tell they'd been sworn at in Turkish.

They tried again, and this time they showed the screen to a hulking man with a blood-smeared apron behind the counter of a butcher's shop. He had a meat-cleaver in his hand and was busy mutilating a piece of meat. His whole demeanor said he was not the kind who would be entering any geniality contests, let alone winning any of them. However, despite his menacing looks, Josh was of the opinion that they'd done nothing to upset the man, they'd come in peace, and perhaps a man who could destroy meat with so much gusto might just be able to speak English. But Josh was about to find out how bad a judge of character he was, at least with Turkish butchers.

The butcher had one look at the screen, uttered a ghastly sound, dropped the meat-cleaver, grabbed his butcher's knife—which resembled a sword more than it did a knife—and stormed around the counter toward Josh and Marissa, who were already making their way to the door with great haste. Fortunately, they had a head start and also moved much easier than this gorilla. The man hurled at their retreating backs what the two of them were sure were strings of expletives and profanities which could've, for all they knew, included nasty things about their mothers and their lineage.

When they were a safe distance away and saw the fuming butcher had given up the chase, Josh said, "Marissa, can I have a look at that screen of yours? I get the impression it's something on there that's upsetting these people."

Marissa handed him the phone, and he looked at the screen. In a box on the top of the screen were the English words Marissa had typed in, and it read, 'We are looking for the Avci family. Do you know them?' In the box below that was what Josh assumed were the Turkish words.

"Hmm, nothing untoward about the English. The million-dollar question is how did the app translate that? Let me see if I reverse the translation." Josh copied the Turkish words to the box at the top and selected to translate it to English from the dropdown menu. He blinked a few times when he read it, looked at Marissa in feigned shock and said, "Another job you shouldn't consider doing…"

"Translator at the United Nations?" She started smiling.

"Yep. Definitely not if you are going to rely on this app to help you. I hope you didn't pay for it."

Marissa grabbed the phone out of his hand, read the translation and started laughing. "Yeah, well I guess asking a man when was the last time he slept with his camel could be upsetting…"

Josh nodded. "Especially if it's a sensitive kind of man, like that butcher."

They enjoyed the hilarious interlude for a little while and then got serious again. They had to find a way to communicate with these people or they were stranded. Marissa wasn't ready to give up on her translation app as yet, so she decided it might be better to just use a single word. So, she typed in the word 'English' followed by a question mark and started showing that to people. They got about ten or so shaking heads and then one person who gestured for them to follow him. The man kept on babbling and talking with his arms and hands as he led them through the passages between stalls. Of course, they had no idea what the man was saying, he looked friendly though, so they followed but made sure to keep a safe distance in case they had to beat another hasty retreat.

Josh mumbled, "For all I know, this guy could be taking us to someone with a gun. How the hell would I know what he's saying?"

Marissa replied, "Maybe he's telling us about his lovely wife and family and how happy he is to see us and wondering if we would like to honor him and his family to come over for a shish-kebab dinner tonight."

"Yeah right, or he could be cursing the insufferable Americans who can't even speak a decent language. And that it's time to make an example of them by having them shot by his friend. The one with the twelve-gauge shotgun under the counter of his shop, locked and loaded for just such an occasion."

Before they could debate any further about what the man was saying, he turned into one of the stalls selling leather jackets, leather bags, and various other leather paraphernalia. There was a young woman in attendance, and to their relief, she looked very friendly and unarmed.

Their helper spoke to the woman in Turkish, and she nodded, smiled, approached them, and to their relief addressed them in perfect English, with a bit of a British accent, saying, "Good morning. My name is Miray. My friend here says you might be looking for someone who could speak English?"

Marissa looked as if she was about to embrace this woman. "Yes, thank you. It would be great if you could help us."

Miray said, "I will try, my English might not be good, but let's try."

Marissa said to her, "Your English is perfect. Where did you learn to speak it?"

"I worked as an *au pair* for a family in the UK for a few years."

She and Josh thanked Miray for taking the time to talk to them and then continued to explain that they were looking for the Avci family who apparently lived in this area.

Miray started smiling. "Yes, I know them very well, in fact. I went to school with one of the Avci children, Hande Avci."

Josh felt as if they'd reached the pot of gold at the end of the rainbow.

Marissa asked, "It would be so kind if you could tell us where we could find her…"

But Josh had noticed the expression of sadness that settled on Miray's face. "She does live around here, doesn't she?"

Miray explained that Hande's parents lived not too far away, but not Hande. Marissa's and Josh's moods soon started turning from expectation to dejection as Miray told them that Hande had left for Saudi Arabia about six years ago in search of a better life. Miray told them that Hande was never happy in Bolaman. She was not happy with how her parents and siblings treated her, didn't like the town or its people, and all throughout their school years had confided in Miray that she was going to leave this place as soon as she was old enough.

Marissa pulled out the photo of Hande she had with her and showed it to Miray who confirmed that it was the same person they were talking about.

It looked as if Miray was relieved to see that photo. She asked, "When was that photo taken?"

"Hmm." Marissa feigned deep thought and then answered, "About a year or so ago, if I remember correctly."

"That's the first good news about Hande in a long time. It means she *is* alive. Well, at least a year ago she was. I've not seen her or heard from her since the day she left… I see her parents and siblings often, and I always ask them if they've heard anything about Hande, but they've also had no contact with her. It's sad." She sighed.

Marissa nodded, "Yes, as far as I know she is alive. I am the one who took that photo."

Miray showed signs of suspicion. "Who are you and why are you looking for Hande? Has she done something wrong? Are you police?"

Marissa and Josh were prepared for a situation like this. Josh left the conversation and started browsing the leather jackets, trying some of them on as if he were going to buy some of them, which he was going to do.

Marissa took over and used all her tact and acumen to put Miray at ease again and persuaded her that they were not police or government or anything that Miray had to worry about. She told Miray that she, Marissa, worked for an aid organization in Saudi Arabia and had met Hande there. They'd known each other for about three months or so and became friends. But then one day Hande told her she was going back home to her family for a holiday. They were going to catch up when she was back, but it was now almost a year later, and she'd had no contact with Hande and was worried about her.

Fortunately, Miray bought the story and relaxed, but she said she was sorry she had no more information about Hande.

"Not even rumors about what had become of her?" Marissa asked.

Miray shrugged, "Yes, but I have no way of knowing if there is any truth in them."

"Like what?" Marissa asked.

"That she was sold into slavery in Saudi Arabia. But from what you are saying that one has been laid to rest.

"There was another one, much more positive. About ten or so months ago a person from here whom I know very well said he saw Hande in Ankara. The man said he spoke to her, and although she recognized him and spoke to him, she was aloof and didn't want to tell him where she lived and what she was doing for a living. Neither did she want to send any message to her family back here. The man said she looked in good condition and she was wearing expensive clothes."

"Can you perhaps take us to this man or tell us where we can find him?" Marissa asked.

Miray smiled, pulled her mobile phone out, scrolled through her contacts, and called a number. A few seconds later, she was talking to someone in Turkish. When the call ended, she told Marissa that the man she had called was her uncle. He was the one who'd seen Hande in Ankara. He had a grocery stall at the end of the market, and he'd agreed to come over to her stall in about twenty minutes.

She offered Josh and Marissa seats and Turkish coffee.

Half an hour later, when Miray's uncle arrived, Josh and Marissa were each the proud owner of an elegant handmade genuine suede leather jacket costing them less than $50 USD, which would have set them back on the order of $500 USD or more back in the US.

Miray's uncle was a friendly man and tried his best to please them by answering, through Miray as interpreter, the barrage of questions from Josh and Marissa. In the end, when they left, they were reasonably sure that the uncle truly had seen Hande in Ankara, and he'd given them the name and address of the shopping mall where he met her. But exciting as it might have been, that was it—they were no closer to finding Rex Dalton than they'd been when they'd left their hotel that morning.

Josh refrained from reminding Marissa about his statement that plans seldom go as planned, but Marissa, in a the-glass-is-half-full mood, said, "Well, at least we sorted that out in less than a day."

"Yes, we did, just like you wished." Josh quipped, "Now we just have to find Hande among the five million inhabitants of Ankara. Piece of cake. Right?"

Marissa playfully punched him in the arm and told him to concentrate on his driving.

Chapter Twenty-Two

Venice, Italy

Two weeks previously

The flight and the ferry ride were unremarkable, so Rex and Digger found themselves in Venice. After enough sight-seeing, taking in St. Mark's Basilica, the Doge's Palace, and the Rialto Bridge, Rex knew he'd enjoy the romantic city and lazy gondola rides with female company. Digger was a wonderful companion, but an arm around him just didn't evoke the same mood as an arm around a beautiful woman.

Like Catia?

Why are you dragging your feet?

Was it because he was afraid he'd find she'd moved on? Or that he wouldn't find her at all? Or that she'd not even remember him?

Shut up and enjoy the trip, he answered himself.

From Venice, they went to Bologna, a three-thousand-year-old city, the capital of northern Italy's Emilia-Romagna region. It boasted not only the oldest university in Europe, attended by famous people such as Dante and Boccaccio, it also had one of the best quality-of-life ratings in Italy. The historic city center had centuries-old piazzas, surrounded by churches, towers, and porticoes topped by terracotta tile roofs.

Rex would have loved to explore the city and surroundings for several weeks, but something urged him to move on after only a few days.

Florence, the cradle of the Renaissance and capital of the Tuscany region was next, with its red-tile roofs, cathedrals, and museums. Digger wasn't allowed into the museums and cathedrals, of course, and it was disappointing he couldn't even go into the lovely Bardini Gardens on a leash and even with a promise that Rex would pick up after him. It seemed Italy's museums and historic sites were not the places to visit with a dog, even one as well-behaved and clever as Digger, though he was welcome and smiled at wherever else they went, even in restaurants.

While staying in Florence, Rex wanted to see the breathtaking Tuscan countryside. Driving a rental car while there, Rex argued with himself. Was it really such a good idea to visit Catia? What if *she* was involved in a mission? Would he distract her? Would his presence endanger her?

And another thought: *What about your own cover? If you reveal to her who you are, it could be a problem—she's probably under obligation to report to her handlers every person she makes contact with.*

But you're going to be in disguise, she won't recognize you.

And what's the use of that?

Well, at least I would've seen her again.

Yeah and then?

Dunno, one thing at a time.

Now he was not only talking to himself but answering back and arguing with himself. Some psychologists would probably have told him it's okay to talk to yourself, but it could be dangerous if you hear voices talking back to you. But Rex wasn't fussed about psychoanalytical babble. He'd been a loner most of his adult life, kept his own council, and when he didn't discuss personal matters with himself, he'd been discussing them with Digger since they'd teamed up.

Since he'd unilaterally declared himself 'dead' and dropped out of the assassin business, he'd regarded it as his prerogative to change his mind as often as he wanted to. *After all, what is a mind if you can't change it?* He often asked himself.

Therefore, when it came to Catia, from one day to the next, he changed his mind three times, at least. He knew he was acting irrationally. He'd noticed that Digger had started studying him with a quizzical look in his dark brown eyes, or maybe the dog was worried about him, which triggered another wordless session.

Have I been talking out loud to myself?

You can't remember? That's a bit of a worry.

Am I going nuts?

What do you think?

Would I even remember any of the sights I've seen, or where I've gone in Italy?

Probably not.

You might as well admit it; this woman has really bedazzled you.

This time there was no response. But Rex took the hint.

In Perugia, a town in the Umbria region, a little over two hours by train from Rome, he turned in his rental car, got back on the train with Digger, and headed for Rome, even though he still hadn't decided precisely what to do when he got there.

Chapter Twenty-Three

Bilaspur, India

Ten days previously

Shortly after starting the drive to Ankara, Marissa had agreed with Josh that even if they ended up returning to Turkey afterward, the better use of their time at this point would be to track down Rehka Gyan, whose home town population was only three hundred thousand, compared to the five million in Ankara. They were months behind Rex, if their information was correct, and the passage of time was now very much on their minds. The trade-off was simple: fewer people to sort through, less time lost in the search. And if Miss Gyan could point them to the where-abouts of either Rex or Hande, so much the better. The odds were with them.

Accordingly, they diverted their route at Merzifon and drove instead to Istanbul, where they caught a flight to

Nagpur, India. There, they rented a car and drove the four hundred kilometers to Bilaspur. Before leaving Istanbul, Marissa contacted CRC's graphic artist and asked for some images to be mocked up. She would have them printed out when they reached Nagpur, if her colleague could work her Photoshop magic in time.

Her request was to have images of Rex, Josh, and herself superimposed to appear together, preferably in scenes where they looked like friends, not mug shots. She ignored the video image of her graphic artist friend smiling broadly as she said the last. CRC name badges, used on-site at the Arizona compound only, did look very much like face-forward mug shots. No one wanted to look friendly among a group of bad-asses like the CRC operatives. But the artist assured her, there were plenty of images on file. This wasn't even an unusual request, as legends sometimes had to be created to include 'family' photos. She had plenty of material.

Marissa's second request, though, was a bit more challenging. She had two images of Rehka from the Mabahith files, and in both, Rehka was wearing Muslim garb, though fortunately her face was not fully covered. If the artist could somehow put Rehka and either Josh or Marissa together in a photo mockup with the same type of friendly scenarios, it would be nothing short of a miracle, or so she flattered her friend. That way, they could convince the people they asked about Rehka that they were friends, avoiding suspicion and eliciting help. The artist, not immune to flattery, said she'd do her best.

The result was the miracle Marissa had hoped for. In one of the photos, which looked like snapshots, Rehka was even smiling fondly at her 'friend' Marissa. Armed with the photoshopped pictures they'd had printed before leaving

Nagpur, Marissa and Josh took to the streets, asking at shops and the marketplace if anyone knew Rehka or her family.

Their initial confidence turned sour when they learned there were many Gyans in Bilaspur and surrounding areas, and they were all distantly related. They met a few members of the extended family, who confirmed that assessment, but most of them did not know to which branch of the family Rehka belonged. There were many shrugs and protestations that the person talking to them either didn't know, or 'try this family', with vague directions to yet another home full of three generations of Gyans.

After a few days, Josh remarked that this was almost as tiresome as it would have been to find the right Smith among the half million Smiths who lived in the UK or the almost two and a half million of them living in America.

Marissa pointed out that Bilaspur had only 300,000 people, they were not all named Gyan. She then told him to stop complaining, remain positive, and continue doing his job of asking everyone on the street about Rehka Gyan.

Josh mumbled something which sounded like, "I'm going to kick Dalton's ass for putting me through all of this when I see him."

It took ten days of frustrating street work and lead-chasing before they found someone who knew something. All the others they'd questioned were correct, he claimed. They were all related, but the family was so large that they couldn't possibly know everyone. However, he knew the woman in their picture. He described a relationship that Marissa reckoned was that of a third or fourth cousin, whom he hadn't seen in years. However, because her family was so poor, she was remarkable and known more widely in their branch of the family—honest but poor farmers of the Vaishya caste—for being very clever, an educated woman.

Even better, he knew who her parents were, and where they lived.

Josh and Marissa followed the cousin's directions, driving out of Bilaspur on a dirt track that led past endless rows of rice paddies. Marissa remarked, "No wonder they call this region the 'rice bowl' of India."

Eventually, they came to a village where the houses were jammed together on small lots. The Gyans' little house was in the center of a street on the outskirts of the village. It was a low rectangle, with a shallow peaked roof of curved terra cotta tiles.

A wooden door of rough-hewn planks in the exact center of the wall facing the street and one window, shuttered, were the only features in the mud-plastered wall. However, the roof overhung the house all along the front, supported by crooked wooden posts set in a knee-high wall and forming a veranda of sorts.

Josh knocked on the door, and a very, very skinny, very, very old man, with a very wrinkled face and not a single tooth in his mouth opened it. He was dressed in a white *dhoti*, a traditional garment made from a single rectangular length of cloth, wrapped and pleated then belted to form a sort of trouser. Over it, a threadbare white shirt billowed around him, suggesting he'd once been more corpulent.

And there their language woes started again. Marissa's mobile phone app was of no use this time. These people couldn't read, let alone speak a second language. Marissa spoke hesitantly. "Mr. Gyan?"

The old man's wizened face broke into what could only be a smile, though so surrounded by wrinkles that it looked as if his face might crack into a thousand pieces. He invited them into the house with gestures, and with more gestures, he introduced them to an old woman whom they thought must be the old man's wife, though she looked much younger than him. The woman, with similar gesticulations, offered them tea. Josh was embarrassed to accept an offer from people in such obvious poverty, but Marissa spoke in a low voice and told him they should accept so as to not offend the Gyans. Then the old man signaled to them to remain seated and keep on drinking their tea and left.

"Where's he going?" Marissa asked, as if Josh had more information than she did.

"Hopefully to get someone who can speak English," Josh answered.

He was right. Ten minutes later, the old man was back with a girl who might have been in her mid to late teens. She spoke English, with an Indian accent, but it was perfect.

"How may my grandfather help you?"

They showed her one of the photos of Rehka, and she showed it to the older couple, with a flood of musical language neither could speak. They got very excited and spoke over each other, until the girl held up her hand for them to stop so she could translate. "That is their daughter," she informed Josh and Marissa. "How do you know her?"

With a pre-determined story and the photoshopped photos, Marissa soon had the couple convinced they were old friends of their daughter's. She explained they had lost touch with Rehka and were looking for her and a man she knew. They showed them the photo with themselves, Rehka, and Rex together, a bonus picture the graphic artist had thought to include.

The granddaughter didn't bother to ask this time. "This is our friend Ruan."

She had to shush the old couple as they got very excited again, while explaining that this was the man who'd saved her aunt and brought her back from the dead.

"Ruan and his dog did that. The dog has a name, but we can't remember what it was."

Concealing her curiosity about the name Ruan, Marissa asked about the dog. The granddaughter continued to translate as the old man gave a long account of how clever that big black dog was and how he was convinced that dog could speak and that was apart from being able to climb into a tree and from there onto the roof of his house. When Marissa expressed surprise, the granddaughter told her proudly that she had seen the dog climb the tree with her own eyes, along with a large number of her cousins.

"Rehka was very private about her life," Marissa said. "Tell us more about her. She will be so surprised when we see her."

The simple folk never guessed that they were being pumped for information a true friend would already have known. Gyan told them how proud he was that his daughter had entered Kurukshetra University and graduated with top honors. His wrinkled face grew sad when he mentioned that after university, although she had a job, she could not pay her living costs and student debt. She entered indentured servitude to work off her debt, and that's when she disappeared. And were it not for Ruan, they would never have seen her again.

He and his wife now spoke in turns to say that Ruan had visited them a few times before he rescued their daughter, and then when he brought her back from a very far place, he visited them a few more times. The old man told them how the two of them played Chaturanga, the ancient game some believed was the predecessor of modern-day chess. The old man gave a toothless grin as he apparently remembered the fun he and Ruan had at playing the game and said Ruan was hopeless at it in the beginning but learned quickly, and eventually, in the last few games they'd played, he'd beaten the old man.

Nodding, laughing, and smiling was all Marissa and Josh could do to pretend to be amused by these anecdotes and in no hurry to know other information. They were burning to ask where Rehka was. But they had to be polite, hide their urgency and wait, letting the conversation naturally get to the point where it wouldn't be rude to ask.

When the Gyans and their granddaughter finally ran out of stories about their hero, Ruan, and his clever dog, it finally came to that point.

"You want to know where to find Rehka, yes?" the granddaughter asked.

"Yes, please. We won't be in India much longer, and we would like to surprise her and say hello."

After questioning the old couple, she recited an address in Mumbai. Marissa begged the old couple and their granddaughter to promise they wouldn't let Rehka know they were coming, since they wanted to surprise her. The family was happy to play along.

By then, though they were ready to leave, the granddaughter informed them they were invited to have lunch.

They had a long lunch and a few more stories about Rehka and about Ruan and the dog. They were beginning to repeat themselves when Rehka's mother looked a bit embarrassed but nevertheless said it, she would've been a very happy mother if Ruan would marry her daughter.

Marissa didn't show any outward signs of what was going through her mind about the Indian custom of arranged marriages, where it was estimated that eighty percent of them were arranged by the bride and groom's parents. Her western upbringing just couldn't fathom the whole concept, let alone the idea that in India the woman paid the dowry to the man's family. Ever since reading about Indian marriage customs, she'd had a hard time believing that these arranged marriages were in fact more successful than the so-called 'love' marriages. She wondered if it was that Indian parents knew their children so well, they knew who the right partner for their child would be, or if it was a matter of the Indian children growing up with the expectation that their parents would arrange their marriages.

She knew Rex's parents were dead, which meant Mr. and Mrs. Gyan would probably have to negotiate directly with Rex. And she struggled to suppress a smile when she thought, *I wonder how much Rex Dalton would be worth? Or would they have to negotiate with John Brandt who apparently felt like a father about Rex?* She didn't envy them if it ever came to that.

By the time the lunch was over and time to say goodbye, both Josh and Marissa felt a bit guilty in the knowledge that all the stories they'd heard about Rehka, Ruan, and the dog were true, but the stories they told the old couple were all made up, except that they were looking for their daughter. If the couple hadn't been so naïve, so sweet, and so obviously happy to be able to help, they wouldn't have given it a second thought. But these were not the usual informants they dealt with.

Mumbai was at least a day's drive away. When they finally made their escape from the Gyan's hospitality, they set out immediately.

Chapter Twenty-Four

Athens, Greece

The morning after the abduction

The Old Timers gathered early for breakfast in the hotel coffee shop. They'd booked a day-trip excursion to Delphi and were to meet the tour bus at 8:30 a.m. for the two-and-a-half-hour drive. But as they soon discovered, one of their party hadn't heeded the wake-up call.

John Brandt was nothing if not prompt, one of the women observed. She'd been half in love with Brandt for half of her life. They'd never had an affair. Both were married to their calling, and it wouldn't have worked out. But she still kept a corner of her heart open for Brandt after all these years. The others agreed. When Brandt hadn't appeared by eight, one was dispatched to go and wake Brandt by pounding on his door. The others looked at the woman who'd spoken, speculating that she might have been the reason for his deeper-than-usual sleep. She noted their interest and thought it would be funny to put on a too-inno-cent air to make them wonder.

However, all thoughts of elderly hanky-panky left the group as the man who'd been sent to get Brandt came back out of breath.

"He didn't answer," the man panted. "I pounded hard. Someone from the next room stuck his head out the door and yelled at me for waking him and his wife. Something's wrong."

The woman who first noted Brandt's absence stood abruptly and said, "I'll get the manager." As she rushed to the front desk, her thoughts turned dark. *What if John has had a heart attack? Sure, he appears fit and healthy, but he's sixty-eight.* The thought spurred her to break into a trot, and she arrived at the desk looking as she was, distraught.

"Our friend... Jonathan Callen. Can't wake him... Call..." She stopped for breath and tried to collect herself as the bewildered desk clerk stared at her. "Don't stand there with your mouth hanging open! Call his room! And then get your manager! Pronto! Move it."

The flabbergasted clerk hastily dialed Brandt's room, but the phone rang without answer until the voice mail system picked up. While he waited for an answer, he'd pressed a button under the counter to summon someone above his pay-grade.

By the time the manager arrived, Brandt's old friend had pulled herself together. Now she was focused and had assumed the role of leader in a crisis. As soon as she saw the manager hurrying toward them, she stepped away from the desk and gave him a brief status report.

"Our friend was to meet us early for an excursion. He is not answering his door or his room phone. He is sixty-eight years old, and I fear a medical emergency. You must open the door."

The manager never questioned her or protested that her friend might just need some privacy, as he might have done otherwise. He nodded wordlessly, stepped to the elevators, and inserted his emergency override key. By then, two of the men from the group had joined the woman, and the three of them accompanied the manager when he first knocked, then pounded on John Brandt's hotel room door.

They didn't wait for the irascible guest next door to come out and complain. When there was still no answer, the manager used his master key to open the door.

Of all the sights the group expected to see, a bed that hadn't been slept in was the last of them. The woman turned white. The men stared at each other mutely, assessing what to say to the manager. They'd known each other long enough to know what the other was thinking. If they indicated they suspected foul play, the police would be called. It would be awkward to explain why someone would want to kidnap the Old Man without revealing who and what he was and the same for them.

It was the woman who recovered first. Setting a cover story the manager would believe, she flipped from shock to feigned anger. "That *bastard!* I knew there was another woman. To hell with him! I'm done." She stalked out of the room, trusting the men to follow her lead.

One of the men turned to the manager. "I'm sorry for the trouble."

The manager shrugged and shook his head and said something in Greek which in the circumstances could only have been translated as "Hell hath no fury..."

Pretending to be embarrassed for their friend, the man

clapped the manager on the back. "Well, at least one of us is getting some action," he answered.

Downstairs, the woman reached the others first as the men had stayed to make sure the manager locked up and left with no further suspicion. It was inconvenient, because one of them would have to pick the lock later, but that was the least of their worries. By the time the two who'd gone to the room arrived in the coffee shop, the woman had explained the situation to the others. She didn't have to tell them her outburst had been for the manager's benefit only, and there was no way John Brandt would have spent the night with a woman—or anything else he might have done —without letting the others know he wouldn't meet them as planned.

"You all agree, something is seriously wrong, and there will be no day-trip?"

Everyone nodded.

The group moved from the coffee shop to the suite the two women shared, and they reached consensus quickly. They'd do what they knew to do, but CRC had to be notified. One of the men went back to the front desk to quietly ask if the clerk could call his opposite, the man who'd been on duty the night before, to ask if he'd noticed Brandt leaving. The group knew Brandt had taken his nightly walk, but had he come back? The clerk made the call, waking the night clerk, whose initial anger quickly dissolved.

"Yes, I saw Mr. Callen leave the hotel shortly after you all came in from your tour," he said. "But I'm afraid I didn't see when he returned. I went off duty at midnight, though."

"It seems he didn't. But don't worry about it. We are checking. Please forgive the disturbance."

The next call gleaned similar results, but the clerk who'd relieved the first one at midnight had just gone off-shift an hour ago, so he wasn't in bed yet. "No, I didn't see him come back. Are you sure he went out?"

The timing was maddening. If Brandt had come back during shift change, it was possible neither clerk would have noticed. If Brandt had been kidnapped, either from the street or the hotel, the perps had several hours lead time on the discovery. The Old Timers pulled out all the stops.

While one man was working to get any information he could from the clerks, the women were working the phones, calling nearby hospitals to inquire about a late-night emergency admission of an older American man. The second man had been tasked with calling Chris McArdle, CRC's second-in-command. He'd have more pull with the CIA and the US embassy.

Chapter Twenty-Five

CRC Headquarters, Arizona, USA

The morning after the abduction

McArdle immediately went into action. He scrambled several teams, one to Greece, one to check in with MI6, and one to Washington, DC. Two more were put on standby to respond to any intel that came in, and the HUMINT and SIGINT teams were called in as well.

It wasn't just their regard for their friend and colleague that had everyone worried. They had to find Brandt, and as quickly as possible. He knew too much. If he fell into the hands of any of several enemies, the whole gamut of them, drug dealers, arms dealers, Islamic radicals, Russians—he had no shortage of enemies, and all were the enemies of the US and her allies—virtually every security agency in the free world would be compromised to some degree.

Brandt had agents who were handling contacts and

informers all over the world, and they worked closely with allies' security agencies. If that information came out, it would set the US and allies' intelligence community back decades. If those agents and contacts were compromised, people were going to die. By the bushel load.

Within two hours of the first alarm, the CIA, the President of the United States, and the heads of security agencies and heads of state of several key allies had been alerted.

Find John Brandt, at any cost.

McArdle next moved to protect CRC's own. He canceled other missions where possible, replacing them with exfiltration orders for as many of their highly-placed informants as they could. This alone would dismantle carefully-constructed information networks, but it couldn't be helped. When their charges were safely on US soil, the agents had a single order.

Find John Brandt.

Everyone who knew Brandt knew he was tough, even at his age. He was not going to give up easily, and he could withstand torture almost as well as any of his younger operatives. If he felt himself on the verge of giving up information that would get people killed, and if given half the chance, he'd rather commit suicide than give up information. The problem was, his enemies would know it soon enough, if they didn't already. They might not give him that chance.

Whoever had him, if it was one of those bad outfits Brandt had affronted in his lifetime, they'd keep him alive and wear him down. Of course, he would lie and cheat and deceive them for as long as he could. He'd drive them crazy, pumping so much BS into their brains they wouldn't know their heads from their asses. But the thing was, they had him, and they could keep him alive while checking out everything and visit more pain on him until they finally had the truth out of him. Everyone, even the Old Man, had a breaking point. CRC and everyone else might have days, or even weeks, to find him, but eventually he *would* break.

It would be better to drop a nuclear bomb on the place where he was held, if they knew where it was and couldn't get to him.

By late that evening in Athens, all innocent explanations had been eliminated. There was no unidentified, older American in any nearby hospital who'd been admitted after ten-thirty the previous evening. Despite the hopes of the Old Timers, Brandt hadn't strolled in grinning and recounting some adventure he'd had. The US embassy was no help, contacting the police or any other Greek law enforcement agency was not an option, and CRC was already doing everything humanly possible with the help of all US and allied security agencies.

John had been missing for twenty-four hours, and there was no ransom demand. That told them everything. Their worst fears, even worse than the fear the Old Man had died or been killed, had come true. John Brandt had been abducted. The people who abducted him wanted to suck information out of him and *then* they'd kill him. They hoped for the best, that they could find him in time. Alive and unharmed was the best outcome, but everyone conceded, it was doubtful he'd be unharmed. The next best outcome was harmed but alive and not having given up any useful information. Not a good outcome, but by no means the worst, was they'd find him dead, still not having given up anything useful. The worst outcome required no discussion, they all knew.

McArdle, after a very long day that had started at 1:00 a.m., had moved into John Brandt's office, temporarily he hoped. He also hoped the Old Man would be around later, insulting him about McArdle getting into his best brandy. It would be infinitely better to take the scolding from the Old Man than to attend his funeral.

Rick Longland, CRC's resident psychologist, sat where he always did when John needed to pick his brain. It was a comfortable old easy chair that had seen better days, and it was within reach of John's desk for his long legs. His feet were propped on the desk, as usual. Rick was not just the CRC shrink with no idea of what the men were doing out in the field. He was a trained Delta Force operator and had passed through the grueling CRC training himself before he was appointed in his role, therefore he knew what made a good agent and what they were up against when on missions. Over the years, he'd become the Old Man's confidant and soundboard.

McArdle knew and understood the relationship between Longland and the Old Man, and it never bothered him. "Have I covered all the bases, Rick? Are we doing everything humanly possible?"

Rick thought for a moment. What he was about to say to Chris was a closely-held secret, one only he, the Old Man, and the two agents who'd discovered it knew for now. Brandt hadn't wanted to alert anyone else, until he'd spoken to the subject of the secret himself, Rex Dalton. It was time to let one more person in on it.

"There is one more thing," Longland began. McArdle tilted his head to the side, alert to the reluctance in Longland's tone. "John had good reasons for keeping this close to his chest, but we've learned Rex Dalton is alive. If there's anyone who understands how John's mind works and can find him and get him out alive and unscathed, it's Rex."

McArdle had sat up abruptly, sweeping his feet off the

desk and nearly upsetting the cut-crystal glass with two fingers of Brandt's hundred-year-old brandy. *"What!?"*

Longland put up his hands placatingly. "I understand you might be upset because he didn't tell you. But let me explain."

Longland went on to tell McArdle of Brandt's hopes and their fears about Rex Dalton. How they'd at one time discussed the possibility that Dalton might one day walk off the reservation for various reasons, and if that happened, they could never feel safe again. And the fact that Dalton and his men were betrayed when they were led into that ambush in Afghanistan could very well be one of those reasons for him to walk off the reservation.

McArdle said, "But I thought Dalton was confirmed killed."

Longland answered, "There was never any confirmation. If there'd been DNA at the scene, we might have known for sure, but the locals destroyed any hope of finding it. Then, just a few days later, something happened that led John to believe Rex had survived." Longland reminded McArdle about the killing of the drug lords and Taliban leaders.

"The fact he didn't report in after that ambush made us assume he was dead. The fact that the attack on the enemy was thought to be the work of one man led John to believe, or at least hope, Rex wasn't dead. But both of us worried that if it was him, he suspected betrayal. If he didn't know who betrayed him, he could be under the impression it was John, and he might just be biding his time waiting for the right moment before he comes for us."

"Why hasn't any of this come out?" McArdle demanded.

"Two reasons. One, we couldn't be sure if he survived

or not. Two, there could be other reasons Dalton didn't report in, if he survived, like maybe he had amnesia. Josh Farley and Marissa Bisset have been searching off and on ever since, and a lead finally paid off. They reported a couple of weeks ago that they have a confirmed sighting of him not long after the whole Afghanistan snafu. He was involved in a one-man mission in Saudi Arabia, where he killed a major illicit arms dealer and all his guards and rescued seven of his pleasure wives.

"Farley and Bisset are tracking down the leads they got during their visit to Saudi Arabia and…"

"Where are Farley and Bisset right now?" McArdle interjected.

"Not sure. They've been in contact with John, and last I heard from him they were on their way to India. They know I've been kept up to date by John, so maybe I can contact them?"

"Agreed. This might be better coming from you. I want them to do whatever it takes, spend whatever it costs, to find Rex Dalton—yesterday!"

Longland checked the time difference. It was mid-morning in Mumbai. He found cell phone and satphone numbers in his records and reached Josh Farley when Marissa didn't answer her phone.

Chapter Twenty-Six

Rome, Italy

The morning after the abduction

When in Rome, so the adage goes, do as the Romans do. Rex Dalton knew the maxim and therefore, as Romans do, he visited the *Scalina Spagna*, the Spanish Steps. The one-hundred and thirty-eight Roman baroque-style steps, constructed in the form of a butterfly, was built between 1723 and 1725 for the purpose of linking the beautiful twin tower *Trinità dei Monti* church at the top of the steps, at the time under the patronage of the king of France, with the *Piazza di Spagna*, Spanish Square, one of the most famous squares in Rome, at the bottom of the steps. The square hosted the *Palazzo di Spagna*, seat of the Embassy of Spain, the famed Column of the Immaculate Conception of the Blessed Virgin Mary, and a fountain depicting a sinking ship, aptly named *Fontana della Barcaccia*, Fountain of the Old

Boat. It represented a legend about a fishing boat carried by the flood waters of the Tiber River in the sixteenth century to this exact spot.

It was an area rich in history, and a great place to sit down, relax, and savor the vibes and vistas of the Eternal City. Since its construction about 300 years ago, the Spanish Steps was a very popular meeting place for people of all walks of life, including artists, painters, sculptors, models, and poets. The house of the famed English poet, John Keats, where he lived at the time of his death in 1821, can be found to the right when ascending the steps. The house had been converted to a museum dedicated to his memory.

But the famous steps not only inspired artists and poets. On March 20, 1986, the first McDonalds restaurant in Italy opened near the Spanish Steps and immediately had the Romans up in arms. They protested against fast food being brought to their country and their beloved Rome. Three years later, Carlo Petrini and delegates from fifteen countries signed the founding manifesto of the international Slow Food movement in Paris, France. Since then the movement had expanded to over 100,000 members with branches in over one-hundred and fifty countries. Rex agreed with the movement.

And of course, due to the intrinsic asinine nature of some members of the human species, visitors occasionally insisted they had an inalienable right to make complete asses of themselves when visiting public places. The case in point was the drunk, young man who, on June 13, 2007, endeavored to drive his Toyota vehicle down the Spanish Steps, causing extensive damage to the steps. Fortunately, he was arrested very quickly.

Those were some of the thoughts meandering through

Rex's mind as he sat on the marble bench surrounding the *Fontana della Barcaccia* staring at the cascading water.

The major part of his mind, however, was occupied with something, or rather someone, else. He knew he was procrastinating, though he still didn't know why.

It had been more than four years since Rex had been to Rome. At the time of his last visit, Rex had been on a mission to stop a major arms for drugs deal between the Camorra and al Qaeda after a CRC agent, Matthew Benedict, was killed by the Camorra. They were a crime syndicate operating out of the Campania region with Naples, its capital. Their territory was ideally located for transportation and distribution of product, with both an international airport and one of the largest seaports in the Mediterranean. The two hubs served a population of nearly four million, the ninth most populous urban area in the European Union.

The transport infrastructure provided a virtually unstoppable highway from the sea to every part of Europe. Whatever products you could get into Naples, including weapons and drugs, you could distribute with ease from there to anywhere in Europe.

Brandt had personally briefed Rex about the mission.

"Just so we're clear," Rex had said at the end of the briefing. "You want me to kill whoever was involved in Benedict's death, as well as stopping the arms deal from going through?"

"You got a problem with that?" Brandt had asked, his jaw thrust forward.

"Not at all. Just verifying mission parameters," Rex said.

During that mission Rex had the backing of a mission support specialist whom he had met a year before when he underwent his European tradecraft training.

Catia Romano was the name she'd given him. Marco was the name he'd given her.

Not since breaking up with his college sweetheart, Jessie, to join the Marines had Rex been so affected by a woman. He'd had opportunities, certainly, on several occasions, but had been always busy, always undercover, always focused on mission tasks, no time for romance.

Catia, however, struck something inside him that he'd thought was dead.

It wasn't just her beauty, though that was undeniable. Tall for a woman, she could stand eye-to-eye with him, and what eyes they were! The color of the Mediterranean, blue at times and aquamarine at others, they changed with her mood and what she wore. But they were always beautiful, large, and expressive, framed by auburn hair and flawless creamy skin, just a scattering of light freckles across her nose to attest to the natural red in her hair. Her smile was enough to set Rex's heart racing, and she smiled often.

Both knew the rules, though. No fraternizing between agents and handlers. It could get both killed. He wouldn't even be able to stay in touch with her when his instruction with her was over. He'd know how to contact her, but the same did not go for her. She couldn't know where he was or what he was doing.

By the same token, he knew very little about her, only that she could be contacted through a complicated exchange she'd set up through a waiter in a certain trattoria. And that she was not one of the 'ordinary people' contacts. She was on the payroll of at least two foreign security agencies. He was told that by his trainer when he was sent to meet her. However, he could only speculate about which security agencies they were. He didn't ask, and she didn't tell, but if asked to guess, he would've said the UK and Italy by process of logical reasoning. The trainer who sent him to meet her was MI6 and she lived in Italy. Rex would've been only half right.

They hadn't discussed their backgrounds. It was one of the rules that would keep both safe from deliberate or inadvertent betrayal by the other. The need-to-know principle at work. No sharing of backgrounds, who they worked for, information about their families, childhood, or where they'd studied. Anything that would allow one to trace the other was forbidden.

On the last day of his training, over lunch, Rex told her, "I'll miss you."

Her eyes warned him that he was straying into forbidden territory. She didn't answer, but the slight blush in her neck didn't escape Rex's eyes. She might as well have said, "So will I."

He had raised his wineglass and said, *"Chin-chin."*

Catia's expression softened. *"Chin-chin,"* she returned. A fleeting smile, then she sipped delicately at the ruby-colored liquid. She looked away.

"Arrivederci." The word used for saying goodbye when there is an expectation of not seeing each other again. The word hung in the sultry air, unadorned. Final.

"Addio." Go with God, she'd added in a whisper.

Rex nodded, downed the few drops of wine in his glass, and left the table without touching her, knowing he might regret, for the rest of his life, not kissing her then. He pacified himself with the thought, *if I ever see her again, I'm going to make up for not doing it this time and kiss her.*

During his flight back to the US, he reflected on the past

six months in Europe, and especially his time with Catia. What was it about her that had broken through the walls he'd placed around his heart? He'd met beautiful women before. He'd met capable women before. He'd met beautiful, capable women before.

He couldn't put his finger on it, but there was something about her, a vulnerability, perhaps. A mysterious pathos that called to something like it in himself. He didn't dwell on it for too long. That train of thought was fruitless.

Then, not even a year later, they met again when Rex was back in Italy on the Camorra mission. This time they met at the Trevi Fountain, she surprised him and kissed him when they met. Before leaving the fountain, they'd honored the age-old tradition when they both took a coin out, went down to the edge of the fountain, turned their backs to the water, and on the count of three threw the coins over their shoulders into the fountain and made a secret wish.

Then they had dinner. Rex had wrapped his jacket around her shoulders when he walked her back to her apartment, and when they arrived, she turned and lifted her face for a goodnight kiss. It was full of promise, but it was not the time, she wouldn't invite him up, and he was okay with that.

Maybe another time, another place, when there was no mission.

Today was not the first time he'd remembered that promise to himself. The entire time he and Digger had spent traveling through Italy, he'd known his objective was to observe Catia and determine whether to approach her. He'd flip-flopped on the decision to even put that plan into action, talked to himself until Digger must have thought he'd gone 'round the bend, and he still hadn't made the final decision.

He called Digger to his side. Digger was reluctant, he could tell. The dog had been making a game of scattering the pigeons, as far as his leash allowed him to go, much to the amusement of the local children. He'd rush at them as soon as they lit on the paving stones, and they'd fly up in a group. Then Digger would sit down and wait for them to land again and make another rush. It was clear to Rex that Digger had no intention of catching the flying rats. He just liked to watch them take flight. Every time the dog sat down, he let his wide grin appear, and he ate it up when one or more of the children ran to pet him.

Kids at home wouldn't be allowed to approach a strange dog. These Romans must know a good dog when they see one just having some fun.

"Come Digger, let's get something to eat, see a few more places, and get a good night's sleep. We'll come back in the morning and then go and see her."

Chapter Twenty-Seven

Bilaspur, India

Two days after abduction

Josh and Marissa decided to fly from Bilaspur to Mumbai. They might have enjoyed the sights on a drive, but now that Rex's trail had become so hot, an eagerness to find him as soon as possible had set in. But after the long lunch with the Gyans, they'd learned they'd missed the last flight out of Bilaspur and had to stay in a hotel that night. When they turned up at the airport early the next morning for their flight, they were told unfortunately, it was overbooked, and as the last ticket-holders, they were bumped. Sitting at the airport for two hours while waiting for the next one, Marissa remarked that they might as well have driven. They'd arrive at about the same time, anyway.

Josh patiently pointed out that the drive would have been through the night and would've taken twenty-four hours, not sixteen. This way they'd be arriving between ten and ten-thirty that morning. It would be a far more opportune time to find Rehka than at dinner time. Marissa had to reluctantly agree, but she still paced until their flight's boarding. If she'd only known they'd be bumped, she could have had another couple hours' sleep.

While waiting at the airport, Marissa bought a box of chocolates and had it gift-wrapped—it was part of a plan conceived the previous night. They'd discussed what to expect when meeting Rehka. They supposed that Rehka's behavior would depend on what the relationship between her and Rex was. They knew Rex was not living with her, at least that's what they gathered from Rehka's parents.

They anticipated that, naturally, Rehka might be a bit reluctant to talk to strangers, and it would be even more so if she'd want to protect Rex's secret. That was if Rex was trying to keep a secret. Nevertheless, they felt the best would be to approach the first contact with Rehka with caution, to first put her at ease, gain her trust, and then broach the matter of Rex's whereabouts at the opportune moment. They agreed that the Photoshopped pictures wouldn't do them much good.

They'd decided to make it straightforward, with just one little white lie. Marissa would take the lead and tell Rehka that she and Josh had just been to Bilaspur, have met her parents there, and have a present from them for her. There were plenty of holes in it, but if it got them a foot in her door, it would be good enough.

Chapter Twenty-Eight

Mumbai, India

Two days after abduction

However, everything changed the moment they got off the plane in Mumbai. Marissa was just turning on her phone to check her messages when Josh's satphone rang. He threw a puzzled look her way as he pulled the phone out of his pocket. It was Rick Longland.

"Hey, Rick, what's ..."

Marissa looked curiously at him as his greeting was cut off and saw his expression turn to shock. Then he said, "What?! When? I've got it. We're following up on a lead right now. I'll get back to you."

Marissa didn't bother to ask. Josh was turning to her, his mouth already forming the words. "Brandt's been kidnapped!"

Marissa knew the rest even before Josh repeated it. "We've got to find Rex, right now!"

"Those are our orders. By any means, and if we can't find him today, we head back to help in the search."

"Back where?"

"He was abducted in Athens. There, I guess, or back to headquarters. Let's cross that bridge when we come to it. Let's hope Miss Rehka Gyan knows how to find him and is willing to cooperate."

They knew the exact address, thanks to her helpful parents. Twenty minutes later, they were knocking on her door. When she answered, Marissa saw Rehka's pictures hadn't done her justice. She was exquisite.

Josh was staring at her.

Marissa elbowed Josh in the ribs, just to get him breathing again, and launched into her cover story. "Miss Rehka Gyan?"

"Yeees... and who are you?"

"My name is Marissa Bisset, and this is my friend Josh Farley." They'd decided it would be best to give their real names, so they didn't have to explain away another lie later.

"We've been in Bilaspur the last few days and met your parents through some acquaintances of ours. When your parents heard we were coming to Mumbai, they were very excited and asked if we would mind dropping off this little present for you."

Marissa held the gift-wrapped box out to her. But both of them could see Rehka was suspicious. She didnt take the present, her gaze shifted between the gift and them.

Marissa thought she would've reacted the same if two strangers came knocking on her door with a flimsy story such as hers. And then of course there was the present itself, wrapped in shiny, opulently decorated gift paper which in no way fit with the destitution in which her parents lived.

Marissa could have kicked herself for not thinking about that more carefully, but it was too late. She turned on all her charm while trying to rescue the situation with another lie. "Sorry, it seems to me you were not expecting us? I apologize for dropping in on you like this. I thought your parents would have let you know we would be coming around."

Rehka shook her head. "No, they didn't."

"Oh, okay. Well, here we are, and here is the present."

This time Rehka visibly relaxed, reached out and took the packet. "Thank you very much. I appreciate the trouble you've gone to, to get it to me."

"Don't mention it, it's no trouble at all. Your parents are the kindest people. They treated us to the best traditional Indian meal we've ever had. It's the least we could do in return for their hospitality."

Rehka took a step back, opened the door the rest of the way and said, "Would you like to come in for some tea?"

Marissa looked at Josh, who feigned a quick glance at his watch, then nodded and said, "That would be nice, thank you."

Rehka asked them if they'd mind having tea in the kitchen. That way they could tell her how her parents were doing while she made the tea.

Of course, Josh and Marissa had no objections.

As soon as the two of them were seated at the kitchen table and Rehka got busy with the preparations, Marissa cleared her throat and said, "Rehka, I have to apologize to you. We…"

Rehka stopped and turned around with a probing look on her face.

"It is true, we've met with your parents in Bilaspur, but it was no coincidence. We went there looking for them to find out where we could get hold of you…"

"Why?"

"Rehka we have to get in touch with the man you know as Ruan immediately. It's urgent, a matter of life and death." Rehka's mouth dropped open for a brief instant, and they could see the fear settling on her face.

She was quiet for a long while as she stared at them in turn. "You've deceived me to get into my apartment. Get out! Get out right now, or I will call the police."

"Rehka, please listen to us. A very important man's life is in danger. We need to talk to Ruan. We mean you no harm."

"I don't know this man… what's his name… Ruan. I've never known anyone by that name. Now please leave my apartment immediately."

Josh pulled out his phone, found a photo of Rex, and turned the screen so Rehka could see it. "This is the man we're talking about."

Rehka took a step closer and looked at the photo. She started shaking her head, but Josh and Marissa were studying her facial expressions carefully.

"I… don't know this man… you must now…"

Josh interrupted. "You aren't a very good liar. You know him. Your parents know him, and they told us you know him. We showed this and other photos to them and they recognized him. I'm sure you know where he is, and you definitely have a way to contact him. We need that information, Rehka, we need it now. If you…"

Marissa threw him an irritated look and gave him a Stop! signal with her hand.

Josh stopped talking and Marissa started speaking in a soothing voice. "Rehka, I want to tell you a story. It's a story about a very good man with a big black dog named Digger."

Marissa and Josh both saw the fleeting moment of recognition and angst in Rehka's eyes at the mention of the dog's name.

"This man had a good heart. He could never walk away from injustice.

"He was traveling around the world and made friends wherever he went. One day, he met an old man and they started talking. He made the old man very happy when he and his dog accepted an invitation to have dinner with the old man and his wife and play Chaturanga with him.

"Then the day after the dinner, the old man's wife told this good man that their very beautiful daughter, their youngest child, had disappeared.

"The elderly couple was devastated and heartbroken. But there was nothing they could do. They were poor and had no means to find their daughter, but they knew she was in some kind of trouble. They even thought she could be dead, or they would never see her again which was the same as being dead.

"But this kind man and his big black dog decided they could not let this go by them without at least trying to find out what happened to the beautiful girl. And they went out in search of this girl.

"The man and his dog went through a lot of danger, but in the end, they found this girl and brought her back to her country and her family."

By the end of the story, Rehka was crying, and Marissa herself had a prickly feeling in her eyes.

Rehka opened her mouth as if to speak, but then buried her face in her hands. "I... I can't. Please, you must understand. I can't... I..."

Marissa told her gently, "I do understand. You don't want to betray the man who saved you, and he's told you not to reveal his whereabouts. And I'm not asking you to do that. I'm asking that you contact him and give him a message, that's all."

Rehka's shoulders were shaking as she cried, "I... I don't..."

"Rehka, Josh and I are going to give you a bit of time to think about it. We'll come back in one hour. All we want you to do is to give Ruan this message; John Brandt, The Old Man, is in grave danger. He needs your help. Please contact Josh Farley of CRC." Marissa wrote the message and Josh's satphone number on one of the pages of her little notebook, tore the page out, and placed it on the table.

Rehka just stared at it and remained silent, the tears were still rolling down her cheeks.

Josh and Marissa stood and headed for the door, but Josh stopped just short of it, turned to Rehka and said, "Rehka, just remember, that man, John Brandt, The Old Man, is an elderly man, who has been the closest thing to a father Ruan's ever known since his own family was killed in a terrorist attack ten or more years ago. That old man now urgently needs his help, and it now depends on you if he lives or dies. That old man needs Ruan as badly as you needed him when he found and rescued you. Think about that. We'll be back in an hour."

Chapter Twenty-Nine

Rome, Italy

Two days after abduction

Catia's apartment was in one of the side streets on the other side of the square—less than 500 meters from where he was sitting. It had taken him more than four years to get back. Four years during which not a single day had passed without him thinking of Catia.

He clearly remembered his last thought when he'd last seen her—*maybe another time, another place, when there was no mission.*

At the time, he knew it wasn't just wishful thinking. There was a promise to himself in that thought, even though, at the time, he had no idea when and how it would be fulfilled.

There was no mission now. As far as he was concerned, he was now free to contact Catia. That he was here now, about to fulfill his promise, was a thought that electrified him.

There were, however, a few stumbling blocks: One, was she still unattached? —he had no idea. Two, did she still work for whatever security agency she'd worked when he last saw her? —he had no idea. If she did, would she be duty-bound to report it to them if he contacted her? —he could only speculate, but probably she'd have to, which meant his cover would be blown. Three, he still had the unfinished business with those who betrayed him and his men in Afghanistan. Was he ready to forego the vengeance he'd promised to visit upon the traitors? —no, he wasn't. He took an oath that day when his men were killed, and he was not going to betray their memory.

So, why are you here then, Rex Dalton?

I just want to see her again.

Sitting there at the *Fontana della Barcaccia* this morning, Rex still had no answer to those questions. What he did know was for four long years he'd been thinking about this day, he'd been longing for this day, and he'd been preparing for this day. Part of his preparations was to find out if Catia still owned the AirBnB apartment above the trattoria and if she was not spoken for. Four years was a long time, and Catia was a beautiful woman, there would have been no shortage of male callers. Besides, it was not as if they'd promised to wait for each other the last time they saw each other.

Therefore, he was considering calling in the help of his IT specialist, Rehka Gyan. Rex had met Rehka in the aftermath of the ambush in Afghanistan, soon after starting a new life in India. Another bad guy, prince Mutaib bin Faisal bin Saud, had offended Rex's sensibilities by buying pleasure wives on the human trafficking market. Rehka, in fact, was one of the victims. Rex had learned of her possible fate from her mother, whom Rex had met by chance. Rex had investigated, found her, and taken her out of Saudi Arabia after dispatching Mutaib, who was not only into human trafficking but also an unscrupulous international weapons dealer.

Rex had asked Rehka to make some very unobtrusive inquiries about Catia but not to hack into her computer or phone. Rehka reported with confidence that Catia still owned and managed the AirBnB business at the same location as four years ago. But she was much less confident about her relationship status, stating, "Searching the social media, as far as I can see, she's not in a relationship. But I have to say she seems to be a very private person, she's got a whole raft of social media accounts, Facebook, Twitter, Pinterest, and more, for her business, but not a single one of those for herself. I've checked government records and couldn't find any one stating that she's married. That's as much as I can tell you without hacking into her computer."

The only choice to know for certain now was fieldcraft. Rex had disguised himself as an old man. The beard was genuine, but the gray in it was not, nor was his gray hair. The walking stick was genuine, but the limp was fake. Catia would not be able to recognize him, he was sure of that, and Digger's presence would make it even more unlikely. His plan was a few days of observation and then work out how, when, and where to approach her. He wasn't sure he would or could do it in the end—for now, it was good enough to just lay eyes on her again.

It had been more than seven months since Rex and Digger had helped a French lady by the name of Margot Lemaire get out of a very dangerous situation and in the process saved the French president and his government from a major scandal. For their heroics, Rex was awarded French citizenship, and Digger got a medal and a big juicy steak.

For the past few months since averting the French crisis, Rex and Digger had been traveling through Austria, Hungary, and Croatia. It was during his visit to the islands of Croatia in the Adriatic Sea, that Rex had often looked across the sea toward Italy and thought of Catia, but his sojourn there had been spoiled by a murder, and he'd moved his island vacation to Santorini, skipping his intention to explore Italy until he'd backtracked in the past couple of weeks.

Rex looked at his watch. It was 8:00 a.m., and if Catia were still in the same routine as four years ago, she would turn up at the trattoria in his line of sight in about half an hour for her daily fix of cappuccino and a cornetto, a sweet pastry.

Rex looked down at Digger who had been sitting patiently next to him for the past half hour studying the people passing by with great interest. There were not many people around yet. The Italians in general were not early risers. They worked on average thirty-six hours per week, starting their workday between 8:30 a.m. and 9:00 a.m. working to between 6:00 p.m. and 6:30 p.m., but enjoying a leisurely hour-and-a-half to two-hour-long lunch break.

"Okay buddy, time for you to be introduced to the fairest of them all. This is the one I've been telling you about for the past fourteen months."

Digger was studying Rex's face intently, as if he understood, with a big dog-smile on his face.

Rex couldn't help but remember Digger's erratic behavior in the past. Like the time in Thailand where the dog went out of his way to prevent any romance between Rex and a very beautiful Thai girl.

And the time in Vanuatu when Digger decided—Rex was sure the dog knew exactly what he was doing— to introduce him to a beautiful French girl. Not that Rex minded the introduction, but Digger's methods left much to be desired. First, he stole the girl's food and Rex had to go and apologize. Then a day or so later, Digger ran her off her feet when he chased a Frisbee, and Rex had to go and apologize again.

Rex, grinned when he thought about that.

That smile on Digger's face was not reassuring at all. "Now, Digger, listen to me carefully. No silly stuff. Okay?" Rex turned Digger's head to look him in the eyes and said, "Look at me and tell me you are going to behave yourself."

Digger just yawned—he was ready to go.

Rex grabbed the leash and with Digger now all excited, right next to him, they headed across the square toward Via delle Carrozze, where Catia's apartment was. He couldn't help but think of another adage; all roads lead to Rome.

He didn't know what made him think about it, but he looked at his watch and wondered what Rehka was having for lunch in Mumbai, where it was half an hour past noon.

He would not have taken another step if he'd known what had been happening in Mumbai over the past two hours.

Chapter Thirty

Rome, Italy

Two days after abduction

Rex was seated at the trattoria, outside under one of the big umbrellas, Digger at his feet, waiting for his breakfast, when Rehka called.

Rex was immediately on high alert when Rehka started speaking. She didn't follow their usual security protocol by asking about the weather, she didn't even greet him, she just started talking anxiously. "Ruan, there were two people at my apartment looking for you. A man and a woman. I have a message from them. They wrote it down for me. It says; *'John Brandt, The Old Man, is in grave danger. He needs your help. Please contact Josh Farley of CRC.'* There is a telephone number."

With a thrill of alarm—had his security been penetrated? —he asked, "Describe them to me."

Rehka continued to describe what they looked like. He recognized the description of Josh Farley, which was bad enough. He didn't know the woman, but he remembered seeing a woman matching the description at a close near-encounter at the Taj Mahal in India about seven or eight months ago.

So, they tracked me down after all. Is Rehka safe?

"Did they threaten you or ask where I was?"

"No, they didn't threaten me at all. But they insisted that I know where you are and how to contact you. I denied that I know you, but they didn't believe me, they knew I was lying. They showed me a photo of you and told me they've been to my parents' house in Bilaspur. My parents told them where to find me and also that I know you and that you were the man who rescued me."

She went on in a panicked rush. "But I didn't tell them anything Ruan. I kept on telling them I don't know you."

Rex could hear her sobs. "Okay, Rehka, I want you to calm down. You are in no danger, please trust me on that. Take a few deep breaths now and then tell me, what else did they say?"

"They said they'll go away and give me an hour and asked that I contact you and give you the message I read to you earlier. They'll be back in an hour to talk to me again. What must I do Ruan? I'm so scared, and I'm worried about you. I…"

"You did the right thing, Rehka, don't worry. I will handle this."

"I got in touch with you as soon as I was sure they were out of earshot. I waited for them to pass below my apartment window before I called you. I hope I haven't done anything that would put you in danger…"

"No, Rehka you didn't. Please stop worrying about it."

Rex's first thoughts were to get Josh and this woman out of Rehka's hair as quickly as possible. She was not trained to handle matters of this nature and stand up to a trained CRC operative like Josh. He was still perplexed about the woman's role in all of this. So, he decided to tell Rehka to tell them to go to a secure place, send her a text message when they get there, and wait until he gets in touch with them.

"You still there, Ruan?"

"Sorry, I got a bit distracted. Okay, I'll handle it from here. When they come back to your apartment, tell them to go to a secure place, send you a text message when they're there, and then they should wait for me to call them. That's it. Don't tell them anything else.

"Then, when you get their text message you forward it to me. I will contact them and make sure that they won't bother you again."

"I'll do exactly as you've said. Oh, Ruan, I hope this is not going to put you in danger." Rehka's voice started shaking.

"Rehka, please stop worrying. I know these people, they don't mean me any harm, and they won't harm you in any way. They need my help." Rex had no way of knowing that, but he had to get Rehka to calm down before she gave away too much about him, if she hadn't already.

"Thank you. Please be careful, Ruan."

"Thanks, Rehka, I will. Take care and say hi to Aarav and his family for me."

When the call ended, it was with a sigh, as Rex admitted to himself that his extended vacation was over.

Just when he put the phone away, Catia was there. Prettier than ever, prettier than in his most romantic dreams of her over the years. He felt his heart beating in his throat—

he didn't realize he'd forgotten to breathe. His eyes flicked to her hands. No rings.

Damn!

"Come on, Digger." He stood, grabbed the walking stick, grabbed Digger's leash, and walked away, with a slight limp in his left leg.

Damn!

Chapter Thirty-One

Mumbai, India

Two days after abduction

Josh and Marissa had a light breakfast a block away from Rehka's apartment, from where they could keep an eye on her front door. No one came out or went in. True to their word, they went back to her apartment an hour after they'd left.

Rehka's demeanor had changed. She'd stopped crying and looked more confident, though Marissa could see in her eyes that she was still under a strain. She let them in without a word and then turned to face them.

"You are to go somewhere secure and text me at this number when you get there." She extended a hand with a slip of paper in it, which Marissa took. "Then wait. You will receive a call from someone who may be able to tell you more about this man you are looking for."

Josh and Marissa exchanged a glance. He stayed silent while she asked, "Rehka, did you contact Ruan?"

Rehka raised her chin defiantly. "I have given you your instructions. Please leave."

Josh shifted and opened his mouth, but Marissa sent him a look of caution, and he relaxed. Marissa said gently, "I hope you are telling us the truth." She linked a hand around Josh's upper arm and firmly guided him out the door.

Outside, he protested. "We should have…"

"Josh, we weren't going to get any more out of her. She's worried and frightened. It serves no purpose to bully her, threaten her, or even torture her. That would serve only to make Rex harder to find. Rehka's a civilian, an innocent bystander. I'm sure she's been in contact with Rex in the past hour."

Josh shook his head. "Other than throttling it out of her, I guess this is our only option for now."

Marissa nodded and grinned. "And it's not as violent as your suggestion."

"Let's find a secure place, then," Josh mumbled. "Should we check into a hotel?"

"Let's hold off on that. I have a feeling we're going to be leaving Mumbai today. A quiet park will be secure enough. I'll keep watch while you talk to whoever contacts you. Let's hope it's Rex."

Chapter Thirty-Two

Mumbai, India

Two days after abduction

Half an hour later, Josh's satphone rang. He looked at the screen, but there was no caller ID or number on the screen, just the words 'Unknown Caller'. *Dalton's using encrypted exchanges and proxies. The call is untraceable. I would've been surprised if he didn't.*

He showed the screen to Marissa and said, "Must be Dalton." She nodded. "Hello," he answered.

"I heard you're looking for me. Why am I not surprised?" Rex's voice, though he hadn't heard it in over a year, was the same as Josh remembered.

"Rex, where are you? We'll come to you. We need your help. It's urgent."

When it came, the answer was in a lower tone, an edge

of roughness to Rex's voice. "Farley, listen carefully. Here's what you have to do right now. Get lost. Go jump off the nearest cliff. Kill yourself. I don't have anything else to say to you, and if I ever have to talk to you or anyone from CRC it will be too soon. Now…"

"Rex, stop it, man! Just listen to me first. We need you, urgently. The Old Man has been abducted."

"What's that got to do with me? I didn't abduct him."

"Rex, we know you're not involved…"

"So, why should I be interested in his health and well-being? Where was John Brandt when I needed him? Where were the rest of CRC?"

"Damn it, Rex, shut up and listen to me! You've got your facts wrong, buddy. Let me set you straight…"

"Buddy? I'm not your buddy. Get that through your thick skull right now. And set me straight, you said? I guess you are now going to try and give me some sob story about how John Brandt was not responsible for sending me and seven of my men into an ambush in which all of them except me were killed? If that's…"

"Rex, please, if you do nothing else today, just give me a chance to speak and finish what I have to tell you. Please. If at the end of it you still feel the same, then so be it. I'll never bother you again."

"I know you won't, I'll make sure of it. I'll kill you. And if you ever come near Rehka Gyan again, you and that woman with you are dead. I will find you, and I will kill you, both of you. Are we clear?"

Josh shook his head. This wasn't going well. "Listen, Rex, you've got to stop and listen to me now. You have to give me a chance to finish. It's just as important for you as for the Old Man."

"I don't know why I'm even bothering, but you've got two minutes. Starting now."

"Okay. I'll start again. John Brandt has been kidnapped, we think. Or killed, we don't know. It happened two days ago in Greece. Yes, we've been looking for you for many months now…"

Rex couldn't stop himself from interjecting, "Yes, I know. I saw you. One day, at the Taj Mahal, you were fewer than two paces away from me. I should have killed both of you then."

How? Where… when? Josh hadn't figured out what to answer before Rex spoke again.

"You're wondering how you missed me. Slipping up, Josh? I'm disappointed. To think I trained you. But just so you know, I know where you are, I know what you're doing, and if you put one foot out of place, I will not walk past you again, I'll get rid of you."

"Okay bigshot, promise noted. Now, can I carry on?"

"Yes."

"Thanks. So, John figured out that you and your men were betrayed and who did it. Marissa and I were instrumental in bringing the low-life to justice. He's dead."

"Yeah. And who did John tell you was the traitor?"

Josh noted the way he said it, implying that Brandt had lied to them. "The director of the CIA, Bruce Carson. He admitted it, Rex. Just before he died."

"And now you're probably going to try and convince me you personally heard those dying words out of Carson's mouth, right?"

"In fact, yes. I'm the one who terminated him."

Rex's mind went back to the time when he'd interrogated Usama and his friends and remembered that Usama had told him that the kingpin in the USA was Winston

Reginald Hathaway, a New York socialite, as far as Rex knew. But he also recalled that Usama had told him Hathaway controlled a senator, whose name he couldn't remember, and the senator had passed the order on to the CIA. He never got the name of the CIA person out of Usama. He wondered if all that information and much more was on the hard drives he'd taken from Usama. It was time to check.

Assuming what Josh was saying about Bruce Carson was the truth, it checked out as far as it went. He remembered seeing the news reports about Carson's death but was sure what was in the media would've had a spin on it.

After a beat, he said, "Yes, I know Carson is dead. The media said he had an accident. Very convenient for you, I'd say. Easy to just link his death to the story you're spinning me now."

"That *'accident'* was me, Rex. I had my gun pointed at him, and he jumped out a window to avoid being taken back to the States for justice. And just so you know, if he hadn't done that, I was prepared to kill him or take him back, whatever it took. Brandt has been distraught about your so-called death."

"Then why did he send you to search for me?"

"Why do you think? Your stunt in Saudi Arabia convinced him you were alive, as if the raid on that Afghan asshole's compound hadn't made him wonder. He'd put Marissa and I on your case a few days after the raid on Usama and his cohorts. According to Brandt, that raid had your name written all over it. Then a month or so later, he got the news about a raid on prince Mutaib bin Faisal bin Saud's compound. Again, Brandt thought that was your work. I thought Brandt had lost his mind, but I don't have to tell you he was right. The only thing we couldn't fathom was this djinn the Saudis talked about. A big, black dog, according to Rehka's parents."

"You interrogated the Gyans? Never mind leaving Rehka alone, I'm going to kill you for that!"

"No, shithead. We don't interrogate elderly couples. What do you take us for? We had a nice lunch with them, and they freely gave us the information about you and where to find Rehka. Oh, and by the way, Mr. Gyan says you are a lousy Chaturanga player, and Mrs. Gyan really fancies you to be her son in law."

Rex smiled at that last remark and was glad Josh couldn't see him. He kept his tone nonconciliatory. "So, after all that bullshit, you expect me to forget everything and all of a sudden care about John Brandt and CRC?"

"Have you not heard a word I've said? John never did anything wrong, Carson was the one who betrayed you. He was the one who gave the orders to the Old Man. Rex, John considers you his son. He never wanted to accept that you could've died in that ambush. Against all the odds, he kept on believing you were alive. He's moved Heaven and Earth to find you and bring you home. He thinks you may have amnesia. That's the excuse he's made for you not checking in after that ambush."

"Okay Josh, your two minutes are up. Here's how I see it. You've been lying to me since we started this call. You've wasted my time. You've prevented me from meeting someone very important.

"So, your search is over. Go back to CRC and John Brandt and I don't care who else. You can lie to them or you can tell them the truth. Take your pick from one or more of the following: You found me, and I am dead. You found me, and I suffer from amnesia, so they have nothing to worry about. You found me, I know I have been betrayed by John

Brandt and others, I am pissed off, and I am coming for them. Whatever spin you put on it, make sure to let them know I am not interested to help anyone at CRC, and definitely not John Brandt."

Josh was on the verge of throwing his satphone to the ground and stomping it in frustration. But then he got an idea and a slight grin broke across his face as he recalled Marissa's brilliant tactics with Rehka earlier. He was now going to try his version of it. "Look, Dalton. If you're not going to help, then screw you. I've got more important things to do than stand here arguing with you. Marissa and I have to get to Greece to join the search for John.

"I'll be sure to let Chris McArdle and Rick Longland know that we found you. You're alive and well, but you've lost your backbone, you've become a spineless jellyfish. I'll let them know that the revered Rex Dalton we at CRC once knew, the fearsome warrior we'd come to respect and idolize, although alive might as well have perished. If we are successful in rescuing The Old Man, I'll also let him know that the man he cared about and respected so much has lost his nerve, his moral compass, and doesn't respect or care about him.

"One last thing Dalton, on a personal note. You trained me. I learned pretty much everything I know from you. We've been on missions together, and I always felt safe when you were the leader. I've admired you, looked up to you as a role model. But today I've lost all of that. I now know you will be of no help to find John Brandt, it's better that we don't have you on the search and rescue team. Enjoy your life, Dalton. I hope you can live with yourself."

"Wait."

Josh paused in the act of ending the call. "What?"

"I'll call you in an hour."

When the call ended, Josh found Marissa looking at him with newfound admiration and a proud smile. "Did it work?"

"Did what work?"

"The Josh Farley version of reverse psychology."

"We'll know in an hour."

Chapter Thirty-Three

Rome, Italy

Two days after abduction

Rex sat on his hotel room bed, his face in his hands, elbows resting on his knees. Digger gave a small whine as he tried to worm his head between the elbows into Rex's lap. Even in his emotional turmoil, Rex understood his buddy was just trying to comfort him. Digger was the best friend he'd ever had, and that included all human friends he ever had.

Did I jump to unwarranted conclusions?

For more than a year, Rex had pushed down the hurt he'd felt that Brandt would betray him, substituting anger. And then he'd pushed that down, too, knowing that eventually he'd have to deal with it. In the deepest recesses of his mind, it festered. Assumptions became certainty, and he'd settled on hate for his one-time mentor and the organization he'd almost given his life for.

He had always meant to deal with the emotions and the retaliation he would have felt necessary, but in his own time, on his own schedule, when he was ready. Now, he wondered if the reason he hadn't been ready was some small doubt in his mind. After all, why would John turn on him? That was something he hadn't wanted to ask himself before, but now he had to.

He wasn't ready, and it wasn't on his schedule, but his hand was being forced. For more than a year, he'd hated and distrusted CRC and specifically John Brandt. Those were strong emotions, not to be flipped at the assertions of someone who had no proof. On the other hand, doubt was beginning to creep in. Where was the evidence against John Brandt? He didn't really have any, unless there were records on those hard drives. Records he hadn't wanted to examine. Why? Because he was afraid they'd reveal it *was* The Old Man who'd sent him knowingly into an ambush? Or was he afraid they'd reveal it wasn't, and that he'd been derelict in his duty to report back?

Seeing oneself in the harsh light of truth could be desolating. But Rex had to face it. He could have been wrong. And if he had been, then maybe everything Josh had said was true. But there was no room for error. It could just as easily be a trap. Self-preservation would dictate he stay ahead of them, let them sort out John Brandt's problems on their own, if there *were* any.

I'm not obliged to help.

Or am I?

Do I have a duty of care?

But since he'd left Afghanistan and set out for a life of peace and quiet, in every country he'd been to he'd landed in a situation where he had to use his special skills to help someone in trouble. Many days he found himself wondering if it was his destiny or his curse for the many killings he'd done over the years. Atonement for his sins? —a standing duty of care to everyone who crossed his path in life.

He sat up straighter, letting one hand fall to Digger's head and gave it a scratch between and behind the ears.

"What do you think, Digger? If Josh is telling the truth about The Old Man looking for me to tell me he knows who got Trevor killed, then I have no reason to be suspicious, do I?"

Digger sat back on his haunches and tilted his head as soon as Rex started talking. He gave a short, soft *yip* when Rex said his former handler's name.

"That's right. The same guy either did or didn't get Trevor killed. Should we help him?"

Digger yawned, ending with a whine that indicated to Rex he was nervous and worried, not bored or sleepy.

"I know, buddy. You can't understand what I'm talking about. And you miss your friend. So do I."

In response, Digger got up and paced to the door and sniffed the floor there, then paced back. He didn't stay, though. Instead of sitting, he nudged Rex's leg and paced over to the chair, where he got hold of his leash, dragged it over to Rex and dropped it at his feet. Then he went to the dresser, nudged Rex's phone, gently took it in his mouth, and took it to Rex.

Rex laughed. Digger was telling him that sitting around talking about the problem wasn't going to solve it—*let's take a walk, get some fresh air, it will clear your mind.* He took the wet phone and dried it on his pants leg. "Thanks, buddy. Just give me a few more minutes. Let me just think this through."

Digger sat down, eyed him for a while, and then dropped down on his belly with a big sigh.

Okay, let's assume what Josh told me is true.

With that assumption, he did have a duty of care, toward Josh, the rest of CRC, and the woman with him, who apparently was CRC, too, though he'd never known of a female CRC agent. His duty especially extended to the Old Man, who'd been like a father to him, he had to admit. It was hard to dismiss fourteen months of distrust in an instant, but if he accepted Josh's story, then it seemed he'd had it wrong. What to do?

Trust but verify.

With that thought came the flip of the emotional switch that put him in full mission mode. While verifying, he'd need to begin assembling an operational team. It couldn't be CRC agents, not until he'd verified that Josh wasn't just trying to trap him. That was his first problem to solve.

Despite his doubts, he'd turned the corner. The Old Man in the hands of his enemies was nightmarish. Rex knew only a fraction of what was in the Old Man's head, and that was scary enough. Even fourteen months out of date, what Rex knew could get a lot of people killed. But Brandt knew about every mission CRC had ever conducted, every one of them still in progress, and every informant across the globe who was handled by CRC agents. He also knew about quite a few, operatives and agents both, who were attached to national security agencies of the US and its allies. It was terrifying to just think about the chaos that would follow if that information in Brandt's head landed in the wrong hands.

He knows about Catia!

That was the thought that galvanized Rex. With a final hope the Old Man could withstand the torture, deceive and misdirect his captors, and remain alive long enough for Rex to get to him, Rex jumped to his feet.

He was under no illusion that he could do it with his meager resources. He'd need help from CRC to set up a major SIGINT, FININT, and HUMINT operation, and he'd need more bodies to do surveillance and information gathering when required.

Maybe I can use Rehka's expertise as well?

Hold your horses, you're getting ahead of yourself.

He first had to personally vet Josh and Marissa. And he wouldn't throw caution to the wind. If they wanted to meet with him, it would be on his terms, in a location of his choosing. He wouldn't totally trust them until he could see them, question them, and let Digger sniff at them.

So, the best idea was to meet them in France. He was now a French citizen, he had the gratitude of the President and Prime Minister, not to mention Margot Lemaire. Yes, he had citizenship under a false name, but that was exactly what the French did for some of their Legionnaires when they received French citizenship after serving the mandatory period. And he might even be able to get some assistance from the DGSE.

All this time, as he was talking to himself about what he'd need for the operation and running it by Digger, he was asking the one important question. *What is the goal of the abductors?*

There was just one logical conclusion. They wanted to suck every bit of information out of the Old Man.

At this stage, it didn't cross Rex's mind that he could be the primary target—again.

He picked up his satphone and called Josh.

Chapter Thirty-Four

Rome, Italy

Three days after abduction

It was early morning when Rex had boarded the plane for Lyon, with Digger in his travel crate in the baggage hold.

He'd had a very busy time after that call from Rehka, making contingency plans and working the phones.

First, he'd called Josh.

"Okay, I'll help. But it will be on my terms. Any problem with that?"

"Depends on the terms," Josh had answered.

"You meet me in France…"

"Why France?" Josh interrupted.

"And you won't ask stupid questions," Rex concluded.

A short, muffled conversation ensued from Josh's end of the call. Rex waited, impatiently.

When Josh came back, he said, "Okay, so far, so good.

But when we see you face-to-face, we reserve the right to question your plans."

"*If* you see me face-to-face, and that remains to be seen, I'll entertain your questions, and you will entertain mine. If I don't like your questions or answers, I walk away."

After another muffled interlude, Josh spoke again. "Done."

"Send Rehka a text message with your flight number and ETA when you're on the plane."

"Will do."

"So far so good," Rex mumbled after the call was disconnected.

Rex then called Rehka and gave her several tasks, and he also called Aarav Patel.

Patel was a Mumbai police detective who had become a friend and supporter of Rex's when he'd first started looking for Rehka, before her rescue. Rex had saved Aarav's life when he was attacked by a gang of thugs working for drug dealers. Rex also quietly and efficiently handled a problem Aarav had with one of the major crime bosses in Mumbai. He and Rex became good friends, and he had given Rex support whenever he needed it. He and his family had taken Rehka under their wings when Rex brought her back to Mumbai. Aarav's wife and Rehka had become good friends. Rex knew he could count on Aarav's help and that he wouldn't ask questions.

Rehka had made travel arrangements for Rex from Rome to Lyon. Shortly before his takeoff, he'd received a text message from Rehka confirming that she'd received a text message from Josh and Marissa that they were on the plane Paris bound and their flight details. She also passed on confirmation from Aarav that Mr. Joshua Wilson and

Mrs. Marissa Elizabeth Wilson had successfully boarded their plane for Paris. He relayed the passport details as well.

In his mind, Rex ticked off another item in the honesty section. Josh and Marissa had followed his instructions to the letter.

As soon as he got the text messages from Rehka, Rex phoned her. He went through their security protocol, and then asked her to sit down.

"Rehka, it's time you knew more about me. You may have guessed some of it, but you've been discreet, and you haven't asked too many questions. I now know I can trust you with the most sensitive information."

"Thank you… ah… Rex," she answered.

Rex chuckled. "Josh or Marissa must have given you my real name then?"

She giggled. "Yes, apparently they did. It's going to take a bit to getting used to calling you by that name. If that's what you want me to call you from now on."

"Some days *I'm* not even sure what my real name is. I'll answer to Rex or Ruan or Rowan." Rex laughed and continued. "Well, with the name thing out of the way, let me tell you some more. You may have guessed that I have a military background. The truth is, I was pulled out of the military and trained as what you might call a spy or a black ops specialist." He left out the word assassin. There was no reason to upset Rehka with details of that kind.

"CRC was my unit, and what I did for you and the other women in Mutaib's harem and for Margot—search and rescue—was one of the types of missions I have been trained to execute. Josh Farley was a colleague, and the Old Man they told you about is the CEO and founder of CRC. They told you the truth about our former relationship.

"Someday, I'll tell you why I left CRC, but now is not

the time. I have only a few minutes before I have to leave for the airport. So, knowing all that, are you willing to help me on this mission?"

Rehka answered cautiously. "Ruan, ah… Rex, you know I will. You didn't have to ask."

"It won't be dangerous for you. But I may need you in France, closer to the operation and more in synch with the timing. You'd get to see Margot again, and the baby, and Digger, of course."

"Ruan, you don't have to sweet-talk me. That's even better. I'd love that! I've never been to France." The energy in her voice told him she was all the way in. Whether it was the prospect of seeing him, Digger, Margot and the baby, or because she'd never dreamed she would be visiting France, she was excited.

"All right then. Is your passport in order?"

"Yes, it's good for five more years before expiry."

"Excellent. Then you can start to pack your bags, keep an eye on the flights, and be ready to leave at a moment's notice. It will be in the next forty-eight hours if it happens. Expect it to happen."

"I'll be ready!"

He was late already. It would take some time to get Digger to his boarding area and into the crate before Rex had to board himself.

Chapter Thirty-Five

Lyon, France

Three days after abduction

When he stepped off the plane in Lyon and went to collect Digger, Rex was still deliberating which of the several approaches he'd considered were best.

Surprise Margot by showing up on her doorstep?

Call her from the airport to warn her he was on the way?

He had no idea if Margot would be able or even willing to help him. The last time they saw each other and said their goodbyes, about seven months ago, it was with the tacit understanding that they would probably not see each other again. Not soon. Maybe never, unless there was a crisis. As far as he was concerned, she didn't owe him anything. That wasn't how Rex operated. He didn't help people so that they would return the favor. He *was* hopeful she would be willing to help, and that she'd be willing to use her influence with the President and Prime Minister. But not because she owed him, and he would understand if they were not willing to help.

I'll cross those bridges when I get to them.

He'd flown to Lyon fully expecting that Margot would at least be willing to see him but uncertain as to how she would respond to his request for help.

If she's not happy to see me, maybe she'll be happy to see Digger.

In the end, by the time his plane had landed in Lyon, he'd decided to call Margot and ask if he could visit. He wasn't surprised when Margot squealed in excitement. "*Of course*, you can come for a visit! Why do you even ask? What a surprise, Rowan!"

"Well, it's not just a social visit, Margot. I have a *big* favor to ask, but I'd rather ask it in person. I just wanted to know whether I'd be welcome if I turned up."

"Of course, you're welcome. You are always welcome, you know that."

"Thanks. Let me rent a car, and I'll be there soon."

"Nonsense. Bertrand and I will come to collect you. Digger is with you, I assume?"

"Of course."

"Then I'll leave Rowena with Adele. You and Digger can meet her when we get back. Rowan, she's so adorable! And strong and brave, like her namesake. She's already trying to explore the world, and she's only two months old!" Breathless, she continued, "Where will we find you?"

Rex chuckled at her enthusiasm and thought to tell her she really ought to pause for breath now and then, but instead he told her that he and Digger would be waiting for them at the NHube restaurant.

Two hours later, he sat awkwardly holding little Rowena

on his lap. Margot, who was living with her brother Bert, his wife Adele, and her niece and nephew on the family estate, watched him with the baby, a fond smile on her face. Digger had sniffed the baby and promptly sat at alert next to Rex's knee. He smiled and wagged his tail at the older children, but he declined to be teased into a game. Clearly, the baby was his major responsibility.

Rex hadn't held a baby in decades. He'd still been a child himself when his brother was born, and not much older when his sister came along. He remembered holding his sister and being afraid he'd drop her. He wasn't precisely afraid of dropping the baby Margot had named for him, or rather for his alias, but he wasn't entirely certain he wouldn't break her somehow. It looked as if Rex was handling the finest piece of porcelain.

Adele, Margot's sister in law, who knew how Margot felt about Rex, couldn't let the opportunity go by to pass on a veiled hint in jest. "Rowan, you're a natural, just look how happy Rowena is there on your lap. You'll make a great father."

They all started laughing at the expression of pure horror that crossed Rex's features for a split second before he schooled them.

Margot also laughed—a little.

He did have to admit that the happy baby was cute. She smiled and cooed at him and waved her arms at Digger when he got his face close enough for her to notice him. She had Margot's brown eyes and a mop of thick, black curls.

But me, a father? Now there's a scary thought. How can I even think to be a father with a history such as mine? What will I teach my children? How to be good killers? No way!

After a little while, Adele excused herself and shooed

the children out of the room, taking the baby from Rex and telling Margot she would change Rowena's diaper and put her down for a nap.

Chapter Thirty-Six

Lyon, France

Three days after abduction

"Now, Rowan, it's time for you to tell us about this favor that was too sensitive to tell us in the restaurant. Although why we couldn't hear it in the car on the way home, I have no idea." Margot let her impatience show, a cover for her sudden surge of emotion as she'd watched him with the baby.

She'd managed to hide her feelings—at least, she thought she had. If the truth were known, she would have been very happy if her lovely little girl were indeed his. But she'd known even before the baby was born that Rowan was not ready to settle. There was unfinished business in his life, she could tell. He didn't tell her what it was, and she never asked. And even if she did, she knew he'd never answer her. If ever a woman tamed him, it would be someone who was just as driven as he was to keep moving and keep making a difference.

Even though she had said she'd return to French politics someday, she wasn't anywhere near ready to do so. She was certain this favor had nothing to do with that plan. Unbeknownst to any but herself, Rowan, Lucien Laurent, the Prime Minister of France, and the baby's father himself, Giles Aguillard, President of France, no one else knew who the father was.

Rowan Donnelly was a knight in shining armor. When the police declared her dead, Rowan disagreed with them. He had gone out of his way to find her because he believed she'd been kidnapped from the island of Vanuatu in the South Pacific. He had protected her when Russian agents tried to kidnap her. He'd prevented DGSE agents from arresting and extraditing her to France. He'd brokered a deal between her and Aguillard. He'd offered to claim the baby as his to help her and to save Aguillard's government from a major scandal. As far as she was concerned, if it was in her power to help him and didn't endanger her baby, there was nothing Rowan Donnelly could ask that she'd be unwilling to agree to.

Before he said anything else, Rowan asked Bert when the last time was that Margot's security detail had swept the house and the room for bugs. Since Margot had moved in with her brother and his family on the family estate in Lyon, the President had seen to it that France's equivalent of the FBI, a DGSI security detail, was assigned to her.

"They do it every day at irregular times. Today it was done this morning shortly before you called Margot from the airport. Would you like me to leave while you talk to Margot?"

"No, Bert. Thank you, but if Margot grants my request then I'd need some favors from you as well."

He then proceeded to tell them what he'd told Rehka. Including his real name and surname. Hearing his real name, Margot looked a bit shocked and Rex noticed.

"No, Margot, you don't have to change her name. I'm humbled, and it remains a great honor that you've named her after me. Besides, thanks to you, Rowan Donnelly *is* one of my legitimate names, and strange as it may sound, I'm proud of that name, especially so since you used the name for that beautiful little girl. So, please don't run off and change her name to Regina, I like Rowena much better."

Margot nodded and started smiling. "I guess you're right. It is as William Shakespeare said so eloquently, 'A rose by any other name would smell as sweet'."

And with that the issues about names, Rex's and Rowena's, were settled.

Neither Margot nor Bert was surprised when Rex gave them a bit of background on his training and his past missions at CRC, although he kept that at a very high level and very vague. Again, there was no reason to get into any of the scary or nasty stuff. As soon as he outlined the operation he had in mind, and assured them that running it from France, if it could be done with the help of the DGSE and DGSI as it would help protect them from any associated danger, they agreed to help.

Moments later, Margot was on Rex's satphone, talking to Lucien Laurent, the Prime Minister and longtime family friend, on his encrypted phone. Laurent didn't need much persuasion once he heard who was asking and what he was asking. He was happy to facilitate whatever he could for the man who'd, in his opinion, saved not only his beloved country from embarrassment but also Margot, his old friend's daughter whom he and his wife loved as if she was their own daughter.

In short order, Laurent agreed to the request, undertook to get the President's buy-in, and inform the Director of DGSE. Rex would meet with Laurent and the Director as soon as he'd arrived in Paris.

Rex was relieved. Now it only remained to vet Josh and Marissa after they'd arrived in France. So far, although they'd passed the first honesty tests, it hadn't been enough to give him the assurances he wanted. Nevertheless, there wasn't time for too much of that. If they were telling the truth, the Old Man had been in custody for four days already. The more time that passed before they found him, the more operations could be blown, and the more lives lost. He had at most another twelve hours to put everything in place.

In Rex's mind there was no doubt the Old Man was alive, and he was going to remain that way until, they, Rex and Digger, rescued him.

———

The next order of business, before getting on the plane to Paris, was to get Rehka on a plane over to France. Rex had decided that it would be best to have Rehka ready to help if he got back to Lyon with Josh and Marissa on board with his plans. If not, he could decide whether to run the operation from there or send Rehka back to Mumbai after a pleasant visit with Margot. She would love to meet the baby, in any case. Either way, no time would have been wasted waiting for her to arrive on the long flight from Mumbai. He made the call with the usual security protocols.

"Rehka, are you ready for that trip to France I mentioned?"

"Yes! Oh, Ruan, I'm so excited! I've been waiting for this call."

"Now, what would you be excited about?" he teased. "Surely not over seeing me?"

"Of course not. I'll be excited to see Digger and meet little Rowena. And to see Margot again."

"Well, thanks for deflating my ego." He laughed. "Okay, Rehka, now before you get on the flight to Lyon, I want you to go to the main branch of the Deutsche Bank in the Bandra Kurla Complex in Maharashtra. You know which one I'm talking about?"

"Yes, I know where it is."

"Good. I want you to go to my safe-deposit box and retrieve the three hard drives and the laptop and bring that with you."

"No problem. I have enough time between now and the next flight, if I can get a seat on the one I'm looking at now."

He gave her the details she'd need to access the deposit box, then told her to text him with her itinerary as soon as she had her flight booked, and again when she'd cleared customs in Mumbai.

"Margot will pick you up," he promised.

Chapter Thirty-Seven

Paris, France

Three days after abduction

Rex had enlisted Margot's and Bert's support and permission, which they were both eager to give, to allow him to set up his operations center in their guest house on the estate, where he'd spent a few days once before.

The next stop was Paris, where he first had to talk to the Prime Minister to get the help of the DGSE if he were able to establish that Josh and Marissa were not trying to lead him into a trap.

Shortly after six p.m., Rex's plane from Lyon landed in Paris. After the usual ritual of getting Digger out of the holding area and out of his cage, the two of them went to the baggage claim area to meet with the person who would transport them to the Prime Minister's office.

Walking into the hall, Rex immediately identified the

man with the dark suit, earpieces, dark glasses, and bulge under the left arm where he had his pistol holstered. Rex started laughing when he saw the little whiteboard in the agent's hands, the words *Messieurs Donnelly et Digger* written on it.

He tried to get over the hilarity of Digger being called mister before the agent would spot them, but then he did himself in when he looked down at Digger and started saying, "Monsieur Digger…" and went into another bout of involuntary mirth.

He bent down to Digger to stay out of the agent's sight.

Dalton, what's wrong with you? You better get hold of yourself or that guy will take you straight to the psychiatric ward and have you put in a straitjacket instead of taking you to the Prime Minister.

Rex couldn't explain to himself what was so funny. He could only put it down to the stress of the last few days, not so much what he had to organize but that he'd been found and maybe the Old Man's situation and maybe…

Just then, the agent saw Rex and Digger and approached. By the time he got to them Rex had his laughter under control. The agent showed Rex his credentials and they shook hands. The agent kept on looking around as if he was expecting someone else to be there.

Rex said, with a big smile, "and this is Monsieur Digger."

The agent started laughing and explained that he was expecting to pick up two humans.

"Okay, Messieurs Dalton and Digger, please follow me, I've got a vehicle outside waiting for you."

By seven p.m., Rex and Digger were seated in Prime Minister Laurent's office. The Director of DGSE was also in attendance and so was one of his deputy directors, Madame Proll, in charge of clandestine operations.

It took about an hour for Rex to first explain to the Prime Minister and Director what he had to explain to Rehka and then Margot and her brother, that he was actually not Rowan Donnelly but Rex Dalton. Then, of course, immediately had to explain why he was going around under a nom de guerre.

Laurent trusted Rex unconditionally, the Director of the DGSE and his deputy not so much. They had many questions.

Rex's problem was he couldn't just spill the beans about CRC and what they did. He felt as if he was doing the egg dance, a traditional Easter game in which eggs are laid on the floor and then you had to dance among them while damaging as few as possible. In the end there was just no way out, unless he withheld crucial information and started lying to them.

When the adage, *to make omelets you have to break eggs* crossed his mind he knew he had to give them more information, and some of it was going to be top secret. But if it helped him save John Brandt then he'd do it. He asked their solemn oath that they would keep what he was going to tell them a secret.

They all agreed.

Rex sighed with relief and continued to tell them about CRC without mentioning the name or the name of John Brandt.

He was still busy providing background when Madame Proll caught his attention. She looked young for the position she held, but a second look brought the realization that she could've been older than the forty or so she looked. A tall woman, athletic build, formally dressed in a charcoal pantsuit, with green eyes and blond hair that didn't look like it came out of a bottle—she was a head-turner. *Attentiveness, intelligence, don't mess with her,* were the words that popped up in Rex's mind as he observed her. Rex had tried to guess her age and gave up somewhere between what could have been, if asked to venture a guess, a compliment or an insult—between forty and sixty-five.

Fortunately, no one asked.

"Monsieur Dalton, to help put your mind at ease, I, personally, and some of my agents have worked with your CIA in the past. We've also worked with some of the outsourced private contractors used by the CIA."

Rex nodded. "Thanks, that helps. Well, so I work for CRC, Crisis…"

"Crisis Response Consultancy, John Brandt? Is that who you're not trying to talk about, Monsieur Dalton?" she asked, her head slightly tilted and a beautiful little grin on her lips.

Rex nodded in astonishment. It took him a few seconds to get his speech back. "Yes, Madame. How…" He cleared his throat. "How do you know the Old Man… ah… I mean John."

Madame Proll smiled. "Careful with the sobriquets monsieur, some people don't like it when you refer to their age, in any manner. But to answer your question, I've known John for a long time. We worked together during the Cold War and after. We still have contact, from time to time."

Contact with John? Working together during the Cold War? That ended in 1991, more than a quarter of a century ago. You're definitely not forty then. You could've fooled me.

She continued. "What is it that John can't pick up the phone for and talk to me?"

"Madame, it's suspected that he'd been abducted in Athens four days ago."

"Suspected? Care to explain?"

Laurent obviously didn't understand the alarm which he saw on the faces of the Director and Madame Proll and asked what he was missing. Proll explained that John Brandt carried a lot of very sensitive secrets in his head, including some of the joint operations conducted between the DGSE and CIA, not only from back in the Cold War days, but also some very recent ones, and some still in progress.

"So, this might hold consequences… a threat to France and the DGSE's covert activities and assets as well?"

"Absolutely, without question, Monsieur Prime Minister," the Director answered.

It took another half hour or so to get all the details out and get the Director to hand the matter over to Madame Proll, with the blessings of the Prime Minister and by then also the President, whom Laurent had briefed via a secured phone call in the meantime. The President had one caveat though; the DGSE's and government's involvement had to be kept on a very strict need-to-know basis.

Rex had no issues with that.

With the proper authorization and backing in place, Madame Proll was very eager to help with any request Rex and CRC might have.

"The first thing you can help me with, Madame Proll, is to vet this Josh Farley and Marissa Bissett after they've arrived in Paris later tonight."

She agreed and immediately arranged for one of her senior agents to meet with Rex right away.

Rex left the meeting with a big smile. He had everything he could hope for and more. And he also had one pertinent question he wanted to ask the Old Man when he'd rescued him, which was going to be, "Tell me about Madame Proll."

Chapter Thirty-Eight

Paris, France

Four days after abduction

Josh and Marissa arrived in Paris just after midnight. They almost missed the sign with their assumed names on it, held by the car hire employee waiting for them. He handed them a sealed envelope with a note that read: G*o to your hotel and stay in your room, use room service for your evening meal, and wait for a call from me.*

In the glove box of the vehicle they found two Glock pistols, which they'd requested Chris McArdle should arrange for them, fully loaded with two spare magazines for each gun.

Josh grumbled that Rex was treating them like naughty children, but Marissa had a cooler head.

"He's testing us, Josh. It's to be expected. You'd do the

same if someone had hunted you down with a story like ours. You'd think it was a trap—admit it."

"You're right. I would. But how are we to know this isn't his idea of a trap for us."

"We don't, but if we're going to get his help with finding John, we have to risk it."

"Time is getting short for the Old Man, if it isn't already too late. I don't like this monkey business. He should have met us at the airport, and we should have been working on the case now, not sitting around in a hotel room."

Marissa was more pragmatic. "There has to be a reason he wanted us in France. What do you want to bet he's got some kind of support here? A network of contacts. He's probably listening to us right now."

Josh looked thunderstruck, and he immediately jumped up, started an app on his satphone, and swept the room for bugs. When he found them, he turned red in the face, brought one to his mouth and spoke in a loud and clear voice, "Rex Dalton, I hope you are listening, you son of a bitch. When I see you, I'm going to kick your ass for this. We've never had any motives but the best. This is what I think of your damn bugs." He threw them to the floor and stomped them.

Marissa looked at him with a big grin. "Feeling better now?"

Josh just growled and got himself a beer from the minibar.

Rex and Digger were in the same hotel, three floors above Josh's and Marissa's. Rex laughed out loud as he listened to

Josh Farley's rants. "Kick my ass, Josh? Not as long as your ass points to the ground. But I'll be a sport and give you the chance."

What Marissa and Josh wouldn't have known was that in addition to the bugs Rex knew they'd expect, locate, and destroy, the DGSE had also employed something they were eager to field-test. The latest and greatest in their spyware had only recently been developed, and foreign agencies hadn't yet discovered and developed countermeasures for them.

Rex thought once Josh and Marissa had found the 'decoy' bugs, they'd relax and talk more openly. And that proved to be the case. He heard them discussing installing the anti-vibration devices on the room window, so no one could eavesdrop on them with a parabolic microphone from the outside. Even though the device, which used the vibrations on the windows caused when people in the room were talking, had been in use for decades, it was still a device used against the uninitiated. But Rex had expected Josh and Marissa would have defenses against it, so he didn't even bother.

Rex listened for a while longer, as Josh grew increasingly vocal about the delay, and Marissa alternately agreed with him and tried to calm him down.

When Rex heard her say, "Let's go to bed. He won't contact us tonight. We need to get some rest," he felt confident there'd be nothing of importance said for the rest of the night.

Even though he'd heard nothing to indicate they had ulterior motives, he wasn't going to take any chances. However, he had no problem admitting that he was paranoid now, especially when he was on a mission. As far as he was concerned, when on a mission, healthy paranoia was a good state of mind. As he closed his eyes, he set his mental clock to wake him in four hours, about twenty minutes ahead of the wake-up call he'd left with the front desk. It would be a long day for everyone.

At six a.m., after a refreshing shower and a room-service meal, Rex checked with the team leader of the DGSE surveillance team that they were ready for the planned operation.

Then he sent Josh a text.

Meet me at Oh! Regalade de la Tour Eiffel, 67 quai Branly, 200 meters from the Eiffel Tower. 7:00. Hope you like hot dogs and ice cream for breakfast.

He had no intention of meeting them there. To the best of his knowledge, it wasn't even open yet for the day. The DGSE team would observe and report back if Josh and Marissa had backup or anything looked suspicious. Then one of them would pay a street kid to take them a note.

Rex watched out his window overlooking the hotel entrance as Josh and Marissa raced out to hail a taxi fifteen minutes later. He grinned.

No time for a shower, no breakfast. They've started off on the wrong foot, I'll keep them off balance and frustrated that way. It will be easy to trip them up if they are up to no good.

At the hot dog stand, at *Oh! Regalade de la Tour Eiffel* the couple stopped short at the Closed sign and started looking around, obviously hoping to see Rex approaching or waiting for them. Rex watched a live feed from the DGSE agent's camera as they waited until the top of the hour, and then Josh threw his hands in the air and could be seen talking rapidly to Marissa, gesticulating wildly. Rex didn't need audio to get the gist of what Josh was saying.

"Send the kid in with the note," Rex instructed a second agent.

Moments later, a skinny teenager slouched toward Josh, holding a note in one hand with the other outstretched, palm up. Marissa dug in her handbag while Josh read the note and then questioned the kid, who shrugged. Marissa handed the kid something, Rex assumed a few Euros, and then took Josh firmly by the arm and virtually shoved him toward a corner, where they got into a taxi a few minutes later.

The next several 'meeting venues' went the same way, until late that afternoon, Josh crossed his arms, looked at Marissa, and said something. Then Josh unfolded his arms raised them both above his head, displaying a middle finger on each hand. He slowly made a three-sixty-degree turn. The message to Rex needed no interpretation or translation —it would be understood universally.

Rex grinned. There'd been no sign that the couple was followed or had any kind of backup. Josh had clearly had a gutful, and the two were showing signs they were at odds.

It was time.

He sent a text to Josh directly. Something's come up. I'll have to meet with you tomorrow. Go back to your hotel and wait for my call.

Josh shook his right fist in the air while making another three-sixty for Rex's attention.

Rex smiled and shook his head. I really need to have a chat with that young man about what is expected of decent people in public places.

Chapter Thirty-Nine

Unknown location

Four days after abduction

John Brandt still had no idea where he was, how long he had been there, or the day or time.

His captors had given him water and some energy bars what felt like every four hours or so, but it was impossible to tell how much time elapsed between each feeding. The stinking bag was still over his head, and no one spoke to him when they attended to him.

The people who untied him and fed him never spoke a word, and though his eyes had adjusted to the dark, there was still very little light. All he could tell when they removed the bag was that they were wearing ski masks.

He was naked as the day he was born. There was no toilet, not even a bucket, and if there had been one, he wouldn't have been able to use it, because they kept him tied down, spread-eagled, all the time, only untying his hands and removing the bag over his head to eat and drink.

With every feeding, they would first hose him down with what felt like a firehose to get rid of the urine and excrement. Then they'd take his pulse and blood pressure and write it down. Only then did they feed him.

All of this was part of the process, disorienting and softening the captive up before the interrogation started. John Brandt knew from personal experience, having used it himself on many occasions and trained his CRC agents in the same methods. He and every agent he'd trained had gone through it during training, more than once, to teach them how to withstand it and prepare themselves for what would come after the first stage.

What he was going through now was the easy part. In a few days, or weeks, or months, if he lasted that long, he was going to miss this time of "peace and quiet."

After what felt like maybe two days—it could have been more, or it could have been less, he had no idea—he was untied and dragged out of the room or container into another room or container.

They removed the bag, and he squinted against the bright light. It had the same proportions as a container, which would fit his theory from the periodic rocking he could feel that he was on a ship. However, it was fitted with wooden panels and a tiled floor. Everything was white, and the lights were extremely bright, uncomfortable after his hours of enforced darkness.

The two men tied him to a metal chair with armrests. Risking an early blow, he tested but found the chair was bolted to the floor. His captors secured his arms with duct tape to the armrests, leaving his hands available to the torturer for all the fun stuff to come. His feet were tied to the legs of the chair making his feet available for more fun stuff.

This will be the beginning. They'll pull a few fingernails, maybe break a finger or two, smash my toes with a hammer. Get ready, old man. Let's see if you've still got it.

Brandt looked around the room and noticed the array of video cameras on the wall, with microphones hanging from the ceiling above his head.

Excellent. I'd hate to think I'll be putting on this performance without an audience in attendance.

What he didn't know was that his audience was not in attendance, not onsite. He was sitting on the other side of the Atlantic Ocean, more than 7,700 kilometers away in New York, watching on closed-circuit TV in real time, cracking jokes at the unenviable situation of his enemy and with great anticipation awaiting the start of the show while sipping hundred-year-old single malt whisky and nibbling on snacks.

As John watched, they wheeled in a stainless-steel trolley. On it were all the tools for interrogation to inflict pain. They placed it right next to him where he could see it. Intimidation, or so they would have assumed. John kept his sardonic grin to himself. He wasn't intimidated. He knew the drill. What was coming would be painful but survivable, until his mind broke and he told them what they wanted to know. That would be days, maybe weeks from now, he silently promised them—and himself. He wasn't looking forward to it, but it's the unknown that intimidates. He knew exactly how it would go.

All the 'surgical' equipment looked clean and sterile, and together with the bottles of antiseptics, it looked like they were preparing for major surgery. Only the anesthesiologist was missing. He had to suppress a small grin again as he wondered how they'd react if he asked where the good doctor might be.

Good work, boys. No use killing your source of information unintentionally with a nasty infection before you've sucked him dry.

However, on closer inspection, he saw that the hammer hanging off the side didn't look so sterile, though. It was full of rust and grease, as dirty or more so than any construction tool he'd ever seen.

That would be for the knees, elbows and feet. Shit, I hope they wrap it in cloth to soften the blows a bit.

He suppressed the grin once more when he thought, *Okay, I'm ready. It seems you're ready, so let's get this show on the road.*

He had some time to wait, presumably to allow the dread to build. Instead, Brandt meditated, putting himself in a serene state. Then a man walked in, and Brandt almost laughed. He was dressed in a suit, white shirt, but no tie. A tall man, with tanned skin, gray hair, and dark sunken eyes; he had a smile on his face.

So, this is going to be my tormentor. Well, buddy, it takes two to tango.

John knew the process. The man would start out friendly, not with what he really wanted to know. He'd hide his ultimate objective, though Brandt had no illusion what the ultimate objective was. The specifics didn't matter. The ultimate objective would be all of the information in his head, and if he gave in, people would die.

"My name is Logan Jones," the interrogator said.

Brandt didn't reply, just nodded slightly. *I'm Bugs, like in Bugs Bunny.*

"I am sorry for the discomfort you've had to endure. I told the men to treat you well and make sure that you were comfortable. But they obviously misunderstood me. Believe me, I'll have a quiet word with them about this and make sure that they follow my instructions to the letter from now on."

Yeah, I can't wait to move into the deluxe suite.

'Logan'—Brandt doubted it was his real name—spoke perfect English but with a heavy Eastern European accent. Brandt couldn't place it, but if he had to venture a guess, it would have been Bulgarian. Brandt was fluent in Russian and French, languages he learned when he operated in Europe during and after the Cold War. He knew a few words and phrases in Bulgarian and some of the other Eastern European languages, but he was not going to let this man know what he understood or not.

Brandt finally spoke. "Oh, that's great to hear. So, this whole thing is a misunderstanding. Right? Then there is no need to have me tied up like this. Right? Why don't you untie me, let me have a shower, put on my clothes, and you and I can find a nice place where we can have a coffee and chat?"

Logan grinned, revealing what had no doubt been expensive dental work, and shook his head. "Sorry, my friend. I see that you are a joker. As you know, I can't do that, not yet. I am going to ask you a few questions, and I hope we can get this over with very quickly. Let's start with your name and who you work for."

Brandt grinned in return. "Oh, okay, so no coffee then. My name you asked. I am sure you know that already. I heard you saying you want to get this over with very quickly. Believe me, I want it over with even more quickly. Maybe we can cut out the unnecessary questions?"

Logan said, "Yes, I know the answers, but I need to first see that you have not received some kind of brain trauma because of the bad treatment you were given, for which I apologize again."

"Right," Brandt said. "How thoughtful of you." *And of course, to check if I'm lying.*

Logan nodded as if acknowledging a real compliment. His flat expression told a different story. They were taking each other's measurements, sizing each other up. The verbal sparring would go on until Logan grew tired of it, and then the real fun would begin.

"I think my brain is good. I've had it since birth and took good care of it for the past sixty-eight years. My name is John Brandt, and I am the CEO of CRC – Crisis Response Consultancy. How was that? Brain damaged or not?"

Logan grinned. "It looks good so far, but there are a few more questions before I'll be able to tell with certainty."

"Shoot."

"I am interested in some of your clients and the work you do for them."

"As the name says, we do consultancy work. As you might guess, my company responds to crises. I'm afraid our client list is private. You see, some of them don't want their customers to know they have had a crisis. Bad for business, you know."

Logan persisted. "I need to know more about some of your clients. For instance, their names, the dates you worked for them, and more specifics about the work you did for them."

Brandt shook his head. "You must be joking! That's not the way to run a business. It's important to keep your customer information confidential. I'll get my ass sued and my company bankrupted before you can say 'thank you'. I signed NDAs, Non-Disclosure Agreements, with all my clients, so I can't divulge that information without their explicit written authorization. As for what we do, we're consultants. We don't really do much other than give advice."

Logan nodded. "Well, John, I think we might have an impasse. You see, I need some information. Until I have it, I'm not authorized to improve your situation. The thing is, if I can't get the information, I'll have to use more… oh dear… how shall I put it? More strenuous measures? I hope that won't be necessary."

"Okay, Logan. Let's cut the foreplay. I'm all worked up and ready. Come to the point. Tell me what it is that you want to know, and I will see if I can remember. But bear in mind, my brain *is* sixty-eight years old, and as you said, it could've been damaged because of the maltreatment by your goons."

"Tell me about the work you did for the CIA in Afghanistan between June 2013 and July 2014."

Brandt was only a little surprised that Logan started with Afghanistan and not with the spies CRC had been handling throughout quite a few eastern European countries, including Russia and the Middle East. During the time period Logan was asking about, in Afghanistan, CRC had at least five operations going. Two of them were to assassinate Taliban leaders, two were straightforward handling of various spies who had infiltrated the Taliban and were providing information to their handlers, and the fifth one was Rex Dalton's mission to study the opium trade to find out their contacts, delivery routes, and anything else he could find.

The last operation had gone south when Rex started eliminating producers and dealers and blowing up their warehouses. Not that Rex had reported his extracurricular activities, but it wasn't a stretch for Brandt to figure it out. Rex had asked for permission. When it didn't come, he'd taken matters into his own hands.

It ended with Rex and his men in an ambush, with seven of them killed, and as he now knew, only Rex and a military dog survived. He'd only days before his capture learned that Rex and the dog did in fact survive.

Brandt, playing for time, gave some vague information about one of the operations, the killing of the Taliban leaders. Those guys had already been killed and there was not much damaging information he could give about the operation. Under further questioning, Brandt told Logan he wouldn't admit or deny that the CIA had been involved. He admitted there had been CRC operatives involved but in advisory capacity. "Information gathering and interpretation," Brandt said. "But they never did the killing."

Which was a lie, of course. One of those assassinations had been carried out by Josh Farley, the guy looking for Rex. *And I hope Josh finds him quickly. The two of them may be my only hope to get out of this alive.*

Brandt could see that his rambling and vague answers were beginning to annoy Logan. It didn't show on his face, but his body language telegraphed it as surely as if he'd started throwing things and shouting. Brandt's strategy was working. It might make the questioning more painful more quickly, but that didn't matter. What mattered was his ability to tie the man in knots and force him to waste time investigating the disinformation.

Logan turned the subject to the second set of missions, the spies in the Taliban. Now this was much more serious stuff. Those operations were ongoing, and the spies were alive and spying. Brandt knew if he talked about this one, he would be placing those spies in real danger. They and their families would die horrendous deaths.

"Tell me about this mission to spy on Taliban leaders. Has that mission been completed? Who are the targets? Who are the spies?"

Though Brandt knew the names of the leaders and key people in the Taliban groups, as well as the names of the spies and his operatives who were handling them, he knew his own horrific death would be preferable to letting his men and their contacts down.

But maybe I can do some real damage to the Taliban.

Brandt shook his head. "No."

"Excellent. You will tell me, then, who are the targets, and who are the spies?"

"I'm sorry, but you know I can't give you that information."

Brandt screamed as the hammer came down on his hand. He'd been so intent on reading Logan's face that he hadn't noticed the man lifting the hammer until too late to steel himself to the pain. He was certain bones had been broken. His hand was on fire, and worse, it was throbbing. Every beat of his heart sent stabbing pain radiating up his arm.

Well, the gloves are off, now. Time for my best acting job.

Brandt allowed himself to fully feel the pain, until involuntary tears sprang from his eyes. He could have ignored it, but the idea was not to accept more punishment than necessary, while letting Logan believe his tactics were effective. It was a fine line, and Brandt hadn't had to dance it for many years. *It's just like riding a bicycle,* he told himself. Let enough of the pain through to be convincing, but not so much that he really gave away anything important.

In the end, after letting Logan inflict what he thought

was a lot of pain, Brandt gave a few names—those of some devoted Taliban leaders—none of them spies for CRC. If Logan passed that information on, those guys would be history overnight. He knew how the Taliban operated—no trials, no please explain, no second chances. The mere fact that a person was named a traitor was enough. If the person were unfortunate enough not to be killed outright immediately, he would be tortured, he and his family, until they got a confession out of him, true or not.

That would cause so much distrust and havoc and fear among the Taliban that it would take them months, more than likely a few years, to regroup.

Brandt was hurting too much to grin, but he would have if he could have, as he thought this could very well turn out to be one of CRC's most effective operations in a very long time.

It was probably only going to cost a few of his finger-nails, maybe a knee, and a few electric shocks in addition to the broken hand.

All part of a successful mission.

Chapter Forty

Paris, France

Four days after abduction

Josh and Marissa were still steaming about the royal runaround Rex had given them when they walked into their hotel room just before midnight. They were jetlagged and tired and grumpy.

But then, there he was, waiting for them—in their room. Rex Dalton, the man they'd been chasing for more than a year.

They stared straight into his Sig Sauer P226. Digger, the big black dog, not a djinn which they heard so much about and only half-believed in its existence, was standing next to him, on alert, his lips pulled back in a snarl, though he was silent.

They froze in their tracks.

Rex had deactivated the remaining bugs before they'd

arrived. The DGSE didn't need to know everything about his business. The need-to-know principle worked both ways.

Rex told his former colleagues to close the door, put their guns and knives and mobile phones on the table, and to take out the batteries. Then he told them to strip, Marissa to keep her bra and panties and Josh his boxer briefs.

Josh scoffed. Marissa was much more vocal, complained and protested, "I've heard a lot about you, Dalton, but no one told me on top of everything else you're also a nut job and a pervert."

"Yeah, well, I've learned a long time ago I can only please some people some of the time not everyone all the time. So, shut up and take it off."

Josh started to open his mouth to support the protest, but evidently something in Rex's expression told him Rex was not playing games, and by the looks of it the dog was getting impatient as well.

With Digger backing him up, Rex searched them, making them lean against the wall, face to the wall, supported by their arms and their legs spread. Rex, being a male and nothing wrong with his testosterone levels, couldn't help but notice what a beautiful woman Marissa was, even before she took off her clothes. He would have apologized to her for the necessity to touch her, but his observations of her during the day told him she was a trained professional and would know he wasn't just copping a feel. Even if she didn't, he didn't care. This was about his security, and he considered it necessary, no matter who it offended.

While he searched them, he paid close attention to Digger's behavior. He'd been with Digger for long enough to know that it was important to pay close attention to the signals the dog was giving when he met people for the first time. Digger was a four-legged lie detector that outstripped any man-made device or human observations. Digger had carefully sniffed at both of them in turn before he took a step back and sat down behind them, about one pace away. He'd looked at Rex and 'smiled,' mouth open and tongue lolling out as if to say, "They're okay, you can trust them."

Despite Digger's assurances, Rex continued to hold them at gunpoint. He allowed Marissa to put on a robe for modesty but left Josh in his briefs. He ordered them to sit down on the couch and to ziptie each other, feet first, then Marissa to ziptie Josh's hands. Finally, Rex commanded Digger to protect, while he took care of Marissa's hands. When he was satisfied they were immobilized, he ordered them to start talking.

Marissa refused to talk, still glaring at him over the humiliation she'd suffered, and Josh looked as if he was on the verge of self-combustion.

"So, buddy," Rex said, after both refused to say a word. "You're going to kick my ass, are you? But I guess you'll have to wait, we have more important matters to discuss right now. Assuming you're telling the truth about the Old Man, he's running out of time. Or are you really going to let a little grudge delay his rescue?"

Marissa spat, "Who's been playing games all day?"

It was Josh who calmed the waters this time. "I get it. You had to learn if we were followed or watched. So, now that you know we're not two-timing you, let's get on with it. Who's helping you?"

"Stupid question. I thought we agreed you won't ask stupid questions."

"Okay, you still don't trust us. At some point, you'll just have to. In the meantime, here's what we know. We don't have a ransom note, and I doubt you know the people who reported him missing. We didn't. We were in Mumbai, on our way to your friend Rehka, when we got the news. Our orders from the Old Man were to find you and decide whether you had amnesia or had gone mad."

"So you say," Rex interjected.

"Yeah, so I say," Josh stuck out his square jaw and stared at Rex, until he gestured for Josh to continue.

"We've been all over the damn place trying to find you. For a long time, Marissa and I believed you were dead and that the Old Man had lost his marbles. That was until six weeks ago when we went to Saudi Arabia and for the first time got confirmation that you were alive and traveling with a big black dog. The Saudis provided us with information about the women, the pleasure wives you rescued, and we started following their trails in the hope that one of them would lead us to you. We went to Turkey in search of Hande Avci but realized it would take some time to track her down. Apparently, she lives in Ankara these days.

"From Turkey we went to Bilaspur where we met with that funny old guy, Gyan, Rehka's dad. By the way, he said to tell you he'll whip your ass at Chaturanga if you dare show your face there again."

Of anything Josh could have said, that took the edge off Rex a bit. That was something Gyan *would* have said, and he would've been cackling as he said it. A faint grin started, before he caught himself and put on his poker face again.

Josh took up the tale. "The Gyans finally gave us the confirmation we needed and told us where we could find their daughter, Rehka, and told us she would know where to find you. Oh, and as I've told you before, Mrs. Gyan reckons you could be good son-in-law material. I didn't set her straight though." And without missing a beat he continued.

"Right when we landed in Mumbai, all the messages we'd missed while the plane was in the air came in. One was from Longland, who, when we called back, told us the Old Man had been kidnapped and then handed the phone to Chris McArdle who filled us in on what he knew."

"Who contacted him? How did they know to call McArdle?" Rex's tone was aggressive. This was the first potential hole in the story. He seriously doubted the Old Man would have told anyone his identity.

"I'm not real clear on that. McArdle said it was some people he traveled with occasionally. He said he got the impression they might have been old friends from his days with the Company, or maybe retired CRC people?"

"Go on."

"That's all we know. McArdle said our top priority was to find you if we could do it in a hurry. Otherwise, we were to get to Athens and see if we could pick up the trail. So, Dalton, you need to make up your mind. Are you going to help us or not? I need to report to McArdle what you've decided."

"Are the police looking for him?"

"Come on, Rex. You know they couldn't involve the police. The Old Man was in Greece on CRC business and under a false name. You think it would be a good idea to go to the police and say to them, 'hey guys, we lost our spymaster in your country, can you please help us find him?'

"It's up to us. And as much as I disagree with him, McArdle thinks you can help us. It seems the Old Man didn't tell him about his belief that you were alive. Longland was the one who told him. McArdle was pretty shaken when he told us to find you. It was just a stroke of luck that we did, considering how long we'd been looking."

"I don't believe in luck or coincidences," Rex stated. His

voice was so heavy with suspicion that Digger growled as if to punctuate the message.

"Neither do I, buddy, but you said you almost bumped into us at the Taj Mahal. What do you call that? If not coincidence, then it must be destiny. Fact is, we found you right at the time when the Old Man was abducted…"

"Never mind that. All right, let's say I believe you. Tell me everything you know about the kidnapping."

"From us, it would be second-hand. What do you say to letting us go and we can all hear it in detail from those friends he was with?"

"From you first. Then them."

Josh sighed. "Dalton, you are the most pigheaded person I've ever met. It's a waste of time."

Marissa, who spoke for the first time since this conversation started, interrupted. "No, Josh, *you* are even more obstinate than he is. Just tell him."

With an irritated glance her way, he complied, telling Rex the bare bones because that was all he knew. "It was about five days ago, at night, in Athens. The Old Man had gone for a walk and hadn't come back. He was not found dead or unconscious, he wasn't in any of the nearby hospitals, and he would have told his traveling companions if he intended to go off on his own.

"Everyone assumes kidnapping, because the Old Man has a valuable commodity—intimate knowledge of every important mission that CRC or its principal clients are running. You know the motto; prepare for the worst, hope for the best."

Rex hadn't needed to be told that. He'd already considered the dire consequences if the Old Man were to talk. And it was only a matter of time before he did.

"So, let me see. There was no ransom demand, right?" Rex asked.

"Yes, none so far." Marissa replied. "And if we're correct in our assumptions about his kidnapping, we are not expecting any. The kidnappers want information, not money or a prisoner swap or release of terrorists or the like."

"That means he could be dead, and they haven't found the body yet, or he's alive and we may or may not get a ransom demand. I take it we are all in agreement that we assume he's alive until we have evidence to the contrary?" Rex asked.

"Absolutely," Josh and Marissa replied in unison.

Rex quickly cut their zipties with his KA-BAR knife. "Okay, get dressed. I've already got an operations center set up, and Rehka will be there to provide IT support by the time we get there.

"No hard feelings?"

"I'm still going to kick your ass." Josh grinned. Only now, I'm gonna do it twice. Once for the bugs, and once for the insult to my woman. And where is this 'there' you're talking about?"

Rex grinned. "Okay, here's the deal. We find the Old Man. When that's over, I will grant your death wish and allow you to *try* to kick my ass. Note the emphasis on the word try. As for where 'there' is, I'll tell you later."

Rex didn't wait for Josh's reply. He turned to Digger and said, "Digger, these are friends. But watch them carefully."

Josh and Marissa both shot nervous glances at the dog and at each other. They had no idea whether the dog could understand human speech that was more nuanced than commands or if Rex was playing the fool with them. They glanced at each other again and wordlessly agreed not to try to find out which it was.

Chapter Forty-One

En route to Lyon, France

Five days after abduction

It was shortly after four a.m. when they checked out of the hotel. They got a taxi to take them back to the airport where they rented a car to drive to Lyon. Rex thought it was better to make the five-hour drive instead of flying so that they could use the time to start planning their mission. Besides, the five-hour drive also gave the DGSE time to set up all the equipment they'd need in the Lemaire guest house and then disappear. Rex still didn't want Josh and Marissa to know who had been supporting him thus far. At some stage they might need to know, and that's when they would be informed.

Rex assured them he'd have state-of-the art computing equipment and secure comms available when they got to their destination. Josh and Marissa asked about the destination. Rex only told them that it was a guesthouse on a private estate outside Lyon, belonging to friends who'd agreed to help but stay out of the way.

Before they got into the car, Josh made a quick call to Chris McArdle, to let him know that they'd finally managed to meet Rex and his big black dog, Digger.

McArdle was excited and told Josh he wanted them all on the first plane back to the US or if necessary, he'd charter a private jet for them.

At that, Josh told him to hold the line, he put the call on mute and told Rex what McArdle wanted.

"Tell McArdle, with my compliments, unless he knows where John Brandt is being held, I'm not going to the US. I'm in France, I'm going to Lyon, and that's where I'm going to stay until we find out where the Old Man is. Also, tell him I'm in a hurry. If he wants to, he can talk to me when I get there.

"Now, end that call, get your ass in the car, and let's get on the road."

Josh just shook his head, turned, and walked about ten or so meters away from Rex, unmuted the phone and spoke in a muffled voice to McArdle.

Rex couldn't hear what was said, but Josh ended the call less than a minute later, walked back to the car, and got in the back seat with Digger without saying a word.

The atmosphere in the car was tense. No one spoke. Rex didn't ask what McArdle's response was—he didn't care. He always preferred to work on his own. If CRC wanted to work with him and supply him with resources, fine. If not, it wouldn't stop him, since he had the backing of the DGSE.

They were all silent while Rex navigated the Citroën C5 Aircross SUV through the streets of Paris to get onto the A6, known as the Motorway of the Sun, which would take them to Lyon. A block away from the A6 onramp, he pulled off at a service station and told them this was the first and last opportunity to grab food and drinks for the road and use the toilet.

Once on the A6, Rex engaged the cruise control at 110 kilometers per hour, took his foot off the gas pedal, and said, "Okay, we should get there in about four hours or so. Let's use the time to brainstorm. I want to know if there is anything about John's disappearance you haven't shared with me yet?"

"No, not deliberately," Josh replied. "We know as much as you do. It's possible that McArdle might've received more information. I can call him if you're okay with it?"

"He's your boss, not mine," Rex replied tersely.

"Ah… wha…" In the rearview mirror Rex saw the look of confusion on Josh's face and the shrug. "Never mind, not my business. Marissa and I were tasked to find you, not investigate your employment status. I'll call him now."

When McArdle picked up, Josh informed him that the phone was on speaker and the reason for the call.

McArdle was on his high horse immediately. "Josh, you and Marissa know everything we know, and I take it you've given all of that to Dalton?"

"Yes, sir. We did."

"Now, and if you're listening, Dalton, you're wasting time. John was abducted more than one hundred and twenty hours ago—I don't need to tell you that every passing hour lessens our chance of finding him alive and… Well, every minute is important. I've got a team of analysts here and a team in Greece. We need all hands on deck. I want you at CRC HQ. This is where you can contribute to the operation, not in France…"

By now, Rex had the middle finger of his right hand in the air waving it in front of Josh. "Tell him what I'm saying."

Josh frowned, harrumphed, and made a few more strange noises but didn't say anything.

"Tell him," Rex said.

"What the hell is it you need to tell me?" McArdle demanded.

"Sir, well… hmm… ah… how can I…"

"Dammit, Farley. Stop hemming and hawing. Spit it out, man!" McArdle yelled.

"Okay, you asked for it. He is showing a middle finger."

"Dalton, you're an insolent son of a bitch. I don't have time for your damn antics. You're really testing my patience. I…"

"McArdle take a few deep breaths," Rex interjected. "Now, get your feet off John's desk, pour yourself another glass of his best brandy, and listen."

By now, McArdle was on his feet, behind Brandt's desk, *how the hell did he know I had my*… "Farley, have you got the video on?" he shouted.

"No, sir!"

Rex started laughing, loud enough so that McArdle could hear, and then he said, "I told you, you can talk to me when I'm in Lyon. Josh or Marissa will call you when we've arrived. Now excuse me, I've got some driving and thinking to do over here. Oh, and see if you can do something to calm yourself down. Okay?"

There was no reply, just the beeping sound on Josh's satphone indicating the call had been disconnected.

Josh and Marissa went quiet again, waiting for Rex to

take the lead. Josh was a bit worried about the way Rex had spoken to McArdle. He would never have done that and didn't understand what Rex's gripe was with CRC's second in command.

Marissa had never met Chris McArdle. She also kept her own council about Rex's treatment of McArdle but decided not to ask. Not yet.

She was one of John Brandt's small group of female agents. At CRC, there were only four people who even knew of them; John Brandt, Chris McArdle, Rick Longland, and for the past fourteen months or so, Josh Farley.

John never wanted to involve women in CRC operations, because of his wife who was a spy with him in the CIA and was killed. But after one of the CRC missions was made infinitely more difficult than it should have been because a woman was needed for surveillance in the home of the target, Longland had persuaded him to rethink it.

He'd recruited four women after that, making sure they were diverse in age, appearance, and ethnicity. He'd trained them in a separate facility and with different skills than his male teams. Naturally, he'd given them defensive training, from martial arts to firearms and explosives, but he'd always tried to use them on assignments where he was relatively certain they wouldn't have to use it. Any of them could pass for anything from a waitress to the CEO of a multi-billion-dollar corporation.

Marissa was the best. She also had the looks. Her shoulder-length, raven hair and azure eyes suggested her French heritage, and her thirty-five years gave her a mantle of maturity that men found alluring, as well as a full figure that women envied, and men coveted. And she was hyper-intelligent.

Rex brought their attention back to task. "Who would want to abduct the Old Man and why?"

"Yes, let's make a list of the Old Man's enemies," Marissa suggested.

Both Rex and Josh started laughing. "Marissa, my dear," Josh started with a smile. "That's going to be a very long list. John Brandt didn't spend his time building up his social capital at cocktail parties like politicians and business people. The Old Man was... no wait, strike that, he *is* a warrior bent on the elimination of the enemies of our country."

Rex nodded in agreement. "So, there's your list, Marissa, the enemies of the US are the enemies of John Brandt."

"Okay, I get it. I've known John for quite a few years, as well, and I agree he's not known for his big circle of friends, but we have to start somewhere. Not being his friend doesn't necessarily mean the person is his enemy."

"Yep," Rex replied. "So, I'd start by grouping them—terrorists, arms dealers, drug lords, human traffickers, and such. Then group them by country—Russia, China, Iran, Syria, Palestine, and so forth."

Marissa nodded. "And don't forget he could also have lethal enemies in the US and other friendly countries."

"Then we get every security agency on the planet who we can trust to start shaking the trees in those groups and see what comes down," Josh added.

"Exactly," Rex replied.

"We'll need SIGINT, HUMINT and FININT teams," Marissa said as she took her tablet out to make notes.

By the time they reached the outskirts of Lyon, they'd agreed on some strategies they'd want to follow.

There was no question about who should be leading their group if Rex got his way and they stayed in Lyon. Rex was the best, most experienced of the three of them, actually in all of CRC. And despite the battle of wills between them, even McArdle had such a high regard for Rex's skills that he was prepared to let Josh and Marissa, two of his best agents, spend valuable time to get Rex onboard. Rex was the leader, no question about it.

"Rehka should have arrived by the time we get there, too," Rex said casually. Digger, relegated to the back seat with Josh, pricked up his ears. Josh noticed.

"So Rehka and Digger are acquainted?"

Rex smiled, the first genuine smile he'd given in the past few hours. "Quite observant, Josh. That they are. Digger loves Rehka, and the feeling's requited. He was…" Rex realized he was about to give away something he didn't want known and interrupted himself.

Marissa spoke gently. "We know about Saudi Arabia, Rex, remember? Rehka was one of the pleasure wives you rescued. And we know Digger was part of that rescue. That's where we learned about him for the first time. Although, some of the eyewitnesses thought of him as a djinn."

Rex relaxed. "Yeah, he was part of it, a big part. There was no way I could've done it without him. He was magnificent. You have no idea how talented he is." He paused. "A djinn, you said?"

Marissa nodded.

"Digger, buddy, did you hear that? Some people think you're an Arabian desert spirit."

Digger was asleep. He only opened one eye, lazily, when his name was mentioned, sighed, and went back to sleep.

"Would you tell us more about Digger?" Marissa asked.

Rex thought without answering for the next few minutes. At last, he spoke. "You probably already know that I, with a group of men working for a private military contractor, Phoenix Unlimited, was ambushed outside Kabul. My team was killed."

Marissa nodded, not wanting to interrupt his thoughts.

"Digger was part of the team. He's a trained military dog. His handler was one of my best friends, Trevor Madigan, an Aussie, former SAS."

"We know about Trevor. We spoke to one of his friends."

"Okay, right. Well, Trevor wasn't killed outright. He was bleeding out when Digger and I found him, no hope to save him. With his last breath, he made me promise to take care of Digger… I did. But let me tell you, if the truth was known, it's Digger who has taken care of me all these months since…"

Rex didn't tell them about his kynophobia. They didn't need to know about his fear of dogs.

Josh spoke up from the back seat. "What kind of military dog? Is he search and rescue or drug-sniffing? I guess not explosives-sniffing, or he'd have…"

"It didn't go down like that," Rex interrupted. "And he's all that and more. He's an Aussie military dog. They're trained in everything. Trevor explained to me, before the ambush, that Australia doesn't have our budget, so their dogs don't specialize like ours do. They train many of their dogs in all of those, including attack. Digger's probably smarter than many Americans."

"American dogs?" Marissa asked.

"No, the human kind of Americans," Rex answered. He didn't need to clarify, because Josh and Marissa would know what he meant.

Rex used the last half hour or so of the trip to ask Marissa to explain how she'd become involved with the search for him, and prior to that, how she'd joined CRC. By the time they reached Lyon, Rex was convinced she'd be an asset to the team.

Chapter Forty-Two

Lyon, France

Five days after abduction

They reached Lyon just before eleven thirty a.m. All three adult Lemaires and Rehka turned out to greet them, and Rex made the introductions between Josh and Marissa and the Lemaires. Rehka was laughing while trying to fend off Digger, who was determined to give her a kiss. He'd torn out of the car and made a beeline for her, almost knocking her off her feet when he jumped up.

Rex said, "Digger, off!", but Digger continued his jumping and ignored him until Rehka bent to allow him to 'kiss' her on the cheek with his wet nose.

"Yes, Digger, I am happy to see you, too."

She turned to Rex and gave him a hug, which he returned. "I'm happy to see you as well, Ru…Rex."

After the introductions, Adele was the first to speak.

"Welcome to our home. We understand what you are here to do is of critical importance. Please don't hesitate to ask for anything you need.

"Your quarters are ready. Rehka has already settled in. Just let me know if you need anything."

"Thank you very much, Adele, Margot. We appreciate your help," Rex responded.

"From tomorrow," Adele continued, "you can prepare your own meals, and you'll find everything you need in the guesthouse. Between Margot and I, we'll take care of your shopping for you. Just provide us with a list of what you need as often as you need it.

"For today, I have prepared lunch for you. I take it you're hungry after the long drive?"

Josh grinned boyishly. "Mrs. Lemaire, I can eat anytime, anywhere, anything."

Adele smiled. "If you keep on calling me Mrs., you'll get nothing."

"Apologies, Adele," Josh replied quickly.

Rex nodded. "I'm starving. And let me tell you," he said, as he looked at Josh and Marissa, "Adele is an excellent cook. You're in for a treat." He turned to Adele, "Thanks, Adele. We accept."

Bert led the way to the big farmhouse kitchen, where everyone but Digger enjoyed a *cassoulet*. When Adele tried to apologize for the plain, country food, Rex waved her off. As soon as he'd swallowed the delicious mouthful, he insisted that it was a perfect dish, and as far as he was concerned, no gourmet meal would have been any more satisfying.

Josh, shoveling another spoonful into his mouth, nodded enthusiastically, too busy enjoying it to stop and talk.

Even Digger, contentedly gnawing on a dried pig's ear after the whole chicken, approved of Adele's homemade treats. He had gone through his food and treat in a few minutes and was then enticed by the children to go play fetch with them in the garden.

It was about one p.m. when the four of them, Rex, Rehka, Marissa, and Josh, thanked Adele for the lunch, and Rex whistled for Digger to come. He obeyed immediately, but the children were disappointed. "We were having so much fun. He's a very clever and friendly dog. When can we play with him again?"

"Okay, tell you what," Rex said. "If your mom and dad agree, you can come over to the guesthouse every morning and afternoon and play with Digger. I'll show you how to play hide and seek with him as well. How does that sound?"

The two kids yelled, "Yes! Yes! Please." Then they remembered Rex's proviso, turned to their parents, and begged in chorus, "*Maman et papa?*"

Bert smiled and nodded. Adele said, "Yes, but only when your homework is done."

The kids promised in unison.

After arriving at the guest house, now turned into a military-style operations center, Josh and Marissa told Rex that it was time to get things with Chris McArdle over with.

Rex felt a frisson of discomfort. He'd avoided any contact with CRC for fourteen months, so it felt like walking into the lion's den. But he shook his head to clear his mind, *the lion's den never scared you in the past. Get it over with and move on. The Old Man is waiting for you to rescue him.*

Josh got hold of McArdle on the satphone and handed it to Rex.

Rex didn't expect it to be a nice conversation, but he was not going to give in on his demand to run at least part of the operation from Lyon. He knew Chris, and Chris was a good guy. Quite a bit younger than the Old Man, and therefore less experienced, but also more prone to reason than the Old Man's sometimes bombastic and inflexible style.

None of them saw the need for any pleasantries, so they got straight to the point.

McArdle said, "Dalton, this operation *will* be run from here at headquarters in Arizona. The three of you need to get your asses on a plane and get here ASAP. You're squandering valuable time."

"McArdle, are you hard of hearing, stubborn, stupid, or all of the above? I told you I'm not going to the US. I will help you find John, but on my terms. Not negotiable."

"You are working for CRC. In John's absence, I'm in charge. I won't have any insubordination, do you understand?"

"No, there's nothing for me to understand. You're the one with the lack of understanding. In case the last fourteen months haven't given you and CRC a clue, I resigned. I've left CRC. That's why you haven't seen me in all this time. No one, least of all you, is in charge of me. This is not insubordination, because I don't work for you, I don't report to you, and I don't give a flying… Well, just get lost. I'll send Josh and Marissa back to you first thing in the morning."

Marissa's jaw dropped, and Josh jumped to his feet. "Now just a minute here, Rex. You can't *send* us anywhere. We don't work for you, either. And by the way, we have minds of our own, as well. Put the phone on speaker," he told Rex. Then, raising his voice for the phone, he said, "Chris, I'm staying here. If you want to fire me, go right ahead. You said yourself Rex is the best asset we have to find the Old Man. I'm sticking with him."

Marissa stood next to Josh and echoed her agreement with him.

A short silence on the other end of the conversation indicated McArdle was considering his options. Finally, he spoke. "Listen, guys. There is no time for this. We need to find John. If you won't come to me, I'll come to you."

Despite their current differences, Rex was impressed. He'd always had a lot of respect for McArdle, and that just went up a few more notches. Under the circumstances it could not have been easy for him to pocket his personal pride and focus on the issue at hand—the characteristic of a great leader.

"Hang on, Chris," Rex said, in a much calmer tone. "Before you jump on a plane, I don't think it's necessary for you to fly here. We live in the age of technology. Let your IT guru talk to mine, and I'm sure within the hour we'll have a virtual office spanning from France to the US. They can setup secure communication lines so we have continuous audio and video contact with each other, as if we are in the same office. If you don't like the setup, then you can fly over here. Okay?"

"Deal," McArdle said. "Make it happen."

Chapter Forty-Three

Unknown location

Five days after abduction

He couldn't be certain, but it seemed he'd been snatched off the street in Greece about three days ago, but it could've been four, even five. He'd given up trying to keep a tally of the times he'd been fed, such as it was, since he'd first come to in the dark. It felt like about every four to six hours, but with a longer period after three or four of the tasteless energy bars they'd given him. Probably those longer periods were the nights, or the days, whenever they slept.

What he did know was that in the beginning, he'd been questioned in a different place, by a different man. He couldn't be certain he hadn't missed some longer period after being drugged. Or had that happened? Yes, he was almost certain of that, unless the sensory deprivation was making him hallucinate.

The truth was, being kept in the dark for twenty-four hours or more was disorienting.

But that wasn't what mattered. What mattered was it seemed to have been too long since his last interrogation. That may have meant that his deceit worked, and they were checking out the names of the Taliban 'traitors' he gave them. And that, if true, was good news. It had bought him some time.

He tried to keep his mind off the maddening and fruitless exercise of trying to work out how long it had been since he'd been captured by thinking instead about what his friends would be doing to find him. They'd have contacted Chris McArdle, and Chris would have done everything necessary to protect their assets and those of their allies. If they knew he was missing.

They'd surely know I am missing by now, wouldn't they? It had to have been days, not hours.

Stop it!

He silently commanded his brain. He didn't dare speak out loud. Though he couldn't sense or hear them, there could be others in the container with him. He doubted it, because the stench was terrible, but he couldn't be certain. He took a bit of satisfaction that his person was disgusting enough to give even hardened criminals pause when they did come in. He almost welcomed the stinging iciness of the firehose-delivered water that washed away the mess he had no choice but to make, tied down as he was.

Time was what he needed. Time so that agents and spies could be moved out of harm's way.

Time so that CRC could launch a search and rescue operation.

Time to recover from his injuries. Time to prepare his mind for the next torture session.

Time for his CRC agents to find him.

The only thing he controlled in this situation, for now, was time. It depended solely on him, how busy he kept his captors with his lies and misdirection, and how long he would be able to keep his mind in such a state that he wouldn't break and give it all to them. He knew if he broke, and they got what they wanted, he'd be killed. For now, the fighting spirit in him was still alive and well.

He turned his thoughts to what awaited him when his captors came back. It may take weeks or days for them to discover he'd lied, but more likely only hours. And then the next interrogation would be rougher. They'd punish him for the lies and try to discourage him from telling more. He just grinned.

I've only started with you numbnuts. By the time this is over, whether I'm rescued or killed, I would've created so much havoc and agony for you, you'll be regretting the day you captured me.

Chapter Forty-Four

Ops Center, Lemaire Estate, Lyon, France

Five days after abduction

When Rex and McArdle finished their call, Rex handed the satphone to Rehka and told her to hang on while McArdle got hold of his IT specialist, Greg Wade.

Within minutes, Rehka and Wade were exchanging information and had started configuring the secured network between the CRC and Lyon ops centers.

While Rehka was busy, the rest of them unloaded their luggage from the SUV, took a quick tour of the guesthouse, and dropped their stuff in their respective rooms. There were three bedrooms, each with its own en suite bathroom and toilet. The rest of the house was one big open-plan containing a kitchen off to one side. What was previously the dining and lounge areas had been turned into an 'open office' space. There was a group of reclining chairs arranged around a large coffee table in the middle of the open space. Against the big glass wall, overlooking the garden and vineyards, were desks and office chairs with desktop computers each connected to two monitors, as well as laptop computers for each of them.

Less than an hour after Rehka and Wade started talking, Rex had just finished brewing a big pot of coffee and poured himself a mug, when the big wall-mounted screen came to life with the almost life-size image of Chris McArdle on it. Rehka hit a few keys on her computer and the screen was split into four equal-sized windows. Each window showed a different part of the CRC operations center.

Rex smiled and raised his coffee mug in a greeting to McArdle and his team in Arizona. "Hi Chris, there you go. It can't be much easier than this, can it? Saved you a trip to France, what do you say?"

McArdle grinned slightly. "Yeah, this is great." And then he was all business. "Okay, let's introduce the teams and get to work."

They quickly did the rounds with everyone getting an opportunity to state their name and what their roles were. Rex knew most of the Arizona team, and without exception every one of them, even those he'd never met, welcomed him back when it was his turn for introduction. Digger was sitting next to Rex during the introductions.

McArdle noticed the dog and said, "And that mutt next to you, Rex?"

"Chris, let's not get off on the wrong foot here. You're forgiven this time because you didn't know better. This here is no mutt. His name is Digger, he's a pedigree Dutch Shepherd, the best friend I ever had. I and many people are alive today because of Digger. He's a highly intelligent military trained dog. I can tell you a lot more about him later. Please call him by his name from now on. And if you ever meet him, be advised he gets really shitty with anyone who crosses swords with me."

McArdle had a big grin on his face, probably because it was the first time ever he had seen Rex as passionate as this about anything.

Rex said, "Digger say hello to everyone."

Digger raised his right paw in the air and smiled.

In Arizona, everyone smiled, started clapping their hands, and shouted, "Welcome to the team, Digger!"

Thanks to the DGSE providing a dedicated and secured satellite link, the video and audio feeds were excellent.

Rehka and Wade declared that they were happy with the initial setup but requested that Rex order a few more pieces of equipment, including more cameras and audio equipment, so they could have the ability to have various separate video conversations going on at the same time if required.

A quick phone call, immediately answered despite the ungodly hour, to his contact at DGSE, followed by an encrypted email with the specifications, and Rex told Rehka it would be delivered by nine that morning.

With the introductions out of the way, McArdle suggested that everyone grab themselves something to eat and drink and get back in ten minutes for the first joint meeting. "I'd like to start by sharing what we know so we can all move forward from the same page."

In the noise and disorder that followed when the teams dispersed, Rex had to smile when he picked up on a conversation, clearly not meant for his ears, when one of the Arizona team said to another, "That Dalton is one lucky bastard. We're here in the middle of the desert with only male company, and he is on a wine estate in France surrounded by the most beautiful women I've seen in years. Shit, I've got a good mind to ask McArdle to send me over there immediately."

Rex couldn't hear the reply, as they were off-screen by then. But he could just imagine that there were going to be more than a few off-screen remarks about Rehka and Marissa among the Arizona team, an all-male group.

Just then, Josh called Rex to the side, and when he was certain Rehka couldn't hear them, he said, "One quick question."

"Shoot."

"Rehka. I take it she doesn't have a security clearance?"

"No, she doesn't."

"Is that going to be a problem?"

"No, I'm sure it won't. Let's ask her in front of everyone when we reconvene."

Josh nodded, "Good enough for me. If you trust her, so do I."

Ten minutes later, when they were all seated and ready for the meeting, Rex told McArdle there was a matter that had to be taken care of before they could proceed.

McArdle frowned but nodded for him to proceed.

Rex looked at Rehka and said, "Rehka, before we start, I need you to give me, that is us, and by that I mean all of us," he waved his hand across the big screen and around the room where they were, "your solemn promise that you will not ever discuss with anyone what you are going to learn here from this moment forward."

Rehka didn't hesitate. She nodded. "You have my word, Rex and everyone." She waved her hand, the same way Rex had done it a minute ago.

Rex looked at Josh and Marissa first, then at McArdle.

"Anything else anyone wants her to say or promise or undertake?"

Marissa shook her head. "That's good enough for me. Welcome to the team, Rehka. It's an honor working with you."

Josh also nodded. "Same for me."

McArdle and the CRC team responded in chorus, "Welcome to the team, Rehka!"

Chapter Forty-Five

Unknown location

Five days after abduction

It began with a shaft of light that fell across his eyes and hurt them. He shouldn't have closed them, though. The blow came unexpectedly, from someone who'd approached so silently he didn't even feel the change in the air around him. It would have doubled him over, if he hadn't been tied down, spread-eagled on the floor or deck, whatever it was.

Then came the kick to his ribs, followed by another kick from the opposite side. The only sounds were his grunts of pain as the kicks were delivered. Only when they thought he'd passed out did the kicks stop. And then they were followed by the stinging cold water and shouts of outrage by his torturers, who'd evidently been caught in the deluge.

"You could have done that first," one of them shouted

in Russian. An answer came from further away, accompanied by laughter.

Oh, good. They're in a better mood.

The fleeting thought didn't give him any comfort that his primary interrogator would be.

He was sure he had broken ribs.

But I'm in for some serious pain now.

With that thought, he did pass out, only to come to with a bucket of cold seawater dashed in his face. He woke sputtering, still tied, supine.

"Look, guys, I appreciate your reviving me and all, but if you don't want me to drown, you've got to quit doing it like that. Try sitting me up first."

When he got no answer, he shrugged. Guess they don't appreciate my advice.

Five seconds later, he felt the back edge of a knife slice through the tape around his wrists and ankles again, and someone brutally jerked him to his feet. He stumbled, and with a curse, another man took his other arm and kept him upright. The two of them muscled him into the paneled room where he'd been questioned before, with the surgical instrument tray and filthy hammer in the same place it had been. Silently, they repeated the process of binding his wrists and ankles to the chair.

His interrogator was already there, watching the men securing him to the chair.

"John, I have to say, you have hurt my trust in you," Logan began. "Worse than that, you have caused some strife between me and some of my best clients. The information you gave me last time was false. That has lowered my credibility with them. I'm not happy about that. You'll have to do much better from now on."

Brandt smiled faintly. "Yeah, I know what you're talking

about. It's very important to keep the clients happy and never lose their trust. Does that mean we're no longer friends?"

Logan lashed out with a closed fist, striking Brandt in the jaw almost before he finished his sentence. Brandt's head rocked back, and with a bloody smile, he added, "I guess not. And I was so much looking forward to having that coffee with you."

Brandt knew he'd gotten under Logan's skin. What it meant for him was more pain *before* more questions. But it also meant his strategy was working.

John Brandt 1, Logan Jones 0.

For the next several minutes, Logan put him through a bit of psychological torture by picking up first one, then another instrument, as if he was debating what injury to inflict. When he finally picked up the long, thin forceps with a curve at the end, Brandt's toes curled. He was about to lose one or more finger or toenail, he suspected.

Logan smiled at Brandt as he opened and closed the instrument.

Brandt was ready for him with a totally new tactic.

"Time for my manicure? Or is it the pedicure?"

Logan shook his head. "No. We're going to play a game, I call it four by five. It's a lot like a TV quiz. We don't play for money, that's too boring, we play for nails. You get four sets of five questions. I get one point for each nail I remove, you get one point for each nail you keep."

"You know, Logan, I'm starting to like you. You're an innovative man. I like people with an entrepreneurial spirit. Did you know you could make a lot of money if you get one of the TV shows interested in this game of yours? I can just imagine how popular it's going to be. I'm all excited, let's get started."

Logan grinned and nodded. "Okay, the rules are simple. I pick a nail, then I ask a question, and you give me an answer. If I like the answer, you keep the nail and get one point. If I don't like the answer, I get the nail and one point. Got it?"

Brandt smiled. "Yep, that's easy enough. I like this game, simple rules."

Logan chose the big toenail on Brandt's right foot and wedged the grip of the forceps in under the nail bed and said, "Okay, here we go. Tell me about the ambush near Kabul, about fourteen months ago, when a team was sent to kill a drug lord named Usama, but were all killed themselves?"

"I know nothing about it," Brandt answered.

Logan wiggled the forceps a bit, looked at Brandt, and said, "Last chance. Answer the question or the nail goes."

"No, wait a minute, Logan. That's unfair. Those were not the rules. You can't change them unilaterally—there are two of us playing here. You ask one question, I answer, and depending on my answer, I score, or you score. Come on, don't be a cheat. You won fair and square. Take the nail, jot down your one point and let's move on to the next question."

Brandt had a hard time not showing his satisfaction when he saw the look of incredulity on Logan's face. It was obvious he never had a captive begging him to rip a nail off. He was hesitating.

"Come on, Logan. Let's move on. The score is one zero in your favor."

Logan clamped the forceps down, moved it back and forth, and then ripped the nail off.

"Shiiiiit!" Brandt screamed and unleashed a string of profanities. It took him a few minutes before he could talk again. "That was exciting. That sting, man. I can't begin to tell you how exhilarating that was. You *must* try it some time."

Logan stood back. He didn't even try to hide his stupefaction. Clearly Brandt had gotten the better of him, probably making him question if he'd gone too far already, and whether Brandt had lost his mind.

He took a sip of water and said, "Tell me about the ambush near Kabul, about fourteen months ago, when a team was sent to kill a drug lord named Usama, but were all killed themselves?"

"Logan, what the hell is this? You keep on changing the damn rules on me. What chance do I have of ever winning this game if you keep on changing the rules?"

Logan stared at him wordlessly. Brandt could only guess what was going through his mind.

"Come on, let's play nice now. Pick the nail, then ask the question. But you can't ask the same question twice, that's unfair. I'm the one who's got the nails in the game. So, each nail is worth one *new* question."

Logan picked the big toenail on the left foot and asked, "Who was in charge of that team who walked into that ambush?"

Brandt started laughing, and it grew louder and louder until it sounded uncontrollable. Tears of laughter were streaming down his face, and his whole body was shaking. It went on for minutes, until Logan slapped him across the face.

"Logan, you must be taking me for a fool. That last question of yours was exactly the same as the first one. I told you, I know nothing about it. You didn't like my answer, and you scored one point. Come on, stop doing that. Just think about it. If it were your nails at stake here, would you want to have the rules changed on you?"

Logan said nothing. He just bent down and ripped the big toenail of the left foot off.

Brandt let lose with another flood of swear words and screaming. When he finally got over enough of the pain to talk, he said, "Okay, I am not interested in playing this game of yours any more. You won, twenty zero in your favor. Congratulations. But you cheated, I'm not going to trust you ever again. Now go ahead—have your nails and leave me alone."

Logan's blow caught him under the eye, giving him a cut that started bleeding immediately.

"That's going to leave a mark," John mumbled.

John Brandt 2, Logan Jones 0.

Bogdan Bogomilov Gavrilov, aka Logan Jones was rattled. He had never been in such a situation where he was not in control of the interrogation. Sure, he could inflict pain, but this John Brandt seemed immune to it, though he put on a good show of screaming and yelling. Nevertheless, most men would have given up something useful by this point in their torture.

Brandt is still joking, making a fool of me.

Logan was the one who needed a break now. Brandt had gotten under his skin and into his mind. *The son-of-a-bitch had been taking me for a ride for the past seventy-two hours. It's as if the man has three or four different personalities.*

The drugs they gave him in the beginning didn't work. They didn't get anything out of him. It was as if he wasn't even there, just incoherent mumbling.

Now, with the physical torture, Logan was worried that Brandt had gone insane. He had never seen or heard anything like this. Or maybe Brandt was insane to start with. Logan couldn't tell whether Brandt had broken more quickly than most, or not at all.

Will he completely lose his mind if the torturing continues? If so, how reliable is his information? Is he playing me for a fool?

He had no idea, because he'd never dealt with a prisoner like this one. It was as if he was growing stronger or crazier with each bit of extra pain inflicted on him, and Logan couldn't tell which.

Maybe Brandt was very, very clever. But that was an enormous lot of pain to go through in the last session just to keep up a charade of insanity, not to mention the hours of solitary confinement, naked, tied up, and the rest of the torture, both physical and mental, he'd already gone through.

Is there really a human on this earth that wouldn't break?

If there is, then this John Brandt could very well be the one.

Chapter Forty-Six

Ops Center, Lemaire Estate, Lyon, France. 4:00 a.m.

Six days after abduction

Josh yawned loudly and looked at the two digital clocks in the bottom right-hand corner of the big screen, showing it to be four a.m. in Lyon, eight p.m. in Arizona. He shook his head and mumbled through another yawn, "I just realized the time difference is not going to be a factor, because we ain't gonna get no sleep."

Rex looked up from his laptop where he'd been studying the data the Arizona INT teams had shared with them. What he saw were three live corpses in the appearance of Rehka, her head nodding, Josh yawning again, and Marissa fast asleep on her arms in front of her computer. It struck him then that apart from lack of sleep the past two days, or was it three, they were also suffering from jetlag.

He looked at the big screen and in the top right window

saw McArdle also studying something on his laptop. "Chris, I'm going to send these three to bed now. They're no use to us in this state."

"Yep. Give them at least four hours, then start rotating them. I've already setup a roster for my guys over here."

Rex shooed the three out of the ops center and told them that he'd wake them in four hours.

They didn't need any encouragement.

Rex donned his headphones so that he wouldn't disturb the sleepers and told McArdle to do the same. "Okay, shall we do a bit of brainstorming with the information we have so far?"

McArdle nodded, "Yes, that might just produce something new."

Since they'd established communications earlier, the teams had gone through the information they had. Rehka had started a list as Rex suggested, of the industries where John's enemies could come from, and they'd identified the countries they thought to target.

McArdle would put out an international BOLO with the help of the CIA, who he'd ask to contact the intelligence and law enforcement agencies of all friendly nations and ask for their cooperation.

At Josh's suggestion, they'd started a link chart on the walls of both ops centers. They already had pictures of some of those individuals who they knew, thought, or suspected could be John's personal enemies. Then they listed all the CRC and related missions, past and present, and linked them with pieces of string where they found or suspected a connection.

Rex and McArdle had to admit that they were stabbing in the dark. This was not just the proverbial search for a needle in a haystack—it was a very small needle in a very,

very big haystack. The investigative team in Greece had been unable to produce any lead. No one in Greece had seen or heard anything, neither on the night of Brandt's disappearance nor in the days after.

The efforts of the NSA and similar organizations of allied nations had come up empty so far—no chatter on the wires, not even a hint. Absolutely nothing mentioned about the abduction on the Internet or telephone conversations or text messages or emails or chat programs. Part of the reason for that could've been that CRC and everyone else had kept the abduction a secret, and apparently, so did the abductors. The CRC, CIA, and FBI analyst teams were collecting and studying every bit of FININT, SIGINT, and HUMINT data they could get, but had not produced any results. Not even a hint.

Rex remarked, "It's as if the Old Man was abducted by aliens and scooted off to another planet."

McArdle nodded and went quiet for a few seconds. "Yeah, it does feel like that. Okay, I'm going to get some of my team onto the analysis of the CRC missions, maybe something will come out of that."

Chapter Forty-Seven

Ops Center, Lemaire Estate, Lyon, France. 6:00 a.m.

Six days after abduction

After waking his team, Rex was standing in front of the refrigerator door, considering what to fix for breakfast, when Josh arrived, dressed casually, his hair still wet from his shower.

"I didn't think I'd ever need to eat again after that lunch yesterday," he said. "But I'm starving again."

"Must be all that exercise your brain got for a change," Rex said, grinning.

"You know it. Can I help with anything?"

"What do you fancy for breakfast? Bacon and eggs, or yogurt and granola?"

"What kind of stupid question is that?" Josh complained. "Bacon and eggs, of course."

"Do you think the girls will want the same?"

Marissa's voice sounded from behind them. "I'll take yogurt and granola, and I'd bet Rehka will want that, too."

"Okay, bacon and eggs for two."

Digger growled, causing Rex to correct himself. "Sorry buddy, bacon and eggs for *three* coming right up."

Digger smiled.

Josh stared at Digger. "Do you mean to tell me he can count?" he said, incredulous.

He got no reply.

"What's for breakfast?" Rehka's lilting voice asked.

"Yogurt and granola or…"

"Perfect," she answered.

It didn't take long for the Arizona team to realize that on the other side of the Atlantic, breakfast was about to be served and for them to start wondering, aloud, whether frog legs and steak tartare—raw ground meat mixed with onions, capers, pepper, and Worcestershire sauce, topped with a raw egg—was served as part of a traditional breakfast in France.

Soon all of them participated in the lighthearted banter as Rex cooked and listened to the jibing about his skills as a chef. Some of them wanted to know why he was not wearing his *toque blanche*—the tall, round, pleated, starched white hat worn by chefs.

At some stage, he took two plates loaded with the bacon, eggs, and toast to one of the cameras and showed the Arizonians a close-up. "Guys, have a look. We're not French."

The raillery continued for a while, and McArdle didn't mind; it was good for the morale to let the troops have a bit of fun.

But as soon as breakfast was finished and the kitchen tidied, it was back to business. All had a mug of coffee, except Rehka who had a cup of tea, and were back at their desks.

"Okay," Rex started. "While you were having your beauty sleep, Chris and I agreed that it might be worthwhile reviewing all CRC missions of the past five years. The four of us will review the missions we were involved in, he will get the Arizona team to do the rest, and then we'll compare notes."

Rehka rolled her chair back to her desk, connected her computer to the projector showing her screen on the nearby wall, and then pulled up a mindmap application. She took notes while the others thought about recent and past missions, what countries and what organizations had been the targets, the names associated with them, and when they'd happened, to the best of their combined recollection. Rex had the most to share, and his recollection was near total because of his eidetic memory. As he recited the details, Josh and Marissa chimed in when their missions intersected with his.

Josh updated the link chart as they talked.

The conversation ebbed and flowed while they combed their memories.

Then Josh asked, "Rex, what was that last mission of yours, before the ambush? You were over there for a long time."

"Didn't the Old Man tell you about it?"

"Yeah, but we never understood the reason for the ambush. You were just there to observe, right?"

"Well…" Rex allowed himself a faint grin. "I may have gone outside mission parameters—a bit." He began to tell them about his frustrations with the CIA's unwillingness to act and how he eventually ran a few unauthorized raids on drug-manufacturing facilities. "I just couldn't stomach allowing all that product to hit the streets back home," he said. As he described them, he made the raids sound funny. Before he got to the ambush, and just when Marissa got up to refill her coffee, Digger's growling indicated someone was approaching the house.

Rex looked at the monitors displaying the feeds from the security cameras outside but saw nothing. He looked back at Digger and asked "What's up boy? What's bugging you?"

The hair on Digger's back was standing on end, and he growled again.

Rex looked at the monitors again and saw the nose of the approaching white delivery van coming around the bend in the road.

"I'll be damned! Did you see that Marissa?" Josh said. "Digger knew about that van before the security system…"

"Amazing. Isn't it?" Marissa agreed.

Rehka and Rex just smiled. "You ain't seen nothing yet," Rex added. "Wait until you see him on a mission."

The panel van pulled up, and Rex saw two men delivering the supplies and equipment Rehka had ordered. He was pleased that the van had no insignia, and that the men were wearing what looked like delivery uniforms. He had no doubt they were DGSE.

Chapter Forty-Eight

Ops Center, Lemaire Estate, Lyon, France

Six days after abduction

When the delivery people had gone, they carried everything inside, and within the hour they had efficiently installed it all and had it operating the way Rehka wanted.

It was time to get back to Rex's Afghan mission. "You already know most of the information about the ambush that my team and I walked into. I only learned about the treachery a day or so after the ambush when Digger had led me to Usama's compound, where I found him and his gang of drug lords partying in celebration of our demise in the ambush. Digger and I broke up their party, interrogated all of them, including Usama, and learned that the ambush was arranged from America. Treason.

"However, treason or not, it was my ego that got seven

good men killed. Men who were my friends. I'll regret that for the rest of my life."

A moment of silence in respect for his loss stretched until Digger, sensing the somber mood, whined. Then Rex brightened. "One thing I won't regret about it, though I still regret the reason, was that Digger and I became partners, like I told you last night in the car."

"Can you recall what Usama and his thugs told you?" Josh asked.

Rex nodded, leaned back in his chair, and closed his eyes as he relived that night at Usama's compound. It was as if a movie of the events were playing in front of his eyes, and he started giving his audience running commentary of what he was 'seeing'.

"He told me his contact in America was Winston Reginald Hathaway."

"I've heard the name and know he's a New York socialite. Over the course of three or more hours, with Usama's reluctant cooperation, I was able to put it together. He mentioned the names of people who were involved in this drug business that would blow your mind away. To me, the size of the conspiracy was astounding, reaching from the highest levels of government to low-level military NCOs both in Afghanistan and at home.

"He told me he'd recorded it all on his computers. I dragged him over to his office. It was like a base of international operations. Several monitors were attached to each of three computers, two desktop models and a laptop. I got Usama to log on to each and every one of the computers, and I got access to all his financial and business data. Not only that but also dozens of names with contact information. I made backups and took the hard drives from all the computers in addition to the laptop.

"The usernames and passwords as well as the encryption and decryption keys for the data were recorded in a small journal, which I took and kept with me." Rex took a little black notebook out of his pocket, about four by six inches, bound with supple leather and containing about twenty lined pages filled with website addresses printed in neat Latin letters, with Arabic passwords including login information to hundreds of sites, including Dark Web and Deep Web locations. He held it up for them to see.

"Then I asked him who'd set up the ambush on my team? He told me they didn't know who I was, that is, who was raiding their warehouses. So, they requested the help of Hathaway. Usama told me that he wasn't sure, but his understanding was that Hathaway put pressure on a senator, whose name he didn't know, who in turn put pressure on someone in the CIA to take care of their problem."

"Bruce Carson," Josh and Marissa said simultaneously.

Rex nodded. "Could very well be. I remember at the time when Usama told me, Carson *was* at the top of my list of suspects. Nevertheless, what I learned from Usama that night made it clear, the corruption was at all levels of the US government, and it had cost the lives of innocent men. He told me that the only aim of that explosion was to kill me."

"How did he know you'd be there?" Josh asked.

"That's what bugged me at the time as well. Usama didn't know my name, but he knew my pseudonyms. I got my orders to set up an ambush for Usama and his cronies from Brandt. So, had Brandt told one of Usama's co-conspirators? Had Brandt told Usama himself? Had Brandt told someone at the CIA? There were so many questions and no answers, only suspicions. I didn't know who I could trust, and to be honest with you, I still don't trust John

Brandt, not until I've saved his ass and looked him in the eyes when I ask him if he had anything to do with it."

"Rex..." Marissa started, but Rex held his hand up to stop her.

"Don't even try, Marissa, not unless you can tell me you've lost seven of your friends at the hands of traitors."

Marissa nodded. "You're right. I can't even begin to understand what you went through and are still going through. But I can tell you John Brandt loves you like a son. He'd die before he'd betray you. But it's as you said, you'd have to look him in the eyes to discover that."

"Okay, so anyway, after that I knew I couldn't go back to the US, not under my real identity, probably not under any identity—not for a long, long time, if ever. In other words, I realized to stay alive, I had to remain dead. That was the turning point for me, and that's when I walked away from CRC and my old life—Digger and I."

Rex stopped talking and a long silence followed.

Rehka wanted to ask what happened to Usama, opened her mouth to ask and closed it when she realized she already knew the answer and that it would pain Rex to tell her the truth.

Josh pointed to the hard drives and laptop sitting on Rehka's desk and said, "I take it those are what you took out of Usama's computers and that's his laptop?"

"Yep," Rex replied. "So far, I haven't retrieved the data from it. I had the devices locked up in a safety deposit box at a bank in India. Rehka brought those with her. I think we should now get into them and have a good look at all of Usama's contacts.

"Rehka, this is your show. Can you extract all the data on this drive first?" He held up the one he'd marked when he took it from Usama. The drug lord had told him it had all his contacts and communications back-ups. Rex handed her the little book with codes and keys to decrypt his files.

Marissa said, "And I think we should get Chris to put some tabs on Hathaway ASAP. I've also heard his name somewhere. He's a rich and influential guy in New York. A bachelor, if I remember correctly, a high flyer with a wide circle of influential friends."

"The type of man we should approach with great care," Josh added.

"Well, I don't really care about his money, status, and friends. I've made up my mind about him a long time ago. His late Afghani friend, Usama, told me the man was the main importer of their drugs into the US. In other words, the man's a scumbag, a drug dealer, and a low-life. Regardless if he had anything to do with the Old Man's kidnapping, I took an oath to pay him a visit at some stage in the future.

"So, I agree with Marissa. I'll ask Chris to put surveillance on him."

Chapter Forty-Nine

Six days after abduction

While Rex spoke to McArdle about putting the tabs on Hathaway, Josh and Marissa went to the kitchen area and fixed a few snacks and drinks for everyone and started talking about what Rex told them.

"The Old Man was right all along. Josh, we screwed up. We…"

Josh interrupted. "What are you on about?"

Marissa explained. "Remember, John told us, as soon as he heard about that raid on Usama's compound, he 'knew' it was Rex. All evidence to the contrary, he believed Rex was the only man he knew of who could have done that single-handedly."

By now, Rex and Rekha had joined them and they engaged them in the discussion.

"John sent us over right away, but the trail was cold. You said you nearly bumped into us at the Taj Mahal," Marissa said. "You left no trace, Rex, so we just speculated that you could've gone to India. To be honest, Josh and I thought the Old Man had sent us on a wild goose chase. We thought you were dead and buried in the ashes of that explosion. You may not know that the townspeople rioted and destroyed the scene and wouldn't allow anyone to get near that place ever again. So, we were never able to get DNA samples from the site to prove you or any of your team were dead or alive."

Josh took up the narrative. "And then, a few weeks later, the Old Man called us in again. It was after that Saudi guy, Prince Mutaib, left to meet his seventy-two virgins in Jannah.

"Again, the Old Man was convinced that the raid on Mutaib's compound had your signature all over it. But we couldn't see any motive for you to be involved, even if you were alive. Truth be told, we thought the Old Man was obsessed with the whole idea that you were alive while there was no proper evidence to support it.

"And then, there was the story about the dog, or djinn. Marissa's favorite. Reports were mixed." He grinned at Digger. "Some of the people, including Rehka's parents and cousin told us he can climb trees. Is that true?"

Rehka's eyes sparkled as she pretended to be offended. "Are you questioning my family's honesty?"

Josh backpedaled fast. "No, no—that's just an expression. It means I find it hard to believe and just want to corroborate…"

By then, Rehka was laughing at him, and he stopped in confusion.

Rex said, "When we have a few minutes, later today, I'll

ask Digger if he'd like to give you a demonstration. I take it you'll be okay with that Digger?"

The dog was too busy trying to get the treat that Rehka had put into his kong to answer.

If Josh or Marissa found it strange that Rex was talking with or about Digger as if he was a human, they didn't make any comments about it. Although, they both had slight grins on their faces.

Rex said, "Okay, let's get back to the business at hand? Marissa, what you're saying is…"

"What I'm saying is, all this time we've been trying to understand that raid on Usama and its relationship to the ambush a few days earlier, if any. But now that I have the full picture, I'm thinking you blowing up their drug warehouses and eliminating the entire Afghan leadership group must have pretty much destroyed their drug empire. It would've stemmed the flow of drugs into the US. And I'd venture a guess that it would've have taken a long while to recover from that. It's quite possible that their business is still in flux."

Josh caught onto Marissa's logic and added, "In other words, you've pissed them off, big time, and they're trying to figure out who took out Usama and his network."

"And if I am not entirely stupid and understand you, you reckon there is a possibility that they could've taken the Old Man because he might be able to tell them who did it?"

"Exactly," Marissa said.

"But Brandt doesn't know anything about that," Rex objected.

Marissa nodded. "Yes, he doesn't have firsthand knowledge, but they don't know it, and what does it matter? John had been conjecturing that it was you since he heard about it—and he was right. Apart from that, he now knows you're alive, we've kept him up to date with our search. We spoke to him last after our visit to Saudi. So, under torture he could tell them what he thought happened, *and* that he has confirmation that you've survived the ambush."

Rex nodded. "And obviously for them it was easier to get hold of John than me."

Marissa nodded. "Josh and I wasted too much time before investigating the Saudi incident, because we didn't believe it was you. If we'd done it a year ago, we might have found you sooner, and…"

Rex held his hand up. "Don't beat yourself up about it. Remember the words of Sophocles; *'I have no desire to suffer twice, in reality and then in retrospect.'* Let's deal with what we have. I think there is merit in your hypothesis."

Rex turned to Rehka. She had not paid much attention to the conversation as she had returned to her keyboard and was hammering away at it to decrypt the information on the hard drives. "Miss Gyan, how are you going with those hard drives?"

"Mister Dalton." She smiled. "If you give me ten more minutes, you can all go onto your computers, and you'll find that I've set up a virtual drive, the U drive, on them. Through that you can access the decrypted files on the server."

"Have you shared it with the Arizona team as well?"

"Yep. I've already told Greg, and he said he'd pass it on to Chris."

"You've just earned yourself another pay raise, Miss Gyan." Rex looked at the big screen on the wall and saw McArdle at his desk. He activated the microphone on his computer and got McArdle's attention.

"What's up?"

"Hathaway," Rex replied.

"Yeah, tell me about it."

"Okay, hang on. Let's do this on the big screen, then everyone can participate." They all dragged their chairs over to the big screen, Rehka pushed a few buttons, and the sound came through the TV's speakers. McArdle and Longland were in attendance on the other side.

Rex started, "Marissa and Josh, please bring Chris up to date with your theory about Hathaway, which you explained to me before."

McArdle and Longland listened attentively as Marissa and Josh laid it out for them. When Marissa finished, McArdle said, "I can't fault your logic, Marissa. We'll treat it as one of the possibilities. It's not as if we have any other or better or hotter leads to act on at the moment. So, I've already, after Rex spoke to me earlier, dispatched two of our agents to New York to set up surveillance on Hathaway. I've also got a few of the INT team delving into his life."

Rex nodded. "Rehka is in the process of decrypting and extracting the data from Usama's hard drives. She's already loaded some of it onto the server. Usama showed me some of the names and details of his business contacts across the globe. It's all on those hard drives. I suggest we get those names out and add them to our link charts and see where it leads us."

"Agreed," McArdle replied.

"Rex, I've got this feeling in the pit of my stomach that we're in for some real nasty surprises on those hard drives," Longland said.

"Rick, you've got no idea, I've seen only part of it, and it was nauseating."

Chapter Fifty

Unknown location

Six days after abduction

Although John Brandt had lost all sense of time, how long he'd been in custody, whether it was day or night, he hadn't lost his resolve. He was well aware that there were no awards for withstanding pain, but he knew there was an award for giving in—he would be a traitor and people would die.

He'd been fighting the ever-increasing notions that he wouldn't be rescued. He'd long since concluded that he was on a ship, probably a container ship. The container where they held him between interrogation sessions was probably one of, depending on the size of the ship, anywhere between eight thousand and eighteen thousand—impossible to detect by surveillance. If his captors hadn't sent a ransom demand, there was simply no way to find him. Or was there? The flame of hope, although waning, helped him to fight those negative thoughts.

His body was breaking down from the beatings. There was not an inch on his body that was not aching or burning or throbbing. He had no more toenails or fingernails to give. Yet, he took solace in the knowledge that in the process of sacrificing those, he'd also driven Logan Jones to the brink of despair more than once and more frequently so, lately.

Clearly, his theory that they wanted the information he had in his head rather than money was correct. And it was as clear as daylight that the information about Rex Dalton's last operation in Afghanistan was what they were after. He found it perplexing that they always, with each session, without fail, returned to Dalton's Afghanistan mission, thus giving away the fact that the other CRC operations were not highest priority.

The thing was, Brandt hadn't sanctioned the operation to kill Usama and his cronies. He would've if he'd had contact with Rex after the ambush, but that hadn't happened. Even if he capitulated, he had no information to give them—the only person who could give them that was Rex himself. He smiled wryly at the thought, *maybe I should tell them that I might be able to arrange for the man who knows all about it to come and visit them. I won't tell them that such a meeting would not go well for them. I'll leave that as a special surprise for them.*

Nonetheless, as long as they were hammering him for information about the Afghan missions, they were not getting to the information that would put so many more in jeopardy.

He expected to be hosed down and taken to the interrogation room any minute, and there he'd begin losing body parts. They'd start small, to take their time to inflict and keep up the pain-levels until he broke. Despite the knowledge of what awaited him, he felt strangely energized by the thoughts of Rex Dalton turning up soon. *Wishful thinking? Maybe. But Dalton had a way of doing the impossible.*

His final strategy was to make them kill him before he would give up life-threatening information. But it was not time for that yet.

He'd sent them on more than just a couple of plausible wild-goose chases already, but they weren't taking enough time to check them out before starting the interrogations again. That meant either they didn't believe him, or they were under pressure to get Rex Dalton's name, and then they'd be done with him.

So, not giving up Rex's name is probably what would keep me alive.

He fought for lucid analysis. Would it be so bad to give them the name? Rex wasn't using it anymore, he was certain. They'd find he was presumed dead, his affairs left as they were fourteen months ago because there was no body, but no trace of him found in all that time, as far as the official record went. Only some crazy old man's desperate belief that the man he'd thought of as his own son must still be alive.

Moreover, the only place where they could get more information about Rex Dalton was at CRC, specifically himself, John Brandt and Rick Longland, the resident psychologist.

He'd hold out as long as he could, and then he'd make them kill him, but if he blurted out the name, it would probably be the end for him. And that realization, giving them Rex Dalton's name could possibly be the trigger that would get him killed, gave him a new weapon. It motivated him to stay alive for as long as it was humanly possible because he now had the key to end it all, when it suited him.

As his mind wandered, it occurred to him that it might actually be a welcome relief if they'd waterboard him for a change instead of cutting off body parts. He'd heard drowning was a peaceful death, though he reckoned water-boarding might be less so. *On the other hand, there are some body parts I value more than others. I wouldn't want to lose those, even though I'd have no more use for them once I make them kill me.*

The thought made him chuckle out loud, and his chuckle had escalated to howls of laughter when the water from the hose hit him.

Maybe they'll think I've gone insane. Let's see where that gets me. I still have plenty of tricks for you in my bag.

Brandt's facility with languages wasn't the equal of Rex's, but he was still better than the average American. He could identify more languages than he could understand or speak. The one thing that hadn't made sense to him before was that his interrogator spoke Bulgarian, he was almost certain, but one of the guards spoke Russian like a native. Yet another sounded like he had some sort of accent when he spoke Russian. And once, another guard had slipped and said something in Spanish. *What country would have a motley crew like this one in its security forces?*

The answer he'd come up with was none, obviously. He was in the hands of a crew of international criminals, then. That, too, could be exploited.

Nothing ventured, nothing gained.

In the interrogation room, something had changed. Instead of being duct-taped to a chair, he was forced supine onto a gurney and handcuffed, ankles and wrists, to the frame.

Brandt couldn't see Logan, though he rolled his head

around as much as he could, looking for the man. He remembered his strategy, and said, "Show yerself, ye dastardly pirate! I'll have ye keelhauled and then ye'll walk the plank. Argh."

"Still joking, John? Now, let's get down to business. What is the name of the man who raided Usama's compound?"

"I dinna remember," Brandt said, allowing a little saliva to drool from his mouth. "Who be Usama?"

"You might as well drop the act, Brandt. Pretending you've gone insane is an old trick."

Brandt rolled his eyes back until only the whites showed, he hoped, and then he intoned, "But I have something I can tell you. This is a big one. I can't just blurt it out in front of everyone. But you and I have become such close friends, I've decided to tell you. I trust you, and I probably don't have to tell you, you can't share this with anyone. Right?"

Jones grinned and nodded, "I promise John, your secret is safe with me. My lips are sealed."

"Okay, come closer, real close, the others must not hear this."

Jones leaned in with his head close to Brandt's, tilted his head to bring his ear closer to Brandt's mouth. Brandt had closed his eyes.

"The US government has been keeping an important secret from the world and even its own people. For decades."

"What?" Jones whispered.

Jones's breath in his face told Brandt he'd leaned in closer for the secret.

"They have a colony of aliens being kept alive at Area 51," he said, and then he spat, and was satisfied that he'd hit Jones in the face when Jones growled in disgust.

Rematch John Brandt versus Logan Jones. Round one: Brandt 1, Jones 0.

To his disappointment, though, Jones didn't lose his cool.

"You'll regret that," Logan said.

The next thing Brandt heard was the *tink* of steel on steel.

Please let it be something I don't really need, like a little toe. Even a big t...

Brandt screamed as his wish was granted. He'd felt the steel surround the first joint of his left small toe, but before he could brace himself, the instrument had sliced through flesh and bone, forcing the scream from his throat. His foot was on fire, but he'd be damned if he said one more thing today.

You could take the rest of them if you feel the need. This is no longer a game—it's all-out war.

Chapter Fifty-One

Ops Center, Lemaire Estate, Lyon, France

Seven days after abduction

The operation was not swift-moving, but it had to be. Neither Rex, nor Marissa, nor Josh had ever been tortured by the enemy, but they'd all been through training to withstand torture. But nothing to the extent which they suspected the Old Man would be subjected to by his kidnappers.

Rex spoke for everyone when he said they were running out of time. If the Old Man wasn't dead yet, he soon would be. If they started hearing about compromised missions, dead assets, and dead or missing agents, they'd know that the Old Man had broken, and his death would be imminent. It wasn't only CRC and CIA missions in danger. Allied countries had been notified, but they weren't as swift to pull agents and informants out of the field. Sooner or later, someone would die, unless the Old Man's heart gave out under questioning before he said anything. That, of course, was preferable to him giving in, but it was an unacceptable outcome, too.

Marissa, looking over some of the background information already available for Hathaway, looked up to respond to Rex's remark. "I think we should pay as much attention to these other names as to Hathaway. We shouldn't put all our eggs in one basket, Rex. Hathaway is a mover and shaker in New York City. He's Old Money, and he has more than enough in his trust funds if you believe the media. Why would he be involved in something like this? It is a long shot."

"Yes, it is a long shot but no less so than any of the others. And don't forget, Usama mentioned Hathaway's name, independent verification that he is or was involved with drug lords and terrorists. So, he fits our profile of a suspect. However, I agree with you, we should get tabs on all the suspects on that link chart. We have to shake all the trees." Rex answered.

Chapter Fifty-Two

Manhattan, NY, USA

Seven days after abduction

Three thousand miles away, in his apartment in New York, Hathaway considered the information from Brandt's last session.

To think, I've always dismissed rumors of aliens landing at Area 51 and the government keeping it a secret as conspiracy theory, believed only by nutjobs.

But the idea that he could profit from Brandt's information seized his attention.

Slowly, he said. "I want you to make absolutely sure you keep him alive. He'll be a valuable asset even after we know what we want to know."

Jones was shaking his head slightly. "This is the toughest bastard I've had to interrogate in my entire life. He seems to be immune to pain. I'm convinced the screaming and swearing he puts up is just to entertain us. Intellectually and psychologically, he's an enigma. He's been playing mind games with me, and to be honest, I'm not sure I'm winning."

"What are you saying? You want to give up? Walk away from it? Want me to get someone else with the guts to do it?" Hathaway snapped.

"No, none of that, I'll get him to talk, eventually, but I just want to manage your expectations. It's going to take a long time. As you can see, we already had to slow down the pace of pain-infliction as it might kill him. His heart is still strong but not as strong as when we captured him. I've got to keep a balance between the pain I mete out and what his body can take. He *will* give it up in the long run, but for the first time, I can't tell you how much longer. It could be ten or maybe even fourteen more days. I don't think it could be more than that. But I just don't know."

"Well, I paid a shitload of money to get you. Do your job, keep him alive, and get me that information. I've waited more than a year to get it. A week or two won't make a difference."

Hathaway was out of his element, though he didn't realize it yet. In the back of his mind an idea was taking shape. He was wondering if he could auction the old bastard off to the Russians or the Chinese. Or maybe he'd just rent him to whoever wanted him for a while, provided they didn't kill him. He was certain the Taliban would be interested. So would Al-Qaeda and Hezbollah and a few others. Or maybe he should save the terrorist groups for the end, after the old geezer was used up. After the Russians and the Chinese, of course. Oh, and he almost forgot his own kind, the drug lords.

Hathaway started to wonder how much he would

charge, and in his mind's eye he was already counting his millions when he ended the call with Jones.

Chapter Fifty-Three

Manhattan, NY, USA

Seven days after abduction

With the help of the INT teams at CRC HQ, the two-man CRC team in New York quickly had the tabs on Winnie Hathaway, as he was known to his friends.

If it depended only on Winnie's social life information, McArdle would have recalled his agents and reassigned them to other tasks. But he knew better. Rex's friend Rehka had decrypted Usama's hard drives, and Winnie's name was on them. There could be no illusions about the major role Hathaway played in Usama's business. Those hard drives revealed that he'd been trading billions of dollars' worth of Afghan drugs for many years in the US. So, the evidence of his 'other' life was there, they just had to find it.

They studied Winnie's spending habits and quickly knew which places he frequented, when he visited those places. One of the places where, according to his credit card records, he'd been spending money on an almost daily basis, caught their attention—Scarlet Manhattan. It took less than two minutes to learn it was an escort agency—a brothel in disguise.

Winnie's email, cellphone, and other internet records made for some boring reading. It was all about hookers, liquor, hookers, drinks, lunches, dinners, parties, hookers. The amount of money the target spent on hookers was staggering, and not just any hookers; for Winnie it was only the best high-class hookers. That's if there *was* such a thing as classes of hookers. It's merely the price that varies, and Winnie had the means to pay the highest prices to get what he wanted.

It was obvious Hathaway was not a man who worried much about his personal safety. He lived in a safe area, in a secured building, and he associated with rich and influential people. So, apart from an opportunistic mugging, there was not really any threat to him. Therefore, he had no bodyguards. Also, as an egotistical sociopath, Winnie probably lived in the illusion that he was untouchable. He also didn't worry too much about his privacy—the part of his life he wanted people to see. He clearly believed the illusion he'd built was impenetrable.

But it soon became apparent when it came to his business dealings, it was the exact opposite. He'd managed to keep that hidden from the public. It was only later, when they had his whole history from birth to the current date, that they understood he had once burned his fingers when he was careless about who knew what about his business dealings. That had earned him a stint in prison. And that explained why he kept his public life separate from his business life. The latter, no one except his business partners knew, and not all of them knew all of it. In fact, Winnie understood the need-to-know principle very well. So, he was the only one who had the entire picture.

The CRC staff assigned to Hathaway's case was getting frustrated with the lack of information that they all knew *must* be there. That was until Rick Longland pointed out that though Winnie was meticulous about keeping his public and business lives separate, he had one weak point—his sex addiction.

The INT team quickly hacked into the books of Scarlet Manhattan, Winnie's sole supplier of amatory entertainment. Within half an hour, they knew what his preferences were when it came to his female companions–Latino-looking girls, nicely shaped, dark hair, with big breasts and full lips, somewhere between the ages of thirty-five and forty-five, and the odd, well-preserved fifty-year-old. He liked them experienced, apparently, but no kinky stuff.

And CRC just happened to have the right fit, as far as age and looks were concerned, one of the CRC female agents, who conveniently lived in New York. The only problem was, Winnie didn't like the courting thing. He wanted what he wanted when he wanted it and didn't want to have to court and persuade any woman. He wanted a sure thing. It was probably below a man of his stature and means to beg anyone for anything. He always got what he wanted—a beautiful lady-like woman on his arm in public, her cooperation later in private, and no strings attached.

So, CRC couldn't send their voluptuous Latino-looking agent to Winnie's social club to have an 'accidental meeting' and get him to take her home for the night.

Instead, the two CRC agents dressed up to impress— black suits, dark glasses, guns in underarm holsters, and visible communications pieces in their ears—and paid the owner of Scarlet Manhattan a visit. After flashing badges and mumbling the name of an acronymed agency that didn't exist but sounded legitimate and very serious, they explained to the owner that prostitution was illegal in New York, and although hers was a so called 'escort agency' and not a brothel, the court and jury might take a different view. In any event, win or lose, a court case with as much publicity as they had in mind to give this case, was going to ruin her business.

The owner at first denied she was in the business they suggested.

The men in black made no reply. They just stared at her.

Then she changed tacks and mentioned a few high-roller names she said would protect her.

It had no effect on the men in black. They still made no reply and kept on staring at her—clearly waiting on her to say something more intelligent.

Then the owner got to the point where she should have started and asked, "What can I do to avoid all that kind of publicity?"

One of the men managed to get a half grin on his face and explained what had to happen to make them leave her alone.

She was a sensible person with good business acumen and was more than happy to work with them as long as she could continue with her business afterward. It was a seriously lucrative type of business, catering to the high-end, deep-pocket socialites in New York, including the mayor, a serious potential candidate for the Presidency next election.

All in all, it took less than an hour from the time the two men in black suits arrived until 'Jennifer Diaz' was a new rising star in her agency.

Ana Rivas, aka Jennifer Diaz, was just the ticket. In fact, her new 'boss' wished her new 'hire' were real. She told Jennifer that she could undoubtedly make a lot more money if she left her current employment and continued to work as an escort. Ana took no offense. She just smiled and made no reply to the job offer.

The owner was instructed to assign Jennifer to Winnie when he made his next order. She was also told that any attempt to warn him would not be received well. In fact, they'd be very unhappy with her and would be forced to arrange the publicity she so desperately wanted to avoid.

Looking at the amounts of money and frequency which Hathaway spent it at the agency, McArdle was confident it wouldn't be too long before the next order came in.

They were not disappointed. It was that very afternoon that he placed his order for the night.

Jennifer was ready.

She met him at a club, one she suggested was the latest place to be seen in New York. They had a few drinks, the 'new' bartender making sure her drinks were heavily diluted with non-alcoholic mixers and Winnie's heavily spiked with extra alcohol.

Then Winnie took her home, and she gave him the time of his life. So much so that when Winnie woke up the next morning next to Jennifer, he had no recollection of what had happened from the moment shortly after he got rid of his clothes and fell onto the bed next to her or was it on top of her?

He couldn't remember. And he was too embarrassed to say anything about his amnesia.

Jennifer, on the contrary, remembered everything. They'd returned to his home, where he became urgent, but she slowed him down with a seductive pout. "Don't rush it, baby. We've got the whole night." She convinced him that a bottle of champagne would do wonders for them. Winnie agreed it was a capital idea. He got a perfectly-chilled bottle from his wine cellar and a bucket of ice, and returned to the bedroom, where Jennifer was artfully posed in the center of his king-sized bed.

As he popped the cork, he asked, "That's great, lover, but why are you still dressed?"

"I thought you'd enjoy the show if I waited for you, baby." She rolled to her hands and knees and stalked him like a tiger, watching his eyes grow wider. When she got to the edge of the bed, she gracefully slipped to her feet and took the champagne bottle from him. "Make yourself comfortable," she said.

She poured for them and handed Winnie his glass.

Winnie gulped his down quickly, while Jennifer sipped hers slowly and then undressed, giving him the strip-tease show she'd hinted. She drew it out as long as she could, and then got between the sheets and beckoned him closer with a crook of her finger.

Winnie had made it out of his clothes and was eager to comply. He scooted closer. Just when Jennifer started worrying whether she had dropped enough of the drug in his champagne, Winnie collapsed onto the bed, unconscious. Jennifer slipped out of the bed, swiftly re-dressed, and gave him an injection just to make sure he'd have a good night's rest.

The drug she'd put in his drink and the injection would ensure he'd forget what happened. As soon as he was asleep, Jennifer retrieved his security swipe card from the inside pocket of his jacket and sent a text to the IT team at HQ, who were standing by to interfere with the condo's security cameras. As soon as they told her the cameras were in a loop, she used Winnie's swipe card to get into the penthouse's private elevator, which she took down to the basement where her two co-agents were waiting and took them back up to the apartment.

They now had the whole night to search Winnie's luxurious penthouse and bug the place, wall-to-wall. It didn't take them long to discover his hidden 'movie theater' with a huge screen and to figure out that it was connected to a secured, private, satellite link.

"No wonder the NSA couldn't pick up anything—this guy is off the grid with his business communications," one of them said.

They bugged the room and tapped into the satellite link and tested that the feed worked to CRC HQ and to Rex's ops center.

They also found his satphone. The HQ IT gurus helped them hack into it and installed a small, unobtrusive app on it which would now make the INT team at CRC HQ part of all his conversations on that phone, with Winnie none the wiser.

The last thing to do was to make a copy of Winnie's security swipe card in case they wanted to get into his apartment again.

By 5:00 a.m. they had done their work and sanitized the place. They'd been wearing gloves all the time but still wiped all areas where they could have touched. Then they did the security camera loop thing again and left through the private elevator.

Jennifer returned, got into bed, and waited. At 6:00 a.m., Winnie stirred. Jennifer couldn't believe it. They'd been out until nearly midnight, with him drinking heavily. So even if he hadn't been drugged, he shouldn't have been awake so early. She snapped her eyes shut and faked sleep.

She knew Winnie must have had the mother of all headaches, judging from the way he moaned and groaned.

Jennifer 'woke' with a groan as well and immediately started to boost his ego. "What a night! I can't remember when I ever had a night as titillating as that. You're a stud, Winston! Four times…. Wow, wow, wow."

It worked. Winnie's ego was stroked enough to stop him from admitting that he had no idea what she was talking about or mentioning his splitting headache. He just wanted her to leave immediately, so he could nurse his headache and get more sleep. He looked at his watch and realized the next interrogation session of John Brandt would start in an hour.

Jennifer observed everything, even the tiny lift of his eyebrows as he looked at his watch. Knowing his head would not recover anytime soon, she was confident he wouldn't want a morning romp, and she was just as keen to get out of there before he rallied. She made an excuse for having to leave so early, which Winnie accepted without protest, eagerly.

He led her to the elevator, pushed the button for the lobby, and swiped his card.

"We must do this again some time, Winston. I had the time of my life."

"Absolutely, ahh…" He didn't even remember her name. "It was fantastic."

Chapter Fifty-Four

Unknown location

Seven days after abduction

In lucid moments, Brandt had vague recollections that he'd talked to them, told them something. But he couldn't remember what it was. Rather than waste time on worrying about it, he tried again to think of what lie he could tell next to send them on another snipe hunt.

When he was hauled out, naked and dripping wet from the hosing, he took the initiative before Logan could speak. "Look, I don't know what you're talking about, okay? I can't answer your questions. Just kill me."

"You'd like that, wouldn't you? We know you're lying, and every time you do that, you're going to lose a non-essential part of yourself. If you don't know what we're talking about, tell us something you do know."

"Why? What difference will it make. I don't know the thing you want to learn, so there's no point in telling you anything else."

Logan shrugged. "I don't know. Those are my orders. I'm to keep you alive, old man, so this will be as slow as I can make it. You could last for weeks, or maybe even months. One thing I can promise you is that although you'll wish I'd kill you, I won't. I'm going to make sure that you never get that lucky. And don't think your fairy tales will be taken seriously. So, talk."

By now, Brandt couldn't be certain he could speak with enough plausibility to make them investigate. Although he'd lost all his finger and toe nails, his finger and toe joints were still intact, and he knew he was about to start losing them. So, he began to rack his increasingly muddled brain for the plots to thrillers he'd read or seen.

He must have taken too long to think about it, because a heavy mallet to one of his knees made him howl in pain.

"I said talk."

"Okay, okay! So, there was this huge emerald... I sent the guy you're calling *al Shaytan* to get it before your boss could... Auggghhhh! Shit!"

The other knee exploded in pain. "How do you know who my boss is?" Logan asked.

Well, that was a mistake.

"Okay, okay, I don't! Some woman contracted us to help her get it. It was deep in the interior of Colombia, and she needed protection." It had been more than thirty years since Brandt had seen the movie Romancing the Stone. Even if it had been recent, the pain would have made it difficult for him to remember the plot, so he went off-script and spun the tale as best he could. It must have been good enough for the day, because he didn't lose any more toe or finger joints before they took him back to his container.

My knees are wrecked. No more marathons for me.

Chapter Fifty-Five

Ops Center, Lemaire Estate, Lyon, France

Eight days after abduction

It was 7:00 a.m. in New York, 1:00 p.m. in Lyon, and 5:00 a.m. in Arizona, according to the clocks arrayed on the wall and labeled with their respective time zones.

Rehka heard the alarm she'd set up on her computer earlier in her day, after the CRC agents had rigged Hathaway's equipment, to let her know when Hathaway's satellite connection was activated. She'd also set it up to start recording the moment the connection went live.

She looked at one of her screens as two small windows monitoring the link came alive. The first screen showed a rectangular white room, by her estimates about ten to twelve meters long by two and a half to three meters wide. She noticed a chair and gurney, and a stainless-steel cart with surgical instruments, as well as a man in a white lab coat putting on gloves. He turned his face to the camera and said, "Good morning, Mr. Hathaway. Hope you had a good night."

Rehka gasped and quickly pushed her chair back in an attempt to get away from the screen and the man talking to her, but then she realized she was seeing what the person on Hathaway's end was seeing. She let out a big breath.

"Nothing good about it," the man who was addressed as Mr. Hathaway grumbled. "And if you *must* know, I had a terrible night."

The man in the white overcoat grinned. "Sorry to hear that. Well, maybe today's session will get us what we want and brighten up your day. He can't be too far away from giving it up now."

"Rex! Come quickly! I think we've got something important here." Rehka was shaking, but she didn't take her eyes off the screen while, with a few keystrokes, she switched the feed over to the big screen and split it into two windows, side by side. One window showed the room with the man with the white coat, the other window showed the man who was called Mr. Hathaway sitting in a reclining chair in a room, which Rehka knew must be in his New York penthouse.

Rex had just woken from his four-hour break. He'd been in the shower when Rehka called, but within seconds he stood next to her with a towel wrapped around his lower body, water still dripping off him on the carpet.

Josh and Marissa had gone for a short walk, and Rehka was about to send them a text message when they came in through the front door.

By then, Rehka had raised the alarm at CRC HQ as well.

They were all still wondering what they were looking at

when two men dragged a naked man with a bag over his head into the white room where the man with the white lab coat stood.

The naked man was in terrible condition. The man they saw on the video screen couldn't have weighed more than a buck-sixty. They could count his ribs just by looking at him. His body was mottled with bruises of every color from the angry red of a recent blow to grey, blue, green, and yellow. His feet and hands bore stained bandages that attested to bloody injuries.

One of the men who dragged him in pulled the bag off his head.

"That's John!" Marissa gasped.

Josh and Rex looked closer. The naked man bore only a passing resemblance to the man they knew. John Brandt had been a hale man of sixty-eight, six-foot-three or so, around a hundred and eighty pounds, with gray hair, a neatly-trimmed goatee, and steel-blue eyes that could stare a hole through a person.

His hair was matted, and his tangled goatee stained with blood. In fact, it was nothing but a ludicrous hank in the beard that covered Brandt's entire lower jaw. Rex was certain the beard hid more bruises, as Brandt's eyes were both swollen almost shut and his mustache was stained a rusty red below his nostrils.

"My God," Rex muttered. It was not only the fact that he recognized John and was disturbed by what he saw, it was also the realization that John's abduction was all about him, Rex Dalton. That was the only explanation for why Hathaway, a drug kingpin in the Afghan opium trade, would've wanted to abduct John Brandt. To find out who destroyed their warehouses and who killed his business partners.

Wordlessly, Josh slammed a fist into the palm of his hand.

As they watched, to their amazement, the Old Man *smiled*, revealing broken teeth and swollen, bloodied lips. His voice was weak and rusty, but it was unmistakably John Brandt's. He wasn't looking at the goons but at someone off-camera, presumably the man in the white coat who'd been seen in the room earlier. "Time for the party to begin again, my friend? We really must slow down, man. The pace is going to kill us."

Rex cleared his throat to get rid of the emotion. "Yep, that's the Old Man, all right. And he's right. The pace *is* going to kill him.

"Rehka, Greg, get a fix on that white room. We need to know where it is. I take it you can do that?"

"Yes, I think we can," Rehka said,

Speaking from Arizona, Greg said, "You bet your ass we'll get it." He turned to his team and said, "Okay guys, we need that location. The first one to get it gets two weeks in Hawaii." He looked at McArdle. "Right, Chris?"

McArdle showed him a thumbs up without turning.

It was horrifying to see their leader in such a state. On the CRC HQ side, the team was all trained agents. Most of them, with the exception of the IT staff, had seen horrible stuff in their careers.

But on Rex's side was Rehka, and he was worried about her. He whispered to Marissa asking her if she could sit with Rehka and give her emotional support and try to keep her focused on finding that location.

Chapter Fifty-Six

Unknown location

Eight days after abduction

The Old Man's interrogation started. It was gut-wrenching to see the proud man they all respected in such a state.

For the first few minutes, it was nothing they didn't expect as the two goons forced him into the chair and duct-taped his arms to the arms of the chair. They then forced his knees apart and duct-taped his legs and feet so he couldn't close them.

The camera zoomed in on his face. The expected look of dread in his eyes wasn't there.

Hathaway must be a sadist of the worst sort, to want to watch Brandt's eyes while they do this, Rick Longland thought. *And he must be disappointed to see no fear in those eyes.*

Rex glanced at Marissa. She nodded, indicating Rehka was focused on her work, but tears were coursing down her cheeks. She'd noticed what the goons did to prepare Brandt for what his torturer would do next. She averted her eyes when the camera view pulled back, to reveal the man in the white coat examining some wires he held.

Every man in the rooms on both sides of the world cringed when the torturer bent to attach the electrodes, and John said, with apparent good humor, "Hey, you're not my type, and besides, we don't know each other that well."

Without speaking, the other man straightened, now holding nothing in his hands, and turned to the cart. He reached for a black box with dials and displays and turned one of the dials.

An inhuman scream froze everyone observing.

The man in the white coat waited a couple of seconds and then spoke calmly. "That was just a sample, John. We are tired of your games. You will tell us something real, or that would've been the most pleasant experience you have had today."

"Rehka, how are you getting on with those coordinates?" Rex's voice was calm and collected.

"Close," she muttered.

Digger had picked up on the change of mood in the room. He was pacing around to everyone in the room nosing them in turn in an apparent attempt to comfort and pacify the members of his pack.

Rex absently patted his head or rubbed Digger's ears each time the dog came to him. He was desperately trying to determine how long *he* could have withstood such torture without breaking and dreading the moment when the Old Man did. He feared they'd bear witness to that event within the next few minutes.

Rex asked Josh to kill both feeds to the big screen and switch them to their individual computers but not Rehka's so that she and Marissa could focus on finding the location of that room without the distraction of the horror playing out on the TV screen.

Rex and Josh had donned their headsets and could hear and see that the electric jolts were infrequent enough to keep Brandt from passing out. Rex and Josh were airing their rage with soft curses. Marissa had her hand over her mouth and didn't even attempt to wipe away the tears streaming down her face.

Rick Longland probably knew better than anyone else what Brandt was going through and already must have gone through on a psychological level, and it gave him the cold shivers, apart from filling him with blinding rage.

Across the room, Josh reported, "He's passed out. I'm switching to the big screen again."

"Logan, what's happened?" Hathaway's voice came over the TV speakers.

As the video came back up on the big screen, the white room feed showed the man in the lab coat speaking directly into the camera.

"He lost consciousness. That's all he can take today, Mr. Hathaway. Any more will likely cause heart failure. Every time we shocked him, his heart raced dangerously. His resting rate when we got him was around sixty BPM, which was quite remarkable for his age. He spiked to nearly one-fifty today."

"I don't know what any of that gobbledygook means. I need results!" Hathaway shouted. "Shock him again."

"I'd be of no use. He's unconscious, he won't feel a thing, and it won't wake him. However, it might just kill him. I told you this was a bad idea. He didn't even give us his usual song-and-dance today. We got nothing. I'm going to give him twenty-four to forty-eight hours to recover, and then we'll do this my way."

"Logan, I'm paying you a lot of money. You told me you're the pro. Don't make me regret my decision to employ you."

The video feed and speaker both went dead.

Rex shook himself and barked, "That's our deadline—twenty-four to forty-eight hours."

Chapter Fifty-Seven

Ops Center, Lemaire Estate, Lyon, France

Eight days after abduction

"I've got it!" Rehka shouted.

Rehka had pinpointed the location on the GPS app on her computer and switched it to the big screen so everyone in the room with her and at CRC headquarters could see it.

"It's in the Aegean Sea, one-hundred and fifty kilometers southeast of Athens, off the coast of Greece in the direction of Crete." She stated the coordinates.

There was a brief silence as everyone studied the map on the screen before McArdle's voice could be heard over the speaker. "Must be a mistake. Check again. Or is it too late? We lost the feed, right?"

Greg answered. "I was about to give you the same coordinates. Rehka beat me to it. I double checked it, that's the right location. I say it's a ship.

"Excellent work, Rehka! Looks like you have a Hawaiian holiday coming up."

Rehka smiled.

Greg turned to McArdle and with a grin on his face said, "I'm the one who confirmed the location. Anything in it for me?"

"What. You want a stint in Hawaii as well?" McArdle was well aware that Greg and Rehka had become fast friends the last few days.

"Yes, I reckon my effort is worth something."

"Okay, you earned seven days."

Greg winked at Rehka and said, "Maybe we can go together?"

Rehka didn't reply, she just blushed and smiled.

However, Rex interrupted the holiday plans. "Chris, we need to get the CIA to divert surveillance satellites to observe that location, ASAP.

"If it's a ship, we don't know whether it's stationary or sailing."

"On it," McArdle said. He'd already picked up the phone and punched the speed-dial button for the office of the Director of the CIA. The next thing the team in Lyon heard was McArdle yelling into the phone. "*Make* him available! Listen Gale, I don't care if he's on the toilet or if he's with the President or in bed with his wife, or his mistress, put a phone in his hand and patch this damn call through. People's lives depend on it. Move it!"

Rex had to grin in spite of himself. It must be lots of fun being the CIA Director's personal assistant.

"Rehka, Greg," Rex said. "We need to know all the details of that ship, the name, the owner, under which flag it's sailing, the layout, including how many people are on it and who they are. And we need to make sure to track it if it's moving."

Josh and Marissa had already placed a red pin on the map against the wall at the coordinates. The ship was about two-hundred kilometers north of the Crete Naval Base. It was a major naval base of the Greek Navy and NATO, located at Souda Bay on the island of Crete, commonly known as the Souda Bay Naval Base. It served as the second largest (in numbers of battleships harbored) naval base of the Hellenic Navy and the largest and most prominent naval base for the United States and NATO in the eastern Mediterranean.

Rex listened as McArdle got through to the Director.

"We've found him. Yeah, he's in bad shape, but we know where he is.

"No, it doesn't sound as if he's spilled his guts yet, but we have no way to be sure.

"Sorry, but we don't have time for all the details now, I'll give that to you later.

"We need two surveillance satellites diverted to the coordinates I'll give you.

"No. *No!* There's no time for that. Get them diverted now and ask POTUS' permission later." He stated the coordinates and went silent for a moment.

"Okay, thanks.

"Yeah, two. We need eyes on that ship at all times from now until... Never mind, please just get those birds diverted, and let me know when it's done."

McArdle put his face in camera view and spoke to Rex and company. "Okay, it's done. Let's get on to the rescue plan."

Rex didn't respond, he was staring at the red pin on the map against the wall and muttered, louder than he thought he did, "Logan and Hathaway, you lowlife scumbags, I'm coming for you."

Marissa and Rehka were staring at Rex in silence. None of them had ever seen him in such a state of infuriation.

Josh had an imperceptible grin on his face. He was the only one in that room in Lyon who had seen Rex in that state of mind in the past. And what he knew was, without exception, it ended very badly for Rex's foes.

His body shuddered reflexively.

May God have mercy on your souls, Logan and Hathaway.

"Rex, are you with me?" McArdle asked but got no response. He tried again. "Dalton! Snap out of it. Sit your ass down and let's start planning."

"Huh? Sorry. Yes, okay. A plan," Rex said.

"We have some serious airpower, naval power, and manpower at Souda Bay that we can bring to bear..."

"Yep, we might certainly want to use some of that. But I guess you'll agree with me, option one is to move in under stealth and get John out alive? And only if..."

"Yes, absolutely," McArdle interrupted. "And let's not talk about ifs for now. Let's work out Plan A first then look at plans B and C."

Rex nodded.

"Okay, you and your team brainstorm over there. I'll do the same over here and we compare notes in an hour. Remember we have choppers, planes, submarines, and ships at Souda bay. I am sure we could also have a few SEAL and Delta Force teams there in quick time as well."

"Good, we'll keep that in mind. See you in an hour," Rex replied.

Marissa and Rehka offered to make coffee and sandwiches while Rex and Josh took a stroll outside to give Digger a bit of time to run around under the trees surrounding the residences on the estate, which included the main house, the guesthouse, a few cottages for housing the seasonal vineyard workers, cellars, and sheds.

"Okay, the first thing to consider is the time we have," Rex told Josh when they got outside. "I am not convinced just because that slimeball, Logan, said twenty-four to forty-eight hours that we actually have that much time.

"If John recovers earlier, they'll be at it again. And we don't know for sure what he may have given away already. I can't believe a man of his age has held out this long if they've been doing… *that*."

Josh shook his head. "I got the impression that was the first time they used electrocution."

Rex shuddered. "You're probably right. I hope so. If he'd given them anything of substance, he'd already be shark food by now.

"Nevertheless, my suggestion is we rather give ourselves an eighteen-hour window, max; quicker if we can."

Josh nodded. "Yep, the quicker the better. We don't have time to launch a big operation with many people involved."

"You know the CRC motto, speed, surprise, and overwhelming force," Rex said.

"Yep, that's the one."

"But the thing is, in this case we don't have time to assemble an overwhelming force. We'll have to rely on speed and surprise only."

Josh nodded in agreement.

Just then they saw Margot, little Rowena, Adele, and her two children.

As soon as Digger spotted the children and Margot, his

ears came up, his tail started wagging, and he looked expectantly at Rex. "It's okay, boy, you can go and say hello to them."

Digger shot toward them, the kids were screaming with delight when they saw the dog rushing toward them. Margot crouched to his level and let him sniff the baby, then stood and handed her to Rex, who'd arrived by then and was quite happy to hold Rowena.

"Is your mission going well?" she asked.

"It's about to. Sorry, Josh and I can't stay for long, we just brought Digger out for a bit of fresh air."

"No problem, I understand," Margot said.

Seeing the look of disappointment on the kids faces when they heard that, Rex said, "I'm okay if Digger wants to stay with you for a while. You can just drop him off at the guesthouse when you get back from your walk."

"Thanks, Rowan!" The children shouted and started running ahead calling Digger to follow them, and he, after looking at Rex as if to get his permission, didn't let them wait when Rex nodded and said, "You can go, enjoy."

Rex gave Rowena a light kiss on the top of her head and handed her back to Margot. "Thanks for letting me hold her. She is so cute, Margot. I'm sorry I haven't been able to spend more time with the two of you."

"I understand, Rex, don't worry about it. I hope and pray you'll be able to find and rescue your friend soon."

"Thanks, Margot. That's exactly what we intend to do —very shortly."

Chapter Fifty-Eight

Ops Center, Lemaire Estate, Lyon, France

Eight days after abduction

When Rex and Josh walked back into the guesthouse, Rehka immediately noticed Digger's absence and wanted to know, "Where's Digger?"

"With Margot, Adele, and the kids, out for a walk. They'll bring him back later," Rex explained.

"I'm sure he'll enjoy that after all the stress among the members of his pack in here earlier," Marissa remarked.

"You should've seen him when I told him he could go with the kids. It never ceases to amaze me how gentle he can be with people, especially children and women, at times, and at other times, how vicious he can be with those that pose a threat to members of his pack."

Rehka nodded, she had first-hand experience with how gentle Digger was with her when he helped to rescue her and how protective of her he was ever since. "There's so much we don't understand about man's best friend."

By now, the four of them were back in their chairs, each with something to drink and a plate of sandwiches in hand.

"Okay," Rex started. "Until we start to get data from the satellites, Josh and I can tell you what we've been discussing while we were outside."

For the next few minutes, Rex and Josh told them about the concerns they had about the actual time they might have before that alarm on Rehka's computer went off again to alert them that John Brandt was going to be tortured again. None of them thought it would happen in the next few hours, but they also didn't believe that it would be another forty-eight hours.

Before they could continue, Greg appeared on the big screen and said, "Rehka, satellite data coming through now. I'm patching a duplicate stream through to you."

Within minutes, Rehka and Marissa, collaborating with Greg's team, were pouring over the data.

Rex and Josh withdrew to the kitchen corner and continued their discussions about the best way to get to John Brandt without getting him killed.

When the time came to talk to McArdle and his team, Rex had an idea of what he wanted to do. He didn't share it with Josh, and he wasn't going to put that on the table right away. He wanted to hear all options before telling them what he had in mind.

While the mission strategy was being discussed by the experienced field agents, the INT teams were hard at work to get information about the ship. One of them got the identity of the ship within minutes, the MEDIT, registered to a company in Malta. "Aha, sailing under a flag of convenience," the tiny, bespectacled, blond-haired, very skinny INT analyst, with the nickname Muscles, said.

"What does that mean, Muscles?" Marissa asked; she was still struggling not to laugh every time she spoke to him, that nickname was definitely everything but descriptive of him.

"A flag of convenience or FOC is an age-old practice whereby ship owners register their ships in a country other than where they live. Most of the times they do it to get away from the taxes, stricter safety standards, bureaucratic rules and regulations, and such, imposed in their own countries. However, as you can imagine, it also opens the door for more illicit purposes, and I'm sure the MEDIT is in *that* category.

"Look here." He switched his computer screen to display on the big screen. "The ship's owner is a company, Casa Pty Ltd, and look there." He pointed with the mouse at the company details. "Registered in the Bahamas. No surprise there, either. And I'm willing to bet a case of Red Bull that Casa Pty Ltd is a front company for another one registered somewhere else and so forth."

"Okay, that may be so or not. And intriguing as it may be, I don't think that's important for now. The thing is, we've pinpointed the ship, and we know John is on it," Marissa said.

Greg agreed and gave Muscles another task to get busy with while he got in touch with the team lead of the satellite operators, whom he'd been given direct access to by the Director of the CIA. When he got the team lead on the line, he requested that the operators start collecting and relaying thermal imaging data of the ship.

Marissa was combing the ship's manifest for who was on board, what the ship was purportedly carrying, and who the ship belonged to.

Rehka was digging into the backgrounds of the captain and crew.

"Unfortunately, the thermal imaging isn't helping much," Greg said after a while. "According to the manifest, there are close to five-thousand containers, stacked several layers high, on her. I'm assuming John is being held in one of them, but which one is impossible to determine. The thermal imaging can't 'see' through the layers of containers."

"Okay, Greg," Marissa said. "We'll pass that on to the mission team when they're done with their meeting. In the meantime, I think we need to find the floor plans or deck plans or whatever it is called. I'm sure those will be required for the team that's going to board that ship during the rescue attempt."

"Agreed. I'll put some of my people onto it now," Greg replied.

Marissa turned to Rehka. "What do we know so far about the captain?"

"He's a shady character it seems," she answered. "I found quite a few hints that he's suspected of smuggling. Chances are this ship is one of those used to smuggle drugs, weapons, and refugees to and from the Middle East and Africa into Greece and Italy and places like that."

Marissa nodded. "Not surprising. A man that'll allow what we've seen on that TV earlier, on his ship, is probably involved in all kinds of criminal activities. Anyone can buy his cooperation, for the right price, and he doesn't care what side of the law he's on."

Greg, who had been listening to the conversation

between Rehka and Marissa with one ear said, "Ladies, we have a thermal signature for three people on the bridge. I suspect they're a pilot, a lookout, and the third probably the captain. I guess he's keeping close watch on the radar for the authorities."

"Anyone else you've picked up?" Marissa asked. "The manifest says they have a small crew, consisting of the captain and nine others."

"So far, we only picked up the three on the bridge. I'll bet dollars to doughnuts John's captors are not shown on the manifest. And the same will go for any refugees they might have on board. There could be many more people in the containers besides John."

"Not much good news so far. I better go and give Josh and Rex an update—they'll want to know what we've discovered so far."

Chapter Fifty-Nine

At the beginning of the planning meeting, Rick Longland suggested a name for the operation—Poseidon. He explained, "Poseidon was the Greek god of the sea, earthquakes, storms, and horses. He was a moody, bad-tempered, vengeful dude who apparently got seriously pissed when insulted."

The entire planning team accepted the name immediately, it was most appropriate, they thought, because that's exactly how they felt—moody, bad-tempered, vengeful, and seriously pissed off.

Rex and Josh then told McArdle and them about their concerns about the time they had to pull the mission off. They argued that the best risk mitigation strategy was not to work with twenty-four to forty-eight hours but rather with eighteen hours.

A bit of discussion followed, but soon everyone agreed that it was prudent to work to the shorter timelines. That however meant their options were limited as they wouldn't have enough time to assemble a group of Special Forces operators, plan, prepare, and execute the operation.

One idea was to send two or more warships out from Souda Bay to the MEDIT, detain it, and board it with a taskforce of Marines or Special Forces Operators. The idea didn't survive, mainly because of the time constraints and that such a maneuver would give the kidnappers time to kill John and also to raise alerts to the Greek or Turkish authorities—something which they'd like to avoid at all cost until John was safe.

The same reasoning sank the idea of doing a similar maneuver with a couple of submarines.

Then followed a bit of back and forth about bringing in a team of SEALS on a submarine or chopper and drop them off in rubber boats or small underwater subs a few miles out from the MEDIT and let them move in stealthily. This idea had merit, but there were two issues. The first was, they had no idea how sophisticated the sonar and radar systems of the MEDIT were and if it would be able to detect the approach of the SEAL team. That was a risk they'd have to take if they had run out of options. The second issue was the timeline again. McArdle had already checked, there was no SEAL team in Souda Bay at the moment. The closest team available was on R-and-R in Israel, after a mission in Syria. They could be airborne in three to four hours and be on base at Souda Bay in five to six.

"Notwithstanding the time issue with getting the SEALS

onsite, I'd like to suggest we don't abandon the idea outright, let's go ahead and get them to Souda Bay irrespective. We might need them, let's make sure they're there when we do," Rex suggested.

McArdle agreed and made the phone call to the Director of the CIA to get the wheels in motion to bring the SEALS in.

Just then, Marissa and Greg joined the meeting and told them what the INT team found, most of which was not good news. Apart from not being able to tell how many people were onboard the MEDIT and how many of them were armed, they also had the challenge of five-thousand containers which, by the sounds of it, they'd have to search one by one to find John. Unless they could persuade the crew to tell them in which container he was held. But before they could even apply their minds to it, they'd had to come up with a plan to take control of the ship and neutralize every one of the crew and captors first.

Catch-22.

Greg had some useful news which just came in. "The INT team found the ship's plans."

"Great work, Greg," McArdle said. "Those plans might come in handy. Let's hope no major alterations have been made since those plans were drawn."

Rick Longland sighed deeply as he leaned back in his chair. Everyone looked at him, waiting for him to talk. "I hate to bring this up, but I think we will be remiss if we don't plan for it. What if… if… man, there's just no other way to say it. What if we can't do it. I mean, if we can't get on the ship silently."

"Rick, now that's where we'd usually tell you that failure is not an option," McArdle said. "But we have to be realistic. Things are not looking very bright at the moment.

You've raised a valid point. It has crossed my mind more than a few times, and I'm sure it's the same for the rest of us.

"My take on it is, only if we can't get to him before the next interrogation session and they torture him again and he breaks, we'd have to take drastic steps and would have little choice but to bomb that ship into oblivion with John on it. But that's a decision way above my paygrade. The Director of the CIA needs to handle that as far as I'm concerned."

Rex shook his head. "Only over my dead body will it come to that, Rick."

Slowly, everyone turned their gazes to Rex. It was clear he had more to say.

"Okay, Chris, I have an idea, but before I go into details, I'd need to have a conversation with a guy in Australia."

"Australia?"

"Yep, that big 'island' in the southern hemisphere, also known as the smallest continent, often referred to as the 'Land Down Under', they have those funny looking jumping rabbits and those cute little black and white …"

"Yeah, yeah, that much I know. Who do you want to talk to and why?"

"I know his name is Mitch, I don't know his last name. From memory, he's the head trainer at their Special Forces canine training facility at a base near Brisbane. Oh, and I don't have a number for him."

"Military dog trainer you say… Mitch… No last name… No number… Brisbane… So, let me guess, you expect me to get him on the line for you now?"

Rex grinned. "That's what I like about you Chris—perceptiveness."

"What can he possibly contribute to our situation?"

"You're wasting time, Chris. My plan involves Digger. I want to talk to this guy because Digger's former handler, my friend, the late Trevor Madigan, told me that's where he and Digger got their training. I have a few questions for this guy."

"Okay everyone, take a break, but don't go far," McArdle said. "I intend to track down that Aussie dog handler in ten minutes or less. I mean, how difficult can it be to track someone down with all of that information? And after Dalton had his powwow with this guy, we might just get the opportunity to listen to the plan."

From the moment McArdle spoke to the Director of the CIA to making contact with Mitch Roberts, nine minutes had elapsed.

The team cheered McArdle when he gave the thumbs up.

Chapter Sixty

Ops Center, Lemaire Estate, Lyon, France and Military Base Near Brisbane, Australia

Eight days after abduction

It took three more minutes for Greg to patch the secured and encrypted satellite video feed through to Rex's computer and kill the feed on the Arizona side so that Rex could talk in private with Roberts.

"Mitch?" Rex asked when the feed came live.

"Yep, Mitch Roberts."

Roberts seemed to be just shy of six-foot, stocky build, number one haircut, steel-blue eyes with an intense gaze, and soft-spoken. He gave a no-nonsense first impression.

"I'm Rex Dalton. I apologize for calling without any warning."

"G'day mate. No worries. My CO gave me a quick briefing. How can I help?"

"I was good friends with the late Trevor Madigan. He told me a lot about you…"

"I hope you don't believe all you've heard, we can't all be perfect you know." Mitch grinned.

Rex chuckled.

"Trevor was a good guy. One of the best dog handlers I've ever trained. And he died way too young. I'd certainly love to get my hands on those bastards who did it."

Rex nodded in agreement and for a brief moment, he was seriously tempted to tell Mitch that he'd already taken care of all but one of Trevor's killers, and that it was just a matter of time before he'd get to the remaining bastard. But instead he said, "You're probably not aware of it, but Trevor's dog survived."

"What! Digger's alive? Where is he, was he injured?"

"He's right here. I'll call him if you'd like to see him."

"Mate, of course I'd like to see him. He's the son of my dog, Duco, who died of an aneurism a few years back." Mitch went quiet for a beat. "Digger's a good dog, one of the best, he took after his father."

Rex thought he detected a tear in Mitch's eye as he remembered his dog Duco. After more than a year with Digger as his constant companion and best friend, Rex understood all too well how deep the emotional bond between these dogs and their handlers went. He found himself having to clear his throat to get rid of the emotion that had welled up in him before he called Digger over and urged him to stand with his front paws on the desk, within view of the camera, and said, "Digger, buddy, have a look there. Remember that guy?"

Rex remembered reading somewhere that dogs could recognize a face on a digital device if the screen was big enough. On the screens of mobile phones and tablets they were usually unable to do so. But Rex's second screen, connected to his laptop, was a 24-inch, and within seconds it was clear from Digger's wagging tail and soft yelps that he'd recognized Mitch.

Mitch was speechless for a long while as he stared at Digger. When he finally spoke, it was with a trembling voice, heavily laden with emotion. "This is amazing. We thought the same fate had befallen Digger.

"Mate, you have no idea how much this means to me. You've… ah… brought Duco *and* Trevor back to life for me in the last few minutes. Thanks."

"Digger was only shaken up by the explosion," Rex told him. "Together we found Trevor, but he was too far gone. I couldn't save him. With his dying breath, he asked me to look after Digger. Digger's been looking after me ever since."

Mitch just nodded slowly.

Rex realized this was a time to be quiet, to let Mitch have an uninterrupted heart-to-heart with Digger.

A few minutes later, Mitch said, "Thanks Rex, I appreciate the moment with Digger. I'd love to do this again some time, but I was given to understand that you're in a bit of a bind?"

"Yes, I am. And I apologize in advance for not being able to give you the full background on the situation we have to deal with over here."

"My CO told me you're US military, and last time I checked, the Aussies and Americans were still allies. I understand the need-to-know thing. So, if I can be of assistance to kick the shit out of some bad guys, you've got my full attention."

"Thanks, I appreciate your willingness to help. It is as you've said, we're in a tight spot here, timewise and tactically. I need your advice. But before I get to that, let me give you a bit of background information."

Rex went ahead and told Roberts enough of what had to be done, leaving out some and adding a few twists in, so that he didn't give away too much of the specifics.

He also told him that he'd never learned the proper commands, but over time he and Digger had worked out their own signals which worked for them. "You know, I have no idea how he does it. It's as if he can read a situation and my mind and just know what has to be done. He's pulled my ass out of the fire more times than I can count. Most of the time I point and gesture and speak in plain English and somehow, I don't know how, he understands me. I'm sure he's got more brains than I have."

Mitch just laughed at Rex's account of how he interacted with the dog. "Okay, by the sounds of it, you two have worked things out. There's no reason to fix what ain't broken."

"Agreed. Now here's the main question. Trevor told me that he'd done HALO jumps with Digger. I've done a lot, but never with a dog. What do I need to know, and how much does Digger need to practice before we do it?"

HALO (High Altitude, Low Open), a parachute jump, also known as Military Free Fall, MFF, was used to get troops, usually Special Forces, on the ground in enemy territory quickly and undetected.

Rex didn't tell Mitch that he intended not to land on the ground but on the back of a moving ship in the middle of the night.

"Digger probably won't need any. Dogs have much better memory than humans. Digger's done many HALO jumps, and he loved it. But if *you* want to get comfortable with the procedure, a practice run wouldn't be a bad idea, if you have time for it. Digger won't be a problem, he knows how to behave during a jump. You're the one who'd have to make the adjustments for the extra weight and balance when you land."

Rex went on to ask him about rigging Digger for the jump, as well as any special commands to use to clear a shipping-container yard not wanting to tell Mitch where the containers would actually be.

Mitch told him how he'd go about it, and Rex made some notes.

After getting a few more pointers from Mitch, winding the conversation down, Rex told him how Trevor had taught Digger to climb trees, and how much children and adults enjoyed watching him do it. He left out the part about how Digger had used that trick in his rescue of the women in Mutaib's harem in Saudi Arabia.

Mitch got a good chuckle at the mental image and made Rex promise to send a video when he had the chance.

"Thanks Mitch, you were a great help. I promise you, if I get out of this alive, you can expect a visit from Digger and me in Aussie."

"I'll hold you to that. Just let me know when I should light up the barbie and get the cold ones ready. All the best with the operation, and don't do something stupid, like getting yourself killed."

Rex knew the 'barbie' was a barbecue, and he guessed the 'cold ones' referred to the beer, without which, according to what Trevor told him, an Aussie barbecue apparently would be a disaster. As for doing something stupid, maybe that's exactly how some would describe what he had in mind. Rex's take on it, however, was that it was the only option they had to save the Old Man without risking him being killed before they could get to him. Therefore, as far as he was concerned, any debate about the wisdom or absurdity of the method he wanted to use was irrelevant.

Both men were smiling, and so was Digger, when the call ended.

Chapter Sixty-One

Ops Center, Lemaire Estate, Lyon, France and CRC HQ, Arizona, USA

Eight days after abduction

When Rex ended the call with Mitch Roberts, he immediately reactivated the big screen and found McArdle and the rest of the planning team waiting for him.

"Okay, Dalton, let's have it," McArdle demanded.

"Piece of cake," Rex said. "Digger and I'll go to the ship, get hold of the captain, and have a quiet word with him. He *will* tell us where John is, we'll fetch him, and a chopper will pick us up."

"Just like that?" Rick Longland gasped.

"Yep, like that. For the sake of time, I've left out a few of the finer details, but in broad strokes, that's my plan."

"Dalton, you've left out quite a *few* of the 'finer details',

I'd say, and I'm very much interested to know those," snapped McArdle.

Rex stopped him. "Okay, Chris let's get serious. Here's how I see it. We've already decided that approaching the MEDIT with a conventional attack force consisting of ships, subs, choppers, planes, and a battalion of Marines will get John killed instead of rescued. We've also agreed the need to get on the ship by stealth, to disable the crew and get the captain or whoever knows, to tell us where John is."

"No disagreement about that. But the issue is how to get *onto* the ship unnoticed."

"By parachute," Rex replied. "HALO."

"In the middle of the night? Onto a moving ship? Are you… no wait, I don't even have to ask, I already know you're crazy. It's good you're over there in France. Back here in the Sates, you would've been hearing the sound of the ambulances coming to pick you up and take you to the looney bin. No, I…"

Marissa wanted her say and interrupted McArdle. "Are you insane, Rex Dalton? To parachute onto the deck of a cargo ship, even in broad daylight in ideal conditions is a suicide mission, let alone doing it at night. What the…"

Rex interrupted her. "I might be crazy but…"

Just then Rehka interrupted all of them. "Hathaway's satellite link has lit up again."

They all stopped talking and looked at the TV screens. What they heard chilled even Rex, who knew his plan, stupid, crazy, insane or not, was now the only remotely viable one. Jones was reporting to Hathaway that Brandt had recovered sufficiently, and he was going to start the interrogation again in exactly eight hours. it would be midnight in the time zone where the MEDIT was.

They had to get on that ship before midnight. Everyone knew it.

McArdle sighed. "Shit…and suddenly we're fresh out of options… Crazy or no, Dalton's wacky idea seems to be the only option we have… But… damn, a HALO jump onto a moving ship at night… I must be losing my mind as well."

Rex nodded. "Yep, and believe me I know the hazards; therefore, I'll be going in alone."

McArdle waved a finger at Rex. "I know you think you're a kind of Lone Ranger, but even he had an assistant, his name was Tonto."

"Yeah, mine's called Digger."

"Yes, of course, I keep forgetting you have a magic dog." McArdle's tone was dripping with sarcasm. "But let me be clear, not as long as I'm in charge. If we decide there're no other options but this loony idea, then it will be done by as many operators as I can get onto that ship unnoticed."

"Of course, that would've been ideal," Rex replied, "*if* we had the time, and *if* we had operators with the skills available right now, but we don't. I'm not asking anyone but Digger to go with me," he said. He looked at Digger and said, "Right, buddy? You're going with me—or do you also think this is a zany plan?"

Digger smiled and woofed.

Rex turned to them and said, "There you have it. That meant *'Yes, of course I'm going, and what are we waiting for?'.*"

"Hold your horses, Dalton," Josh said. "Looks like you forgot about me. Was that deliberate?"

"Deliberate, Josh. No use in getting both of us killed."

"I'm moved by your concern for my safety, however, if you're going on your own, you'll be out there without backup. A single point of failure. Despite your bravado, you know as well as I do how many things could go wrong with that parachute jump alone. One of them, *if* you manage to actually land on the damn ship and not in the ocean, is that you could be injured on landing. Mission over right there—big failure—John Brandt dead. And *if* you manage to land okay, you'll have to deal with nine crewmen and an unknown number of kidnappers. One mishap, just one lucky shot from them, mission over—big failure—John Brandt dead.

"I agree it's a crazy plan, but if it's all we have and no time to find another, I go in with you, that way we're improving the odds a bit. So, end of discussion. Let's start packing."

Rex knew he'd be seriously outnumbered after he'd landed on the ship, though Digger would even the odds quite a bit. In his heart, he'd welcome Josh, though he'd almost always worked alone. Lately, it was him and Digger, and Digger was a better partner than any human being he'd ever worked with. But he wouldn't ask anyone to do what he proposed. If he hadn't desperately needed Digger, he wouldn't even have taken him. Of course, the others were right—it *was* insane. But sometimes it was the insane move that gave the much-needed advantage of surprise. Therefore, he was willing to take the risk.

The chances are that the captain and his crew and the captors, if they'd be expecting trouble, would be expecting it to come to them on the water, not from the air.

"Digger and I are going, alone, and that's that. It won't take long. Digger and I'll persuade that captain to tell us, and if he can't be persuaded, I'll get Digger on the scent, he'll sniff the Old Man out in no time."

But Josh had more to say about it. "No, you aren't going in alone. No disrespect man, but the Old Man has a better chance if there are more of us to handle the bad guys. I'm going with you. Chris agrees with me, right Chris?"

McArdle nodded slowly. "I still think it's nuts even with the two of you going in. Although its only marginally less so if Farley goes as well. I can't see another option. If anyone has any idea, and I mean any idea, as long as it's better than Dalton's, now's the time."

There were none.

McArdle sighed deeply and shrugged. "I hate this plan. Dalton, Farley goes with you. Not negotiable."

Rex nodded. "We're wasting time, accepted. Now I need to get something with John's smell on it, a piece of clothing would be good. I take it the team over in Greece would still have his luggage?"

"Only one way to find out," McArdle said and turned to Longland. "Rick, can you get hold of them and arrange that John's luggage is sent to Souda Bay? If it can't be done post haste, let me know, I'll ask the CIA to pull some strings to get it over there. I'm sure they have a private jet sitting idly over there in Athens. They have jets stationed all over the world."

Longland nodded and left to take care of it.

McArdle and Rex looked at their watches as if they'd pre-agreed to do so.

"Seven hours," Rex said.

"Yep, two hours to get you and Farley airborne, about three hour's flying to Souda Bay, two hours to prepare *and* get to the MEDIT," McArdle noted.

"I'll organize a ride," Rex said, with Madame Proll in mind. "You organize the welcoming committee at Souda Bay."

"Onto it the moment I have that flight information."

Chapter Sixty-Two

En route to Souda Bay, Crete, Greece

Eight days after abduction

En route to Souda Bay, in a private jet owned by the DGSE through a shadow company, courtesy of Madame Proll, Rex and Josh were able to communicate via the plane's secured video connection with McArdle and his team in Arizona as well as Marissa and Rehka in Lyon.

By the time they landed at the US Naval base in Souda Bay, they had thrashed out a three-stage plan, and the support they required was waiting for them, ready, willing, and able, already briefed by Chris McArdle with the assistance of the Director of the CIA.

The first stage, getting to the ship, would involve the high-risk HALO jump. Rex, Josh, and Digger would be flown in on a military plane at commercial altitude—thirty-thousand feet—nearly six miles up. At that altitude, all three of them would need to be wearing oxygen masks to make the jump. Without it they'd all be dead in minutes from hypoxia, lack of oxygen. Rex and Josh would be wearing night-vision goggles, body armor. They'd be carrying silenced Sig Sauer P226 pistols and a Colt M4A1 each. The Colt was one of the SEALs primary assault weapons featuring a quick-attach suppressor, grenade launcher, shot-gun, various optics, lasers, and illumination tools. It was capable of both semi-automatic and full-automatic firing at a rate of between seven hundred and fifty and nine hundred rounds per minute.

They'd open parachutes at four-thousand feet and steer to the rear of the ship, an area which, from the satellite images, seemed to be undetectable from the bridge, yet close enough to get there very quickly after landing.

If they missed the ship and landed in the water, the first backup plan would come into play. The first backup plan was to have two Chinook Helicopters hovering about thirty miles from the MEDIT at five-hundred feet above the water.

Radar could detect an object at a height of one-thou-sand-five-hundred feet, at a maximum distance of fifty miles. Hovering at five hundred feet, the choppers could be positioned much closer to the ship without running the risk of detection. And at a top speed of one-hundred and ninety-six miles per hour, they could be onsite within six to seven minutes.

The choppers would drop Recon Marines onto the deck who would take control of the ship and search for John Brandt.

Their rules of engagement were simple, *get the captive off that ship, and shoot anyone who stands in the way.*

The second backup plan, the backup to the first backup

plan so to speak, was to bring in the two submarines with a contingent of Recon Marines on board to seize and search the ship. They sincerely hoped and believed that the operation would not go so pear-shaped that it would be necessary to fall back on the second backup plan.

Nevertheless, they felt it sagacious to have such a plan in place.

The subs would be moved to a position out of range of sonar detection of the MEDIT. The maximum detection range for the best sonar equipment was about thirty miles. It was decided to have the submarines stationed at the thirty-five mile mark. At a maximum speed of forty knots, about forty-six miles per hour, it would take them less than an hour to reach the MEDIT if called upon to do so.

Their rules of engagement were the same, *get the captive off that ship and shoot anyone who stands in the way.*

Back to plan A. Assuming the first stage, Rex, Digger, and Josh landing on the ship unscathed, was successful, the next stage would be for them to subdue the crew, find out where John was held, and rescue him. They knew the layout of the ship, thanks to Rekha's and Greg's expertise. They knew how many crew members were aboard thanks to the manifest. The big unknowns were how many kidnappers they'd have to deal with and where they were all located.

They knew the Old Man was in a container, and they thought the interrogation room was set up in one, too. Where were the interrogator and his goons quartered, though? In another container, or in crew quarters, which could have held twice the crew that were listed on the manifest? A few more days of satellite observation might have given them a hint. Now they'd have to wing it.

The operation had to go down quickly, because the chopper would be in the air waiting for their signals. No signal five minutes after expected landing time, and the backup plan involving the choppers would be executed.

If nothing went wrong, or if the three of them could handle anything that did, stage three would be their exfiltration by the Chinooks.

During the entire operation, irrespective of which plan was in play, two surveillance drones fitted with night vision video and thermal imaging and two-way radio equipment would be circling overhead to provide reliable communications between the team on the ship, as well as the teams in the ops centers at Souda Bay, Lyon, and CRC HQ, Arizona.

Rex had kept an eye on Marissa during the discussions. It was clear that she was deeply distraught about seeing the love of her life going off on a potential one-way mission. And although Rex knew that she was a trained CRC agent, and she knew the perils of the job, he felt it was necessary for her and Josh to have a few minutes of private conversation before landing at Souda Bay.

He typed a text message on his satphone to McArdle requesting that he organized it with Greg and Rehka.

McArdle immediately texted back that he was more than happy to oblige.

Josh was a little surprised when McArdle told him that the line was his and Marissa's. He looked at Rex, saw the slight grin, and must've realized he and McArdle must've conspired. He thanked the two of them, donned the earphones, and started talking to the woman he'd fallen in love with over the past fourteen months, while Rex went up to the cockpit to chat with the pilots.

Chapter Sixty-Three

Aegean Sea, near the island of Crete, Greece

Eight days after abduction

Less than three hours before John's next interrogation would start, shortly after 9:30 p.m., the trio were greeted by the commander of the Recon Marine unit at Souda Bay who'd be supporting them, along with the chopper crew. To a man, the officers who were going to be in charge of the support teams were in a state of disbelief that Rex and Josh were even contemplating to parachute onto that ship.

Learning of the plan to take Digger with them, the dog-lovers among them were muttering under their breath that one of them needed to spirit Digger away and keep him safe while the crazy humans jumped to their deaths if that was what they wanted.

Digger, of course, was friendly but only up to the point when someone put his hand on his harness, and then he made it plain that he was in mission mode, and no one was to touch him but Rex.

When the time came to board the chopper, though, the chopper crews and Recon Marines were all business. This mission was going to happen, whether they approved or not, and they were going to be involved, one way or another. Either these two lunatics and that big black four-legged sonofabitch were going to pull this impossible stunt off, in which case they'd be called upon to extract them or, if the first plan failed, they'd be called upon to land on the ship and find the captive. It was their duty to support the mission to the best of their ability, and that was exactly what they were going to do.

The HALO jump was Rex's biggest concern. He had no doubt he'd be able to hit the target if he were on his own. Given the right conditions, he could land on a dime if he had to. He'd done it before, many times. But he'd never jumped with a dog, let alone a sixty-pound dog, strapped to his chest before. He didn't know how Digger's weight and movements might affect his ability to steer the parachute.

He had only Mitch's assurance that Digger loved parachuting and knew what was expected of him. What if he struggled? Would that throw the 'chute off course? When they landed, assuming they hit the ship instead of the water, who would land on top if he couldn't gain his feet at the last minute? Would it injure Digger if he landed awkwardly?

The questions were endless, and they had no answers. No one in their Marine support unit or all of the base had experience with it. Just rigging the tandem harness was worrisome. What if it wasn't done right? What if Digger was released too early, or not soon enough if they landed in the water? Rex knew he and Digger had to somehow stay afloat until a chopper could pick them up. Landing with a parachute and all that equipment in the water was perilous. Adding Digger to the equation made it lethal.

When the alarm sounded, and the plane's cargo door opened, Rex stepped into the opening, and when he saw the green light, he jumped out of the plane, with Digger strapped to his chest in his harness. All of those questions were still unanswered. All he could do on the way down was to adjust to the extra weight hanging from his chest.

When they reached terminal velocity, after about five seconds, they were free falling at a hundred and twenty miles per hour in a belly-to-earth orientation. Rex looked to his right and saw Josh a few yards away. He gave him the thumbs up, and Josh returned the signal.

After another ninety seconds of free fall, they were at the opening altitude, and Rex pulled the cord. His parachute canopy burst wide overhead, jerking him in his harness.

Digger did his part, just like Mitch said he would, he was calm and unmoving.

Rex looked to the right and saw Josh's parachute had also opened without problems.

With a three-quarter moon, no clouds, bright stars in the sky, and no wind, the conditions could not have been more ideal.

Some things have to work in our favor, Rex thought as the MEDIT came into clear view through his night vision goggles.

And in the last few seconds, Rex knew he'd be landing right where he wanted to, unless there was sudden wind shear.

There wasn't.

Rex hit the deck with a little more force than he was hoping for, doubtless a result of the extra weight. In the seconds it took to release Digger from the harness and the oxygen mask, remove his own mask, and release the parachute, he realized he'd sprained his ankle. It might slow him down but testing his weight on it reassured him it wasn't serious and wouldn't stop him.

Josh had landed awkwardly on a stack of containers about twenty feet away, but he was okay. They tested the communications between the two of them. It worked perfectly. Josh quickly disengaged himself from his parachute and clambered down to join Rex.

They had their Sig Sauer P226 pistols with silencers fitted out and were scanning around them for any signs of trouble. Rex looked at Digger for any signs that he might have detected trouble. There were none.

Rex thumbed the switch on his throat mic and addressed McArdle. "Eagle Charlie, Poseidon One. All hands, feet, and paws on deck safely. No signs of trouble."

"Good news, Poseidon One. Now go get them."

Rex and Josh smiled at each other. They knew back in the ops centers people were high-fiving each other. The three of them had just cleared the first, and what some believed to be the riskiest, hurdle of the operation.

Thanks to the drones circling a mile above, the communications between them and the ops centers were working perfectly, as well.

Their first objective was to take the bridge to prevent an alarm being raised and to disable intra-ship communications. While Rex interrogated the captain, Josh would put the rest of the crew to sleep by means of aerosol delivery of remifentanil into their quarters.

Remifentanil was one of the volatile analogs of the drug fentanyl, a potent opioid, used by Russian Special Forces to disable Chechen terrorists who had taken hostage of a theater full of patrons. It wasn't advised as a 'knockout gas', having killed fifteen percent of the hostages in that incident.

However, Rex and Josh were not concerned about that, they were there for John Brandt and their rules of engagement were the same as for the backup teams.

That had all been planned—there was no need to rehash it. The two men efficiently took stock and then began to carry out their assignments.

Rex and Digger rushed to the bridge where the lookout must have picked up something was going down and informed the captain. The captain had time to order him to sound general quarters before Rex was on him. Digger went for the lookout. The pilot leaped for the alarm switch, but Rex shoved the captain into him before he could activate it.

In the tight confines of the cabin, Rex and Digger were almost in each other's way. They managed to keep their three opponents from gaining an advantage, however neither of them could gain much of an advantage to disable someone, either.

That was until Digger, enraged by a blow to his snout, jumped up and got hold of the pilot's throat and ripped. The man fell, clutching his throat and gurgling, right into Rex's legs. Digger then turned to the lookout, who shrieked something in Turkish and finally got hold of the alarm switch and flipped it down.

A hideous screeching sounded from the ship's speakers.

Shit. That wasn't supposed to happen.

Rex had the fleeting thought that he hoped Josh had been able to deliver the gas to all the crew as he delivered a savage blow to the captain's jaw, rendering him unconscious.

In short order, he'd ziptied the captain's arms behind him and told Digger to guard the lookout. The pilot was in his death throes, bleeding out from a tear to his carotid artery. Rex managed to shut down the engines and then helped Digger when he kicked the lookout in the face breaking his jaw, taking him out of the fight. While he ziptied the lookout, he told Digger to go and help Josh.

Then he turned his attention to the captain, slapping him to bring him around but with no luck. Then shouts and gunfire from below drew him to look down and find Josh and Digger pinned down behind a stack of containers by three men with guns. Drawing his own, he dropped the captain and stormed down the ship's ladder, a set of narrow, nearly vertical steps.

He'd almost gained the deck when one of the men must have heard something behind him, turned, and fired off a wild shot toward Rex.

Rex saw the man a split second before he fired and had just enough time to duck, but the bullet ricochet off the railing and hit him in the back of the left thigh.

He almost went down.

He caught sight of the two men shooting at Josh and fired off two shots. One of them took a bullet to the head and the other to the neck. The one who shot Rex was distracted by the crossfire, but Josh had a clear view of him, rose, and precisely nailed him with a bullet to the back of the head.

Rex spoke into his mic, "Is that all of them?"

Josh answered, "Yeah. I got the gas to the rest, but these got out of their quarters after that alarm went off and were waiting for me. Is there any way to turn that damn thing off?"

"Don't know, pal. I was too busy saving your ass to try."

"Well, why don't you go back and turn it off now?"

"Afraid I can't do that… I'm hit."

Rex tried to stand up, but his leg failed him, and he tumbled the rest of the way to the deck. His wounded leg snapped like a dry twig a few inches above the ankle upon hitting the deck.

He had just enough time to say, "Oh, shit. Another thing that wasn't supposed to happen," when the blinding pain hit him, and he had to clench his teeth to stop him from screaming in agony. It took him almost a minute before he could say to Josh, "Listen, the captain's out cold. Can you get up there and try to revive him, before the goons decide to find out what's going on? And while you're at it, turn the alarm off."

"What about you?"

"No can do. Just broke my leg. I'll do a bit of first aid on myself and be ready to help when you find out where the Old Man is."

"I think we'd better go to Plan B."

"What, you mean calling in the choppers?"

"No, I mean sending Digger to find the Old Man. Let me help you with those injuries."

In the ops centers the observers could hear every word between Rex and Josh. They could not say anything, it would distract the operators, nor could they do anything but hold their collective breaths. In Lyon, Marissa and Rehka had their hands over their mouths. Rehka had tears in her eyes. In Arizona and Souda Bay they stared at the grainy images on the screens, some were biting their nails, others were pacing, others were swearing softly—it was obvious, with Rex injured, the success of the operation was balancing on a knife's edge.

McArdle started contemplating bringing in the choppers but wouldn't do so unless Rex told him to do it.

During an operation you always trust the judgement of the man on the ground above your own or anyone else's – John Brandt.

Rex called Digger to him and refreshed his scent memory with one of John's shirts which they got from his suitcase flown to Souda Bay earlier. He retrieved Digger's communication harness from his pack, rigged him up, and said, "Find him, Digger."

In the meantime, Josh had rushed up the stairs, found the alarm switch, and flipped it off.

Digger had taken one more sniff at the clothes, whirled, and headed for the stacks of containers.

Josh arrived back at Rex's position and started working feverishly to get Rex back on his feet. They still didn't know how many kidnappers they had to contend with. Three at a minimum, which would have been the best-case scenario.

While Josh attended to Rex's wound and broken leg, to take his mind off the pain, Rex quipped, "Josh, buddy, as you can imagine, these injuries have slowed me down a bit now. I won't be able to handle more than three to five of them. I'm sorry to dump this on you, but unfortunately, you and Digger will have to take up the slack."

Josh just grinned as he pressed a cotton pad from his first-aid kit against the bullet wound and wrapped it with gauze. "There's no exit wound. You still have a slug in there, and I don't know where it is. If it shifts and nicks a major artery…"

"Yeah, yeah, I'll have a problem, I know. But I can't worry about that now."

Josh dug into the emergency kit again and came up with a rolled foam emergency splint. With Rex gritting his teeth, Josh pulled the leg as straight as he could, then injected him with local anesthetics close to the point of fracture and applied the stiff foam with hook-and-loop closures. It wasn't going to take the place of surgery and pins, but it would give Rex enough maneuverability to fight if necessary.

"Thanks. Now let's see if Digger found what we came for," he said when Josh finished his ministrations.

The element of surprise was gone, thanks to the alarm. Any bad guys on the ship would be hiding or stalking them. Rex activated the little computer screen strapped to his left forearm. The device was linked to Digger's harness via a wireless connection. On the small screen the video feed from the night vision video camera on Digger's harness showed a container.

The image was stationary. "Looks like Digger found the container," Rex said.

"Did you find him, buddy?"

Digger's soft, low growl came back in response.

"He found John!" Rex told Josh.

"Clever boy!" Rex said to Digger.

Back in the ops centers another round of spontaneous applause broke out.

"Okay Digger, come back now."

Rex and Josh adjusted their night-vision goggles and waited. Less than a minute later, Digger was back, his tail wagging happily.

"Come to me, clever boy!" Rex praised him. He took Digger's head in his hands and rubbed noses with him. "You're such a clever boy."

Digger was bathing in the praises.

Josh watched in astonishment. His mouth was literally hanging open as he observed the interaction between Rex and the dog.

With Josh's help, Rex managed to get onto his feet and then said, "Digger, show us where he is."

Digger immediately turned and led the way, stopping every so often to allow Rex and Josh to catch up with him as they made their way through the maze of containers stacked strategically on the deck to balance the load.

Rex had his arm around Josh's shoulders leaning heavily on him to keep the weight off his broken leg as much as possible.

Digger suddenly slowed down and went into a crouch, he looked back at Rex and Josh as if to say, *shhh we're close*. He carefully rounded one more container and sat down. He looked at Rex, then back at the container and back at Rex again as if to say, *he's in there*.

Three containers sat side by side with no others stacked on top of them. It gave the impression of a fort in a narrow box canyon, with stacks of other containers looming high above them. The three Digger had found were oriented lengthwise and butted up against each other on the short sides.

Digger was intent on the one in the middle.

"Digger says the Old Man is in the middle one," Rex said quietly to Josh. "Any bets on which side the crew's quarters are?"

"Nope. Let me circle around and see if there's any hint on the other side."

Rex held his hand up to stop Josh and whispered softly, "I'll send Digger with you. It worries me that with all this noise we haven't seen any sign of them. Surely they must have heard that alarm."

Josh nodded.

Rex pointed to the far end of the three containers and said, "Digger, scout, hide."

Digger started moving to the right in a low crouch.

Rex told Josh, "Okay, follow him, but stay well behind him. I'll track his movements on the screen here and keep you informed."

Digger stayed in the shadows as he scouted the sides of the cluster of containers and Josh followed, they found the door on the other side, and Rex called them back.

Rex ruffled Digger's ears and praised him when he and Josh were back. Then Josh helped Rex to get around to the other side, where they took up positions close to the door.

The hair on Digger's back was standing on end as he stared at the door and back to Rex, telling him in no uncertain terms, there was trouble on the other side of that door.

Now to breach that door and get the Old Man out.

For a moment, Rex thought about using the Colt M4A1 hanging off his shoulder but then thought better of it, not knowing where the Old Man was, it wasn't a good idea to storm in with a gun blazing on automatic.

He and Josh were still thinking of the best way to make their entrance when Digger's low growl alerted them. A second or two later, the door opened slowly, and the barrel of a shotgun came into view followed by the body of the man holding it. The man stood quiet for a moment, looked around, closed the door behind him, and started moving.

Digger was closest to the man, and Rex whispered into the dog's earphones, "Attack!" The next moment, out of the shadows, a jet-black rocket of pissed-off Dutch Shepherd flew through the air in a full, frontal attack. He hit the man square in the chest and knocked him off his feet. The back of his head crashed into the side of the metal container with a dull thud. He didn't get a shot off. The shotgun clattered on the ground. He was out cold.

Josh scrambled and dragged him back around the

corner and ziptied him. He wouldn't have wasted time on that if he'd known the man's skull was fractured—he was not going to get up, ever. He returned to Rex.

"Okay, let's move in," Rex said. "No shooting. We don't know where the Old Man is."

Josh nodded.

They still had no idea how many more thugs were on the other side of that door. When they threw the door open and went in, it was with the hope that their sudden appearance would be such a surprise to whomever was there that they wouldn't shoot at them for a few seconds, at least.

They were wrong, though.

Josh, who entered first, took a hit to his body armor, which almost threw him off his feet. Rex was right behind him and got rid of the shooter with a double-tap, center mass then head.

Digger burst around Josh with Rex hobbling right behind him, and the two of them hit the far door leading into the middle container.

The smell almost dropped Rex, but Digger was forging ahead toward a door on the far side.

Rex suppressed his gag reflex and followed as fast as he could, each time he stepped on the broken leg was a new experience in pain. They surprised the goon opening the door into the middle container. But Digger was expecting him, he jumped up and got the man's face in his jaws and took him down before he could fire his gun.

Rex quickly stepped around Digger and his charge, burst through the door, ignoring the pain from his injuries, as he leveled his gun at the man he'd seen on-screen—Logan.

Logan threw one glance at Rex; his eyes were wide with

shock and surprise. He twisted around and went for the figure on the gurney, scalpel in hand.

Rex didn't hesitate. The shot from his Sig Sauer blew Jones's right hand, holding the scalpel, to smithereens before he could cut the Old Man's throat. Rex immediately followed the first shot up with another which blew a hole through Logan's left shoulder.

Logan sunk to the floor screaming in pain.

Josh had recovered from the blow to the chest and made his way to the door where he saw Rex and Digger had disappeared. He found Digger standing and growling over a man with a face bleeding profusely. He said to Digger, "Back off."

Digger immediately obeyed and took a step back. Josh raised his gun and shot the man between the eyes. He then stepped into the room where Rex was, gun ready, looked around, and lowered his gun.

From the gurney, the Old Man said something in a croak. It was incomprehensible. It could've been, "What took you so long?" It was only a guess, that's what they usually say in the movies.

Then the Old Man started making strange noises which Josh and Rex recognized as laughter.

Rex, keeping his gun trained on Logan, thumbed the switch on his throat mic and reported. "Eagle Charlie, Poseidon One. It's done. Ship secured. We've got him. He's in bad shape but alive, and you won't believe it, the old coot is laughing."

McArdle had just enough time to say, "Great work, Poseidon One. I'll send in the choppers now," before the deafening cheers of jubilation erupted in the three ops centers. In Arizona, McArdle let it go for ten or so seconds and then shouted at the top of his lungs, "Quiet all! I'm still talking here."

"Eagle Charlie, Poseidon One. Negative, I repeat negative, no choppers yet. I'll let you know when you can send them."

McArdle grinned. He knew Rex and Josh had a few errands to run that they didn't want to advertise too widely.

"Poseidon One. No problem. Standing by for your call. Take your time, as long as you do it in a hurry."

Chapter Sixty-Four

Aegean Sea, near the island of Crete, Greece

Nine days after abduction

Digger was nosing the whimpering man on the floor curiously.

Logan cursed and swiped at him and that offended Digger who leaped forward and got hold of Logan's right hand, or what was left of it.

Jones shrieked.

"Good boy. Guard," Rex said.

Though Rex suspected Logan could bleed out if they left him untreated, he wasn't in the least bit concerned about it. He busied himself with cutting the Old Man's restraints. That's when Brandt recognized who'd rescued him. His eyes grew big and round, but he didn't have the words to express what his face was saying.

"You're welcome," said Rex. "Let's get you out of here."

Josh went into action and started carrying the dead captors to the side of the ship and dumped their bodies unceremoniously over the rails into the sea. Then he ran to the stairs at the bottom of the bridge where he and Rex had the firefight with the crew and did the same with the three bodies there.

The sharks are going to have a feast.

He came back to Rex in the interrogation room and lifted the Old Man in a fireman's carry onto his shoulder and ran with him to the deck, placed him in as comfortable a position as he could and went back to get Rex.

While Josh was away, Rex had time to study the interrogation room and the others more carefully. The walls and ceilings were padded with foam rubber. Why?

Aha, I know. You soundproofed the place. You didn't want the crew or anyone else to hear what's going on in here. Well, thanks for that asshole. It worked both ways. That's why you didn't hear the alarms or gunshots.

Josh arrived and helped him to his feet. Rex told Logan to get up and start walking.

Logan refused.

Rex grinned and looked at Digger. "Buddy, did you hear that? I think you need to go over and persuade him to get off his ass and start walking. What do you say?"

Digger didn't need a second invitation when Rex pointed at Logan. He started growling and approached Logan with a vicious snarl.

Logan scrambled to his feet in one movement, screamed out in pain, but started walking immediately. Digger was right behind him growling, making sure Logan knew he shouldn't try anything silly.

On the way to the deck, Rex and Josh took stock. The

captain, they assumed, was the only one of the crew who really knew what was going on aboard his ship.

The rest of the crew they'd leave to their fate. Maybe they'd wake up none the worse for wear from their heavy sleep, and maybe they wouldn't.

The pilot was dead, and his body would be dumped overboard, same as the others.

The lookout was injured but alive and ziptied. He would be left alive with the rest of the crew who managed to survive.

The Marines could take care of everyone who was still alive when they arrived.

The captain was their only concern. Josh retrieved him from the bridge. He had regained consciousness and was talking rapidly and nonstop in Turkish. Rex and Josh didn't understand a word but guessed he would've been telling them how much trouble they were in and probably also hurling profanities at them about their ancestry, as well as their mothers and sisters.

Rex held his hand up, raised his gun, and pushed the barrel into the captain's mouth and said in English, "Shut up."

The captain went quiet.

"You know about the person kept on your ship and tortured by that man?" Rex pointed to Logan.

The captain had his mouth full and couldn't speak but nodded.

"He paid you?"

The captain nodded again and mumbled something incomprehensible.

"Shut up."

He and Josh held a quick court-martial, sentenced the captain to death, stood him at the rail, and shot him, then tipped him overboard to join the other bodies already in the water.

Finally, Logan was the only one left. He was still moaning and groaning in pain. He'd watched the captain meet his end and must've known what was awaiting him. It was possible that he'd been reflecting on the horrible physical, mental, and emotional abuse he'd inflicted on John Brandt. It was also possible that his sick and twisted mind was incapable of remorse. It didn't matter because he would've realized that he was in the wrong company to be begging for mercy.

Nonetheless, he began screaming and begging as Josh ziptied his hands and feet. and maneuvered him to the side of the ship where the captain went overboard a few minutes ago.

He begged to be shot.

Rex said, "Okay Logan or whatever your real name is, I might have a deal for you. You tell me who hired you, and I'll shoot you before we dump you."

"Winston Hathaway, from New York," Logan said immediately.

"How did it come about that you ended up working for that low-life?"

"I got contracted by a broker."

"Name?"

"I've got no idea. It's always done anonymously, through a site on the Dark Web."

"So, you're doing this for a living?"

Logan didn't answer.

"How much?"

"Hundred and fifty-thousand Euros."

Rex nodded at Josh to throw him overboard.

"Please, you promised you'd shoot me!"

"Karma's a bitch, Logan."

Logan screamed as he plummeted to the water.

"Say hi to King Neptune, asshole." Josh mumbled when Logan's body splashed into the sea.

Rex thumbed his throat mic and said, "Eagle Charlie, Poseidon One. You can send in the choppers."

"Poseidon One, Eagle Charlie, doing so right now."

Rex and Josh sat down on the deck next to John Brandt. He was unconscious from the tranquilizer injection Josh had administered to him earlier.

Digger sat down next to Rex with a big smile on his face.

"Thanks buddies, mission accomplished," Rex said to Digger and Josh. Digger sidled closer to Rex, put his head on Rex's lap and sighed with contentment.

"Rex, I know you told us how clever that dog is, and I've always been a bit skeptical, but tonight I've become a true believer."

Rex grinned. "You ain't seen all of it yet. There's a lot more he can do."

"I'd like to see that. But one thing is for sure, if we didn't have him with us tonight, you and I would've been fish food by now."

Rex nodded slowly.

Minutes later, the Chinooks were overhead. A rescue cradle was lowered from one of them to the deck for Brandt and Rex. Digger refused to leave Rex, so he rode up stretched alongside in the cradle.

Josh stayed behind to help the Marines who were

descending on rappel lines to the deck from the second Chinook.

The forty-five-minute flight to Souda Bay was tolerable to Rex, but John Brandt was in bad shape. The support team had brought a corpsman along from the health clinic, however he was neither qualified nor prepared to treat the Old Man's major injuries. The best he could do was advanced first aid.

When they arrived at the base, Brandt and Rex were immediately taken to the clinic, where Brandt was stabilized, and Rex's injuries treated with new bandages and a better splint. Then they were airlifted to Athens, and thence to the US. Final destination: Phoenix, Arizona.

They arrived in Phoenix less than twenty-four hours from the time Rex, Digger, and Josh parachuted onto the deck of the MEDIT in a death-defying maneuver to rescue John Brandt.

Chapter Sixty-Five

US Naval Base, Souda Bay, Crete, Greece

Early morning, a few hours after the rescue

With Rex and the Old Man needing to be airlifted to Athens, Rex was told Digger couldn't go with them. Rex had no choice and asked Josh to take care of Digger until they could make a plan to bring Digger to him.

Josh had to stay behind at Souda Bay for the inevitable debriefing but had no problem at all to look after Digger.

The problem was Digger. He had a different view of the arrangements. He wasn't at all happy to leave Rex's side. Josh had his hands full to restrain him on the leash when Rex was pushed onto the plane on a gurney. Digger must've realized he was not going with Rex.

He caused such a commotion, Josh was worried the dog was going to attack him. Rex had to stop the men pushing him on the gurney and asked Josh to bring Digger closer and leave them alone for a while.

Digger stood with his front legs on the gurney, his face inches from Rex's, whining.

Rex spoke to him in a soft and calm voice and explained at length what was going on, that he was going to be okay and that he, Digger, would have to go with Josh for just a few days. Rex promised him that they'd see each other soon.

There was, of course, no way Digger could've understood any of what Rex was saying. But then, to everyone's surprise, when Rex finished talking and Josh said, "Come Digger," the dog turned and looked at him, and when Rex said, "It's okay buddy, you can go now," Digger left Rex's side, jogged over to Josh, sat down next to him, and watched as Rex was rolled into the plane.

Twenty-four hours later, Josh and Digger were flown back to Lyon on a DGSE jet, courtesy of Madame Proll.

Digger was not entirely himself, it was clear that he was 'worried' and troubled by Rex's absence. Fortunately, he didn't take it out on Josh, which Josh appreciated very much. And he made sure that he kept the dog at his side at all times and gave him his constant love and attention.

Marissa ran up to Josh, threw her arms around his neck, and kissed him passionately when he stepped onto the tarmac off the plane in Lyon. She couldn't stop the tears of joy.

"Seems to me I need to go on missions more often," Josh quipped and got a punch in the arm for his stupid remark. He pulled her closer and said, "I love you, Marissa."

"And I love you, Josh Farley," was all she got out before he kissed her.

Digger and Rehka stood a few yards away, watching and waiting patiently.

Back at the guesthouse on the Lemaire estate they were met by Margot. Josh gave her a brief overview of the mission leaving out most of the sensitive detail and told her that the mission was a success. He told her that their friend had been rescued and by all accounts so far would pull through, that Rex had sustained a few injuries, nothing serious, and that he'd soon be okay.

Margot invited the four of them, including Digger to stay for a few more days. But Josh and Marissa told her they'd have to leave the next day at the latest. In the end, Margot succeeded in persuading Rehka to move to the main house and to stay for at least a week longer.

Chapter Sixty-Six

Manhattan, NY, USA

Twenty-four hours after the rescue

Winston Reginald Hathaway was a seriously troubled man. He hadn't heard from Logan Jones at the time he expected to for the next interrogation session. All attempts to make contact with Logan via the video link and satphone ended in frustration—the lines were dead. Short of getting on a plane and flying over to Greece, there was nothing else he could do. He decided to contact Uwe Krause, the Austrian broker, to get an explanation, and if there was none, to demand his money back. But before he could get that far, two of the contacts he'd made to offer John Brandt to the highest bidder—after Logan extracted the information he wanted—contacted him and made it clear they were getting impatient at the delay.

In truth, even before things went quiet, Winnie hadn't

been happy with the progress, either, considering what he'd already paid to Jones, the supposed pro. And that wasn't even considering what he'd paid to Krause and the exorbitant amount he'd had to pay to the captain of the MEDIT.

Pressure was building from all sides. His Mob partners wanted to know when courier routes would be fully restored. His partners in the drug importation side of the business saw their coffers being drained for information, yet no information was forthcoming.

A nasty, nauseating feeling had settled in the crop of his stomach as the possibility dawned on him that CRC could've tracked John Brandt down and rescued him.

Another possibility was almost unthinkable. Jones could've broken Brandt and was now offering the information he'd received to the highest bidder. That would've been the ultimate betrayal, and Jones would know that would cost him his life. He'd probably not be that stupid.

Yet another possibility was that the MEDIT met with a natural disaster and sunk with everyone on board. But a search of news from the region and weather at the coordinates he'd been given revealed the weather was calm and no shipping disasters reported.

After considering all the angles, Hathaway reached one conclusion, irrespective of how it happened, the operation had failed miserably, and it was time to reinvent himself again. Perhaps retire to a new location with a new name where he could live out the rest of his life in luxury with the money he had stashed away.

As soon as the banks with his various safety deposit vaults opened, he would begin liquidating his US assets, and then he'd high-tail it to somewhere without extradition agreements and with beautiful women.

He had a few social obligations to deal with to conceal

the fact that he was about to disappear, and he had to arrange for a different identity and face.

There was a lot to think about, but he'd done it all before, and this time he had more than enough money to do it right.

The CRC agents keeping tabs on him picked up the increased traffic from Hathaway's communications. He'd called a lawyer, several bankers, and a courier service.

"He's getting ready to rabbit," Greg reported to McArdle.

"Tighten the watch, but don't interfere," McArdle told him. "We're hands-off the bastard. Someone else has dibs on him."

Greg's team kept on collecting all the information flowing out of Hathaway's frantic communications and fed it to McArdle.

Hathaway continued his frantic calling. One of them was to a plastic surgeon in Cancun, and he emailed a picture of a famous actor he wanted to look like to the surgeon's office a few moments later. He called one of his underlings and ordered the man to arrange for a private jet to Cancun a few days later.

As other calls went out, the CRC team picked up intel on who would be creating his new identity, what that identity would be, and which of Hathaway's associates were warned by him to make similar arrangements.

Rex hadn't advertised what he would be doing with Hathaway. McArdle assumed Hathaway would be a casualty, and he didn't care. In fact, if Rex didn't eradicate the vermin, he, Chris McArdle, was going to take care of it, personally.

Chapter Sixty-Seven

Maricopa Medical Center, Phoenix, Arizona, USA

Three days after rescue

John Brandt woke and did what he'd been doing every time he woke since he'd been snatched. Before opening his eyes, he assessed his condition.

What hurts? Am I hungry? Am I thirsty? Am I cold?

For more days than he could remember, the answers would have been, *everything, yes, yes, yes*.

This time, surprisingly, they were *everything, no, no, no*.

He opened his eyes and immediately snapped them shut.

The room wasn't pitch-black.

Gradually, he became aware of a soft beep nearby, that he was lying on something much softer than the cold steel floor of a shipping container. A soft, warm blanket covered him.

What the hell?

He opened his eyes again, and this time he kept them open as he swiveled them back and forth, up and down, to observe his surroundings. A telemetry machine was to his left, with a rotating display he assumed showed his vital statistics. As he watched, the display switched and showed a jagged line with a pulsing heart-shaped icon to the left.

His heartbeat, he saw, as he could feel it going in rhythm with the pulses.

Well, I think that means I'm alive.

Cabinets arrayed on a wall above him, a set of window blinds to his right, and a TV high on the wall opposite confirmed his guess. He was in a hospital room, but he had no memory of getting there. Also, no memory of how long he'd been there.

He risked turning his head, and saw he probably had a roommate. There was no one in the bed, but it was mussed, as if someone had been in it recently. He immediately began to worry about his security.

Where is this hospital? Am I in the US, or still in the hands of whoever grabbed me? No time like the present to find out.

He patted the bed next to him with both hands, noticing they were bandaged, and located the call button lying there. Now, to try to work the button with his hands wrapped like a mummy's.

He did what he could, and then waited.

It must have worked, because in short order a nurse in a set of colorful scrubs rushed in.

"Good morning, John! Glad you've decided to join us among the living."

He tried to answer, but only croaked.

"You're confused about all this, I'm sure. I'll have the doctor and your friend come in as soon as possible to tell you all about it. Meanwhile, are you in pain? I can give you some medicine in your IV if so."

Brandt shook his head, no. He lied, but he wanted a clear head. Something had happened to rescue him from the desperate straits he remembered being in. He needed to know his current situation, and he needed to know it quickly. One thing, at least, set his mind somewhat at ease. That bubbly nurse's accent was pure California. It didn't prove he was in the US, but he leaned to thinking that anyway. But California? Why would he be in California?

He didn't have long to wait. The nurse had hurried out of the room, and within five minutes, someone he didn't know accompanied by a man on crutches whom he thought he'd never see again but had been praying he would, rushed in.

Brandt's jaw dropped.

Rex felt a prickle at the back of his eyes when he saw that Brandt recognized him. The Old Man was back, and it appeared his ordeal hadn't affected his memory.

The doctor was speaking. "Mr. Brandt, I'm Dr. Shawn Neely. You are at Maricopa Medical Center in Phoenix, Arizona. Let me first assure you that you are in a private wing, there are armed guards outside, and we have been informed that your presence here and your identity are top secret. Do you have any questions?"

Rex noted with amusement the expression that crossed the Old Man's features. He gave a croak in answer, but the expression clearly said, "Hell yes, I have questions! About a million of them. Beginning with, why can't I talk?"

The doctor was evidently as adept at reading facial

expressions as Rex. "You may have a little difficulty talking at first. You were intubated when you came to us, which has bruised your throat a little. It should pass in the next twelve hours or so. Now that you're conscious, we can start you on liquids by throat. Would you like some ice chips?"

The Old Man nodded, and Rex did the honors, spooning a couple of small chips into his open mouth.

"Doctor, I'm sure he'll want to know how long he's been here and how he got here. If you don't need to examine him right away, I'll fill him in. But I'll need you to step out of the room."

"Of course. I'll be right outside. Just call me in to give him a rundown on his physical condition."

John was glaring at him when Rex turned back to face him.

"I know, I got the order wrong. Well, I can tell you that you're going to recover just fine. You're missing a few parts, but nothing vital, okay? I'll give you the details when you're able to ask questions, but long story short, Josh, Digger, and I were able to get you off that accursed ship. You were in bad shape, and we suspected you'd had a minor heart attack. We airlifted you to Athens, where you were stabilized at a US military hospital. Then we flew you to Bethesda, to the National Naval Medical Center. From there, it was decided you should be flown here. Maricopa is one of the top trauma centers in the US, and we didn't want to draw attention to you so close to Washington, DC. So, here you are. You've been here three days in an induced coma.

"Shall I call the doctor back in?"

John had relaxed his face, and Rex could see he'd answered the most pressing questions. He nodded, and Rex stepped to the door.

Dr. Neely came back in and turned to Rex. "Now I

must ask *you* to step outside. I'm sure you understand that Mr. Brandt's medical condition is private information."

Rex said, "Ask him."

"Mr. Brandt, do you know this man?" The doctor pointed to Rex. "He says his name is Rowan Donnelly. Is it your wish that Mr. Donnelly be present when I discuss your condition?"

Brandt's eyebrows had shot up when he heard the name and proved again that his mental faculties were all there when he nodded affirmatively.

"Very well. In order of seriousness, you have had a mild heart attack, you have a lacerated liver, a broken tibia and cracked patella, your small toes have been removed by pincers of some sort, and you have no toenails or finger-nails. You also have some broken bones in your fingers, and deep bruising almost everywhere else on your body.

"The good news is that your heart is operating at ninety-nine percent optimal. You must have been in very good shape for a man of your age before your, er… acci-dent. We were able to repair your liver, and you will recover fully from that injury. Unfortunately, we cannot replace your toes. You'll need proper inserts in your shoes to maintain correct balance and gait. As soon as the amputations are fully healed, we can help with that.

"Everything else will grow back or heal in its own good time. You're a very lucky man, Mr. Brandt. You will recover fully, except for those toes.

"Is there anything else you'd like to know?"

Rex spoke up. "I'll bet he'd like to know how long he'll be here and when all these machines he's hooked to can be dispensed with."

Brandt nodded in agreement with what Rex said.

"Now that you're awake, Mr. Brandt, we can discharge

you to a rehab center within a week. I'd like to be sure the sedatives are completely out of your system. Your liver needs a few days to heal before I want you out of bed and walking around. We've got you rehydrated, so if you feel up to sitting up, you can get rid of that IV for nutrition and start on soft foods, let's say tomorrow. Okay?"

Brandt frowned but nodded.

When the doctor had left, Rex went to the other bed and sat down, then hefted his injured leg with his hands as he rolled backward into the bed. When he looked at Brandt again, he noticed his eyebrows up like before.

"Okay, Donnelly is one of my identities, and it's legitimate. But you are too old and too drugged to make sense of it, so I won't even bother to explain. As for what I'm doing in this hospital bed, I sustained a gunshot wound getting your ass off that ship, and it got infected. I'm sure you're not going to worry about it. I'll recover. In fact, they would have discharged me to rehab already, but I told them I wanted to be here to keep an eye on you, so they let me stay. You're welcome."

In answer, Brandt rolled slightly to the right, literally showing Rex the cold shoulder, and pressed the call button again, and the nurse came after a short delay. Brandt showed her with looks, nods, and opening his mouth that he wanted more ice chips.

Rex sighed. There was a duel raging inside of him. On the one hand, it was the pent-up aggression and doubt and hate of more than fourteen months. On the other hand, there was the love for this man who used to be like a father to him. But up till now, the aggression still had the upper hand. He couldn't wait for the Old Man to regain his speech.

Chapter Sixty-Eight

Maricopa Medical Center, Phoenix, Arizona, USA

Four days after rescue

By the next morning, the Old Man had recovered enough of his voice to drive the nurses and nurses' aides crazy with his demands and complaints. Rex just grinned and let them deal with the old bastard. He didn't need the aggravation.

Fortunately, Chris McArdle turned up at the hospital to see Rex for an hour or so and to then spent the rest of the morning with the Old Man while Rex watched TV in the lounge.

It was sometime after lunch when Rex went back to the room, and Brandt finally addressed him.

"So, Josh and Marissa found you. How hard did they have to twist your arm to come find me? I ought to dock your pay for all the time you've been AWOL."

Rex was used to Brandt's brusque mannerisms, and it

had never bothered him in the past. But today it got under his skin. He hadn't expected tear-filled gratitude, or even overt gratitude, though a quiet *thank you* might have been nice. But a full-frontal attack wasn't called for, either. Stung, he answered just as angrily.

"I haven't expected pay since I *had* to go off the grid after that ambush. I've been told, only a few days ago, you had nothing to do with it. Just keep in mind, I didn't know it then, and I didn't know it for the past fourteen months. And I still don't know, because you, John Brandt, haven't yet looked me in the eyes and told me about your role in that ambush. All I know is that the last time you spoke to me you sent me and my men to our deaths.

"So, in case you haven't figured it out yet, I resigned, effective on the day of the ambush.

"Oh, and by the way, I volunteered to find you and get your ass out of a sling as soon as I heard about your kidnapping. How'd you let that happen, anyway? Slipping, old man? Or was that your ruse to get me out of hiding?"

Brandt refused to answer, and as far as Rex was concerned, started pouting again.

Rex had a nice nap until dinner time. He wanted to get things sorted out with the Old Man sooner rather than later and then leave. He missed Digger, who was being cared for by Josh at CRC headquarters. Marissa had gone back home to Washington, and Josh was just as eager for Rex to get out, because, as he told Rex, he had a big question to ask Marissa, and it had to be done in person.

And Digger was driving him nuts, he told Rex. He was sure the dog was well aware that Rex was alive, and that Rex would come back to him, but he acted like a spoiled brat, refused to eat at times, was picky about his food, refused to go for a walk, and most concerning of all, the last day or so had been ignoring the kong, with or without treats stuffed in it. He'd also left Josh a malodorous 'gift', right where he put his feet when he was getting out of bed.

Rex laughed when Josh said, "He's worse than that girl in grade school I broke up with."

Rex had called Rehka and Margot every day to give them an update about his own and the Old Man's progress but didn't tell them how bad the relationship between him and Brandt was. He expected it would get worse before it would get better.

Brandt had some thinking to do. He and Longland had speculated that Rex wouldn't have known who to blame for the ambush, but he hadn't really, in his deepest heart, expected Rex to suspect him. He thought of Rex as his own son and often thought of him when he thought about his successor to run CRC someday. Rex's words had hurt him deeply. But he'd never admit to that, and besides, he wasn't ready to reveal to Rex or anyone else that he was even considering who would succeed him.

He didn't intend to retire. However, he was no spring chicken, as he'd discovered. He had to face the inevitable. Someday, CRC *would* have a new director.

I've got to get out of this bed ASAP, and I've got to square things away with Rex.

He looked at the other bed, and saw Rex was asleep.

Okay, it could wait until the nurses came in to wake him for dinner.

A couple of hours later, both men were sitting up in their beds with food trays in front of them. Rex had sat all the way up on the side of the bed, his feet on the floor, facing Brandt.

Brandt took up the conversation as if no time had passed. "For your information, I was kidnapped because I let my guard down. Happy? The more important issue is your absence from duty. You work for me. You still work for me. You haven't formally resigned, and I haven't fired you, although I should. You can't just go AWOL and expect me to condone it."

Brandt couldn't regret his words or his tone. It was the way he'd always operated. But he did wonder if there would have been a better way to handle it when Rex answered, stubborn as ever.

"Wrong. If I'm working for a company that's trying to kill me or can't protect me properly, you know, not creating a safe and healthy work environment for me, such as deliberately or negligently sending me and my men into an ambush, I don't have an obligation to work for them."

At first, Brandt thought the statement ridiculous, and he had no doubt Rex knew it was, too. He'd known the dangers when he signed up with CRC. But on the flip side, admittedly, Rex had a point about the negligence. However, the insinuation that he'd deliberately sent Rex and his men into that ambush was hurtful. Brandt didn't interrupt, although that's how he felt.

Rex was still talking.

"As far as a formal resignation goes, here." He pulled a notepad and pen bearing the hospital logo from the bedside table. He spoke the words aloud as he wrote furiously. "I resign, effective immediately. There." He scribbled something else and hobbled to Brandt's bedside to hand it to him. It said what he'd quoted, and he'd signed and dated it.

Brandt growled, "You can take that piece of paper and wipe your ass with it. I'm not accepting your resignation."

Rex didn't reply.

Brandt took the paper, ripped it up in pieces, and tossed it into the emesis basin on his bedside table. "There, that's what I think of your resignation."

Rex calmly re-wrote the resignation, signed and dated it, and handed it to Brandt, who tore it up again. The third time, Brandt had had enough. His bellow belied his weakened state when he shouted, "God damn it, Rex Dalton! Do that again, and I'll climb out of this bed and whip your ass! I've told you I won't accept your resignation, and that's the end of it. You stay in CRC, that's an order!"

Rex's voice was only a little quieter when he yelled back, "You can't order me, you dimwit! Nor can you force me to work for you. And if you think you can whip me even when you're healthy, you've got a sad lesson coming. The minute I get out of here, I'll hand my resignation to someone who has half a brain left in his head. I don't know why I thought it was necessary to keep an eye on you. I'm getting a different room."

Rex stormed out on his crutches, almost bowling over an agitated nurse who was coming in to admonish them about the noise they were making.

Chapter Sixty-Nine

Maricopa Medical Center, Phoenix, Arizona, USA

Five days after rescue

It was a testament to the Old Man's fitness before he was kidnapped that he was ready to be discharged to the rehab center only five days after being rescued.

Much to Rex's dismay, he had not been able to get a different room. His doctor had told him he could go to the rehab center early, or he could stay where he was, but they couldn't have guards disrupting another floor.

For the entire time, Rex and Brandt bickered or refused to speak to each other. Mostly it was Brandt picking fights and Rex refusing to answer. Nurses and other staff would scurry in to take vitals, give meds, or bring food, and then scurry out again, unsettled by the thick air of tension.

Rex was ready to climb the walls when the day came that the Old Man's doctor announced with surprise that his ultrasounds and x-rays showed remarkable healing already, and he could go to rehab. Soon afterward, Rex's x-rays showed the same thing.

The orthopedic surgeon couldn't believe it. He walked into the room to talk to both men. "I've never seen anything like this. You both had serious breaks, and you both show accelerated healing. Are you related?"

Brandt just growled at him, while Rex let out an explosive "No! I am human, Homo sapiens, as in 'wise man', he's a primate, as in ape."

The doctor's eyebrows went up. "Well, can you explain this?"

Rex's surly answer was, "For me, clean living. I have no idea about him, you'd have to go ask his relatives swinging around in the trees in the jungles of Africa."

The doctor shook his head. "Well, in any case, we're discharging both of you to the rehab center. The paperwork will be done in an hour or so. You'll need to call someone to transport you unless you want an ambulance. Neither of you is cleared to drive."

Chapter Seventy

Rehab Center, Phoenix, Arizona, USA

Five days after rescue

Upon Rex's discharge from the hospital, Josh and Digger were a welcome sight at the hospital entrance when Rex, under protest, was rolled out in a wheelchair. As soon as Digger saw him, he pawed frantically at the window until Josh went around the car, put him on leash, and let him out. Digger pulled him forcibly over to Rex, who had to laugh as the dog tried to swarm into his lap.

"Easy, boy! I'm glad to see you, too. I've missed you. Okay, that's enough kisses. Josh, let me get out of this contraption and into the car. Come on, Digger, off."

With the last firm command, Digger settled down and watched anxiously as Rex maneuvered out of the wheelchair and into the front passenger seat of the SUV.

"What about the Old Man?" Josh asked.

"He's going by ambulance. Lucky for him, because I'm ready to give him a good pounding, injured or no."

"Uh, oh. What's the problem?" Josh responded. He'd urged Digger into the back seat and climbed into the driver's side. As he pulled away from the curb, he stared curiously at Rex.

"Stubborn old goat won't accept my resignation. Every time I hand it to him, he tears it up."

"Ever considered *not* resigning?"

"No. I'm done, I'd not say forever, not yet, but for now and the foreseeable future, I'm out."

Josh nodded. "I can understand. Oh, just to let you know, Digger has been such a pain in the ass that I made sure the rehab center would let you have him with you."

"Hey, that's good news! I've missed him like crazy."

"He's missed you, too. Half the time he mopes in a corner somewhere, whining. The other half, he tears around the compound looking for you, I guess. It's as if he must've picked up your scent there, but that would be impossible. You were at HQ more than two years ago. Is it not?"

"Yeah, something like that. But don't be surprised to learn that after that time it's not impossible that he could still detect my erstwhile presence there."

"Well, after seeing him in action on that ship, saving our asses, I'll believe anything I'm told about him."

"He is amazing, is he not? Thanks for looking after him, Josh. I really appreciate it."

"You're welcome, buddy. But please don't make me do it again." Josh laughed.

Digger got off the back seat and stood awkwardly in the small floor between the back seat and the backs of the front seat. He nuzzled Rex's elbow and then, just as Josh laughed, licked the back of Josh's ear. Josh's reaction caused the car to swerve and Rex to laugh, too.

Digger let his tongue hang out and stretched his lips in the biggest smile Rex had ever seen.

But Rex wasn't as happy when they got to the rehab center, and he learned he'd once again been assigned to a room with John Brandt.

"This isn't going to work," he told the intake staff. "Brandt and I have been arguing for days, and he won't be happy about my dog."

"Sorry, sir. We heard from the hospital that there are to be armed guards for both of you, and like them, we can't have more than one hallway disrupted in that way. Our patients practice ambulating in those hallways. We're putting you at the far end of one hall, in one room, and that's the best we can do."

Still grumbling, Rex allowed himself to be wheeled to his room. Josh brought in a dog bed for Digger, his food and water bowls, his kong, and a week's supply of food, arranging all on Rex's side of the room.

By the time Brandt arrived, complaining and moaning loudly all the way down the hall so Rex and Digger had fair warning, they were settled in, and Digger was curled in his bed, contentedly gnawing on the Kong.

Brandt was rolled in by a burly orderly. As soon as he spotted Digger, a flood of cursing erupted form his mouth, growing louder. The orderly helped him into his bed and then left, rolling his eyes as he glanced at Rex.

Brandt wasted no time in small talk. "Since when does an agent of mine need a damn dog to protect him?"

"I'm not your agent, and he's not a damn dog. He's a friend, and my friend has a name. Digger. The best partner I've ever had, and the only partner I'll accept now. And he has never betrayed me."

"Stupid name for a dog. Digger." He said the dog's name with such animus that Digger, who'd gone on full alert when the noisy human came in, stiffened and trembled, waiting for Rex's command to attack.

"Tell your stupid dog that threats are a weak play. We don't threaten, we act."

"Believe me, you do not want Digger to act. You'd be back in the hospital with a lot more injuries, or more likely you'd be in the morgue, if he did."

"Digger, stand down. Friend."

Digger slowly sank to his haunches and gave Rex such a look of disbelief that Rex laughed.

"Hmph." Brandt made a noise of disgust. "Am I going to have to stay awake all night?"

"Not if you can start behaving yourself. I'd advise you to settle down and act like a civilized person. He won't attack unless I tell him to, but you've succeeded in making him distrust you. I wouldn't approach this side of the room if I were you."

"Great, now I'm held in a hospital room with an idiot and his dog."

Digger growled.

"I can always arrange a shipping container for you if you'd prefer that."

They stopped talking and had an uneasy truce. Brandt was still fuming—Digger and Rex ignored him. But when the dinner trays came, Rex had regained his even disposition.

Over dinner, Brandt contained himself enough to

appeal to Rex's patriotism in an almost normal tone.

"You once wanted to fight America's enemies, son. What changed?"

"I didn't change, I've just been too stupid to realize America doesn't know who's a friend and who's an enemy. The damn politicians have no will or can't agree among themselves to defend our country. They can't even agree what to call the damn enemy. They can't agree to stop the drug trade at its source in Afghanistan, which is killing three hundred US citizens per week from heroin alone. The thing is, no one cares about the American people anymore. And those who do, get betrayed and persecuted."

Brandt conceded that Rex was right in many ways. "But that's the very reason we need outfits like CRC and men like you. We get the things done that need doing."

"Yeah, look what that got me."

"Look Rex, that ambush should never have happened, and I will regret my part in it until the day I die."

Rex's voice took on a dangerous tone when he asked, "And what *was* your part in it, John?"

"Bruce Carson deceived me when he had me set you and your support team up to raid that fake meeting."

Brandt dropped his gruff demeanor and let Rex see the sorrow he'd carried for once. He had tears in his eyes when he spoke. "When we thought you were dead, I felt like I'd lost my only son. And when we had the hint you might be alive, that raid on the drug lord's compound, I was over-joyed. But then you never reported in. It hurt, Rex."

"You can surely see my side of the story, John. I didn't know who had ordered that ambush, but *my* orders came from you. I trusted you to watch my back, and good men died because you didn't."

"Yes, I see how that could have confused you. Trusting

that traitor has been the greatest regret of my life. If it's any comfort to you, I had Josh terminate the son of a bitch."

"It isn't much comfort, frankly. It didn't bring back my friends."

"What's it going to take to get you back into the fold, Rex?"

Rex was silent for a long time, mulling over what to say to Brandt to get him to accept he was never 'getting back into the fold'. True, it had been more than a year since the events that kept him looking over his shoulder all the time. The habit of thinking he wasn't safe if anyone at all knew he was alive, or his location, was a hard one to break. No matter how much his mind told him he'd been wrong, his heart told him he couldn't ever trust Brandt or CRC again. Brandt might not have ordered the ambush, but he'd still failed to recognize a threat.

Then there was Catia. He *had* to see her and learn if there was any future there. If so, the time was now.

After some time, Rex realized he'd left Brandt's question hanging to consider what working for CRC would mean. But the fact remained that, Catia or no, he wasn't at all sure he wanted to go back to work for CRC. Nor did he have to. He was a relatively wealthy man now. He didn't need a job, and he rather liked going where whim took him and doing what he wanted.

As the discussion went back and forth, anger sometimes surfaced, but every time it did, Digger shut it down by growling at the Old Man if he raised his voice. It was nearly midnight, and the orderly had come and gone with the detritus from their dinner and their medications, when John Brandt finally conceded he'd met his match.

"All right, Rex. You're right. I can't force you to work for

CRC if you don't want to. You've more than fulfilled your contract. I'm damned sorry to see you go, though."

When Brandt stopped pushing back, Rex stopped his aggressive stance and told the Old Man that he had some personal errands to handle, and he had no idea how long they'd take. "After that, though, I'll get in touch. Maybe we can..." Rex didn't complete the sentence.

Brandt, no doubt finally realizing that was as much as he would get, said, "Okay, I'll take that, for now. But if I really need you, I want to call you."

Rex said, "Okay, but only as long as I have the option to ignore you."

Brandt lay back on his pillow and smiled wearily. "Get some rest. We've got a long day ahead of us tomorrow."

Chapter Seventy-One

Rehab Center, Phoenix, Arizona, USA

Six days after rescue

Rehab was uncomfortable for Rex but excruciating for Brandt. Rex could hear him panting heavily, moaning, and occasionally calling his therapist some choice names as he was stretched, forced to walk on a treadmill, and every one of his sore limbs manipulated to regain and maintain range of motion.

They were returned to their room for lunch and told to rest. There'd be another session later in the afternoon. The Old Man groaned as he was helped into bed. Rex waved off help and got himself in a comfortable position to eat. He'd lie down afterward.

However, he and John Brandt had more talking to do.

"If we're going to work together on any level, John, I need you and CRC to do something for me first."

"What is it you want?"

"First, none of it is negotiable. If you won't do it, you'll never see or hear from me again."

"Never say never, son. Just tell me what you want."

"Okay. First, I have provided Chris McArdle with a list of names of US citizens, including high-ranking politicians, officials, and some high-ranking military personnel. They've been involved in the worst corruption you can imagine. Illicit arms dealing, collaborating with terrorists and other enemies, drug and war lords, human trafficking, spying on the US, that sort of thing. Have a look at that list and it'll make you hair stand on end. To save our country you'd have to clean out the vipers' nests. *You* need to bring justice to them, in other words, no lengthy trials, media BS, or country club prisons."

"No problem with that," Brandt replied without hesitation.

"I'm going to take care of Winston Hathaway myself. He's the guy who had you abducted and tortured. The same man who used his influence with a Senator from Georgia, whom I believe passed away a few months after the ambush, and Bruce Carson whom you had killed."

"Ahh, the Senator from Georgia who died of a heart attack last year was a crooked guy. Why am I not surprised?"

Rex continued. "Next condition. I've raided Usama's safe and offshore accounts. I want the proceeds distributed anonymously to the families of my teammates who were killed in the ambush."

"Done."

"Next condition. I also have something a little more difficult to distribute and impossible to hide. I don't want my name on its registration, so I'd like you to figure out how to expunge its history, rename it, and CRC will take possession. CRC will then lease it to me, under an assumed name, for $1 per year for the remainder of my lifetime or until it's no longer seaworthy, whichever comes first."

"A yacht? Where the hell did you get a yacht?"

"Jeez, John, keep your voice down. Let's try not to advertise it to all of Phoenix."

Brandt lowered his voice to an intense whisper. *"Where the hell did you get a yacht?"*

"There was a certain Saudi prince, a human trafficker and illegal arms dealer, who had no use for it anymore."

"What will you do with it?"

"None of your business."

Brandt sputtered a bit, until Rex reminded him that the terms weren't negotiable, and then agreed that of course his legal team could find a way to get it done. "Is that all?"

Rex grinned. "One more. You want me to take your calls anytime you need me, and I'll come and help you, right? Well, it has to be reciprocal. I want your agreement that any time *I* need your help, I can pick up the phone and CRC will come running."

The agreement was sealed with a feral grin on the part of the Old Man. There was a twinkle in his eye when he replied, "Sure, but only as long as *I* have the option to ignore *you*."

It occurred to Rex that he'd have to build his own support team anyway. And he already had some candidates in mind, Rekha he was sure was already on board. Josh and Marissa's images popped up in his mind as well. But he knew there'd be hell to pay if he'd talk about it now. Not that he expected that John's reaction would be much better if he'd headhunt the two of them in the future.

I'll worry about it when the time comes, if it comes.

They agreed on a code phrase to employ that would alert each other they were calling for help. Brandt agreed he didn't need to know where Rex was all the time, so long as he had his satphone number. If either invoked the code, the other would respond.

That evening, after another grueling therapy session for Brandt, he asked Rex what the personal errand was that he'd mentioned earlier.

"You ask a lot of nosy questions, John Brandt. Not that it's any of your business, but there's a woman…"

Brandt snorted. "Son, you don't want to get mixed up with a woman. You can't do that to a woman. In this line of work, when you're on missions, you'll always be distracted, worrying about her. Better leave that alone."

Disgusted with himself for revealing so much and with Brandt for being a stubborn old coot, Rex exploded. "You don't know *this* woman."

At the thought of Catia, he grinned.

From his bed, Brandt waved a dismissive hand. "Yeah, yeah. I've heard it all before. Famous last words. Now shut up. I want to rest."

"On that note, I've got a question for you."

"Make it quick, I'm tired."

"Tell me about Madame Proll."

The Old Man shot up into a sitting position and glowered at Rex. "Christelle Proll, deputy director of DGSE clandestine operations? What…"

"Ahh, on first name terms, I see. So, my suspicions were right."

"What suspicions? What's she got to do with anything?"

"Suspicions now confirmed after seeing your reaction at

the mention of her name, that you and the madame have the hots for each other. And for what she's got to do with anything, well, I'd say quite a lot. In fact, you owe her a debt of gratitude, John. You'd better give her a call and thank her as soon as you get out of here."

"What for? You spoke to her?"

"Of course, I did, and just the mention of your name had her eyes glistening and committing on the spot all resources at her disposal to help rescue you."

"Out with it, Dalton."

"Well, as you know, we had an ops center in Lyon, and it was fortuitous that we did. Because from there we could get to you very quickly when we knew where they kept you. Madame Proll not only made her agents and technology available to us, she also provided us with the ride that took us to Souda Bay."

"Mhh, I see. Okay. I'll call her."

Rex started laughing.

"What's so damn funny, Dalton?"

"I was just wondering if I should now lecture *you* about not getting mixed up with a woman. And how, in this line of work, a woman will be a distraction and that it's better to leave that alone?"

"Get lost. I'm going to sleep now."

Rex shook his head. He and John Brandt had made their agreement. The past had been buried, and if he stayed any longer, he and the Old Man were going to go a few more rounds, and then their agreement would blow up, and it would start all over again.

He left the room, marched into the administrative office, and discharged himself against doctor's orders and over the therapy staff's objections.

"I've dealt with worse without being pampered by you

guys. I've got work to do. Thanks for treating me with so much care. Send the bill to John Brandt, I'm leaving."

What he didn't say to them was that the work he had to do involved putting seven bullets in a man named Winston Reginald Hathaway.

Chapter Seventy-Two

CRC Headquarters, Arizona, USA

Eight days after the rescue

Rex wasted no time. His delayed visit to Catia was uppermost in his mind when he left CRC headquarters after discharging himself from the rehab center and handling a few legal and financial issues. He still limped, and although he didn't need two crutches to get around anymore, he still required an elbow crutch.

He'd spent the first day at CRC HQ, reporting to Chris McArdle about John Brandt's condition. He related the agreement reached between him and Brandt to McArdle who wasn't happy to learn that Rex was no longer going to be in the employment of CRC and had no intention of changing his mind. In fact, he'd called John to confirm what Rex was saying was correct. Only then did he order the CRC accountant to release all of Rex's pay which they'd kept in trust since he'd disappeared more than fourteen months ago. John had also authorized McArdle to pay out a handy sum of one and a half million dollars in severance pay to Rex.

With all the administrative matters taken care of and his resignation letter on file, Rex collected all the information which the INT team had assembled about Hathaway, said goodbye to everyone, and got onto the private jet that would fly him and Digger to New York, and after he had taken care of his business there, he and Digger were to be flown to Rome. All of it courtesy of John Brandt.

He'd be met in New York by a CRC agent who would bring the gear he'd requested and transport him to a location near Hathaway's building. His request that the bugs in the penthouse be disabled as soon as he was dropped had been approved. All CRC involvement would be sanitized within an hour of Rex's signal that he was done with Hathaway. No one knew exactly what he had planned, but everyone had a theory that didn't fall far from the truth.

Manhattan, NY, USA

Nine days after the rescue

At nine p.m., the day after Rex's arrival in New York, the door in Hathaway's penthouse opened, and a man of athletic build, black hair, dark brown eyes, and tanned skin walked in, leaning slightly on an elbow crutch in his left hand. Next to him was a big black dog.

And Hathaway immediately got the feeling that his hour-glass had run empty.

As he opened his mouth to scream, the man raised a pistol with a silencer and quietly said, "Don't."

Hathaway, shaking with fear, closed his mouth again. The trade-off he'd made in not having armed guards in his home but rather relying on building security and certain electronic devices didn't seem prudent now. Somehow, this man had gained access to his private elevator. There was no time to think about that now.

His eyes darted in search of an escape. The man's limp gave him hope that he could somehow gain the advantage, but then he looked at the dog and gave up on the idea.

"You and I had this meeting scheduled about fourteen months ago," the man said. "Let's get started."

Hathaway moved quickly, hoping to catch the intruder off-guard. But he'd taken only two steps when a sharp pain in his calf gave him an abrupt lesson in why the dog was there. The damned beast had bitten him!

The man said, "Don't try that again. You offended my dog. Sit."

If Hathaway had thought the last command was for the dog, he was quickly disabused of that notion. His eyes went to the gun, which was again gesturing—for *him* to sit.

"I have some questions for you."

"I don't know anything about anything," Hathaway ventured.

"Digger, bite."

Digger obliged by chomping down on Hathaway's hand as he tried to fend it off his leg. Rather than scaring Digger, it made him mad.

"Who are you, and what do you want? Get that damn

dog away from me. Next time he tries to bite me, he'll get a few broken ribs."

"Is that so? Digger, did you hear the man? He doesn't want you to bite him, or he'll kick you in the ribs."

Hathaway couldn't believe the look of intelligence and disgust the dog gave him. It curled its lip and gave a low growl, almost as if it could understand what the man was saying.

Rex was quietly amused that Digger had taken matters into his own hands, or mouth as it were. Apparently, his buddy just didn't like the slimy creature before them.

Rex didn't come to Hathaway for a powwow. He wanted to get it over with quickly and leave, so he got straight to the point.

"I want to know how you got to John Brandt. Who helped you find someone to kidnap him, who was involved in that operation, and who did they work for?"

Hathaway's eyes widened. "I have no idea what you're talking about."

Rex said the name, "Jonathan Nichols," and shot Hathaway in the left knee.

Hathaway screamed, but Rex knew there was no one to hear him if CRC had kept their word. He studied the shattered knee and the blood flowing from it. "That's one," he said.

Sobbing, Hathaway said, "All right, I'll tell you. But you have to get me to a hospital, man! I'm losing a lot of blood."

"*Winnie.* I don't have to do anything, and I'm waiting for your answer."

Hathaway hesitated.

Rex said the next name, "Bill Sullivan," and shot him in the right knee. "That's two."

After another bout of screaming and vulgar language, incredibly, Hathaway tried to lie again. "I don't…"

Rex shook his head and said, "Peter Daniels," and shot him in the left shoulder. "That's three."

Hathaway rolled off his chair in agony, crying. Rex watched dispassionately as a stain appeared at the front of his trousers and began to spread.

"Your answer."

"I… I worked through a guy in Austria. A banker. I'd have to get his name from…"

Rex said, "David Smythe." The fourth shot went into Hathaway's right shoulder. "That's four."

Hathaway was still moaning and groaning but less so than before. He was obviously getting weaker quickly.

"His name."

"His name is Uwe Krause."

"And where did you hear of him?"

"Ahh…"

Rex said, "Don Murdock," and shot him in the stomach. "That's five."

"My God, I can't tell you that! They'd kill…"

Rex said, "Frank Millard." The bullet entered Hathaway's hip at an angle, shattering the joint. "That's six."

Hathaway, who had to have realized by then that he wasn't going to survive this 'meeting' and that he didn't have to worry about it, gave up the name of the mob boss who'd given him the banker's name.

"What are those names you're saying?" He asked in a weak voice.

"I didn't come here to answer questions, but I'll answer

that one. They're the names of seven good men you had killed just to get to me. Those were my friends killed in the ambush you and Usama arranged through Bruce Carson."

"You are... you're the man..."

"Yes, I'm the guy you wanted. *Al Shaytan*. The Ghost. Whatever name you knew me by. I'm the one who blew up your drug warehouses. I'm the one who killed Usama and his band of drug lords, your suppliers. Those seven men had nothing to do with the warehouses I raided in Afghanistan. They were innocent."

"Seven men?"

"Yes, seven. He stepped closer and pressed the business end of the pistol into Hathaway's forehead. "The name of the seventh man was Trevor Madigan. He was a good man and a dear friend." Rex pulled the trigger.

Digger whined when he heard Trevor's name.

Rex stared for a moment into the sightless eyes of the man responsible for the death of his seven friends and the deaths of countless others, killed by the drugs Hathaway had provided to them.

"It's done. Rest in peace, my friends," he whispered.

Suddenly Rex felt tired. There was no joy, no satisfaction, just an inexplicable emptiness inside of him.

Slowly, he holstered the pistol, looked at Digger, and said, "Come on, buddy. We're done here, we're going back to Rome."

Next in the Rex Dalton K9 Thrillers Series

www.vinci-books.com/donna-teresa

**In the heart of Rome, a conspiracy unfolds. Rex Dalton
and his loyal dog are the only hope.**

As Rex Dalton and his loyal companion, Digger, witness a
suspenseful chase unfolding before their eyes in the iconic Piazza
del Popolo, Rex's instincts kick in, setting off a chain of events that
will test their resolve and skills.

Turn the page for a free preview…

Donna Teresa: Chapter One

FASCINATION WITH HEMINGWAY

Port of Civitavecchia, Rome, Italy

Sunday August 30, 2015

Rex Dalton was a man who could behold a thing of beauty and enjoy it. She was magnificent. He had seen a picture of her, but that was a long time ago. Seeing her in real life took his breath away.

"Digger, would you look at her? Is she not the most beautiful thing you've ever laid your eyes on?"

Digger responded only with a big dog-grin on his face and a wagging tail, which Rex was sure meant, "It's only a boat. We've seen many of them. What's got you so stirred up, buddy?"

The *TOMATS* was exactly what she looked like—a luxury superyacht. Two-hundred and seventy feet of it, three-quarters the length of a football field, and thirty-seven feet wide. A masterpiece, custom designed and built by some of the world's leading exterior and interior designers.

It had only one previous owner, the late prince Mutaib bin Faisal bin Saud, an international black-market arms dealer and human trafficker. A scumbag whom Rex had killed more than a year ago. It was only a few months later that he had learned about the existence of the yacht and appropriated it, along with much of Mutaib's other hidden wealth. He had distributed the money, either directly to Mutaib's victims or to be held in trust for their future needs.

Other matters had then captured his attention, until he and John Brandt, the Old Man, CEO of CRC, his former employer, had landed in a hospital together after Rex was instrumental in rescuing The Old Man from kidnappers. One of the loose ends Rex had found the time to handle while he was laid up was the disposition of this yacht at which he was now staring. He'd signed the yacht over to CRC and agreed that the Old Man would instruct his lawyers to erase the yacht's history, rename it, and hide its new owner's name through an untraceable maze of dummy corporations. In return, Rex would have a permanent home on the yacht for the token amount of one dollar per year for life. Otherwise, CRC could use it as they wished.

The Old Man had kept his word; that he accomplished it in four weeks, was remarkable.

Now, Rex and Digger were on the pier at Roma Marina Yachting, the first marina to be built in Rome's historic, 2,000-year-old port of Civitavecchia, also known as the Port of Rome, about fifty-five miles from the city center.

His reverie was broken when he noticed a sinewy man about six feet tall, with silver-gray hair and sun-tanned skin, dressed in black jeans, dark-blue shirt and matching color windbreaker, with a black baseball cap, descending the gangplank making his way to him and Digger.

This must be the guy the Old Man told me about two days ago. Declan Spencer, the Old Man's best friend and captain of the yacht.

He was right.

When the man was a few yards away, he smiled and said, "Hi there, I'm Declan Spencer, the captain of the *TOMATS*. And you must be Rex Dalton?"

Rex hesitated for a split second before extending his hand to shake Spencer's. He had been living under assumed names for so long, he still found it somewhat unsettling to hear his real name, especially from strangers.

"Yes, I am, and this is my friend, Digger."

Digger, always up to a bit of grandstanding when humans paid attention to him, sat down and raised his right paw.

Spencer laughed and shook Digger's paw. "I've heard all about you, Digger. Apparently, you're one clever boy."

Ah, the Old Man must have changed his mind about the 'damn dog' then.

Brandt and Digger met in the hospital a few weeks before, and there was no love lost between the two of them then. Brandt kept referring to Digger as the 'damn dog', which of course, neither Rex nor Digger appreciated. Brandt kept admonishing Rex about how stupid it was for an agent of his to go around with a 'damn dog'.

But now, Digger was basking in the praise, and Rex immediately relaxed.

Rex was trained to pay close attention to people's micro-expressions and detect when they were deceitful, but since he and Digger had teamed up, he had come to realize that Digger was much better at it. The dog was a living, breathing, four-legged lie detector that outstripped any man-made device or human observation.

Spencer and Digger were off to a good start. And therefore, so were Rex and Spencer.

He invited them to come on board and meet the crew and get a tour of what was going to be Rex and Digger's abode for... well, as long as they wanted it to be.

Rex picked up his grip bag and followed. "*TOMATS*. Peculiar name," Rex said as they approached the gangplank.

Spencer smiled. "I have no idea what went through John Brandt's head when he chose that name. He refused to tell me. I've given up, don't even have a clue what it means. However, he said you would ask, and I should tell you to try and figure it out."

Rex stopped and stared at the yacht and the name painted on the side in gold cursive letters, mumbling softly, "*TOMATS*... hmm *TOMATS*..." Then he started grinning. "The old geezer had to get the last word in, didn't he?"

"What is it?"

"Ernest Hemingway, the first letters of his short novel, 'The Old Man and the Sea'—*TOMATS*. John Brandt is obsessed with Hemingway. He has read everything the man ever wrote and devoured every scrap of information about him. And let me tell you, just between us, I am convinced some of Hemingway's rudeness and abruptness has rubbed off on Brandt."

By now, Spencer was doubling over with laughter. He had known John Brandt all his life. They were bosom friends, born in the same year, in the same hospital, lived in the same neighborhood, grew up together, went to the same school, same university, and joined the Navy SEALS at the same time. John was recruited into the CIA, and Spencer retired as a colonel in the SEALS at the age of sixty-five. Both lost their wives. John's wife, a fellow CIA field agent, had been killed in an operation gone bad. A heart attack took Spencer's wife five years ago. He knew all about his best friend's fascination with Hemingway.

"That's John Brandt for you," Spencer said when he recovered from the bout of laughter. "He always gets the last word."

If Rex knew Declan Spencer as well as John Brandt did, he would also have known that Spencer always had one dream for his retirement—to be the captain of his own yacht and sail the world. This was not Spencer's yacht, he couldn't afford her, neither to buy nor to maintain. But in terms of the deal between John and Rex, he didn't have to worry about any of that, CRC would take care of it. To keep overheads low, he would not get paid for captaining the boat. And that didn't bother him at all; his military pension and savings, as well as the rental income from a mortgage-free house in DC, provided much more than he would ever need. Besides, he had no board and lodging to pay while on the yacht.

What Rex also didn't know was when Brandt had contacted Spencer to offer him the captaincy, he had also asked for his advice and assistance to get the yacht transferred to CRC's untraceable dummy corporation. Brandt wasn't sure at the time how CRC could put the yacht to good use. Spencer came up with the idea that the yacht could be used for R&R by CRC agents and Special Forces operators—free of charge—in exchange for fulfilling crew duties.

Brandt shook his head. "I don't know if that'll work, but you're the captain. Enjoy yourself. Oh, and keep in mind, from time to time, we might want to use it as a base for a quick reaction team, if the need arises."

Spencer had a big smile. "This deal is getting better all the time. Not only will I be out on the sea, I'll be part of some action as well. Music to the ears of a retired SEAL."

"Yeah, I am glad you're excited about it," John said. "But, unfortunately, I have to rain on your parade; you're not a spring chicken anymore. So, don't you start planning on kicking down doors and shooting bad guys. Our use-by dates are gone."

"Yeah, well, we'll have to see about that."

A few days later, Spencer was back in touch with Brandt and told him the registration had been completed; the yacht had its first crew and would be ready to sail in another week or so.

"Who did you have to bribe or lie to, to get it done so quickly?" Brandt wanted to know.

Spencer laughed, ignored the question, and explained that to get the crew all he had to do was let a few of the US Special Forces commanding officers, former colleagues, know about the exceptional holiday deal for Special Forces operators where they could spend some of their R&R on a luxury yacht, free of charge, food and accommodation included, but not alcoholic drinks.

Brandt was shaking his head when Spencer told him, since putting the word out, he had become inundated with applications. Apparently, Spencer's biggest problem now was to manage the waiting list of very keen operatives who wanted to spend time on a luxury yacht, even if it meant they had to attend to menial chores. Obviously, the fact that they could bring a wife or girlfriend with them as long as she performed crew duties, made it even more appealing. Even the chefs were military personnel.

"Okay, Declan, that's great news. Just keep in mind that whatever waiting list you have; my CRC agents always get highest priority."

"Yep, that goes without saying."

The *TOMATS* had three decks, was equipped for ocean travel with ultra-modern stabilization technology, advanced communications equipment, a helipad, and every nod to comfort that one could think of. It had a range of six-thousand nautical miles, a top speed of seventeen knots, and a cruise speed of fifteen. It was powered by two Caterpillar diesel engines producing close to five-thousand horsepower.

Rex was astounded by what he saw as Spencer took him on a tour of the yacht after meeting the crew. He had never seen so much luxury and comfort and elegance in such a small space. Apart from the very comfortable lodgings for the seventeen crew members, including the captain, there were accommodations for fourteen guests in seven luxurious staterooms. There was a hot tub, sauna, Turkish bath, infinity pool, gym, dining room, and several lounges. One of the lounges had been repurposed to house the sophisticated electronics gear and computer equipment that could be concealed when necessary. Another was turned into a secured communications room. Inside the latter was, among others, an impenetrable encrypted satellite video system, the latest technology in communications.

Grab your copy...
www.vinci-books.com/donna-teresa

About the Author

JC Ryan is a bestselling author renowned for his intricate espionage, archaeological thrillers, and conspiracy mysteries. With over 30 acclaimed novels, including the popular Rex Dalton K9 Thrillers, Rossler Foundation Mysteries, and Carter Devereux Mystery Thrillers, Ryan has captivated readers around the globe.

Drawing from his diverse professional background—as a military officer, lawyer, and IT manager—Ryan creates compelling narratives that skillfully blend historical accuracy with thrilling adventure. He is celebrated as a master storyteller, known for crafting riveting plots, meticulous historical details, and engaging, multidimensional characters. Ryan's meticulous research lends authenticity and depth to each story, immersing readers in richly constructed worlds filled with intrigue, suspense, and adventure.

Fans of David Baldacci, Lee Child's Jack Reacher, Tom Clancy's Jack Ryan, Nelson DeMille's John Corey, Vince Flynn's Mitch Rapp, Mark Greaney's Gray Man, Gregg Hurwitz's Orphan X, Robert Ludlum's Jason Bourne, Daniel Silva's Gabriel Allon, Brad Taylor's Pike Logan, Brad Thor's Scot Harvath, James Rollins' Sigma Force, Steve Berry's Cotton Malone, and Dan Brown's Robert Langdon will find JC Ryan's novels equally compelling and unforgettable.

When not writing, Ryan enjoys spending time with his college sweetheart, whom he married in 1978. They are proud parents of two daughters, have two sons-in-law, and are grandparents to two grandchildren.